The Colour of Mo

After his first two nov
Earth – both made int
writing books and
University. In 1978 he left
again. *The Queen's Gambit* derives from a
that which produced *The Hustler*, but deeper and older.
learned to play chess as a seven-year-old in San Francisco and still plays in his fifties in New York, when not writing novels and short stories.

Also by Walter Tevis
in Pan Books

The Man who Fell to Earth
The Queen's Gambit
The Hustler

Walter Tevis

The Colour of Money

Pan Books London and Sydney

First published in the United States of America 1984 by Warner Books
First published in Great Britain 1985 by Severn House Publishers Ltd
This edition published 1985 by Pan Books Ltd,
Cavaye Place, London SW10 9PG
9 8 7 6 5 4 3 2 1

ISBN 0 330 28604 8
Printed and bound in Great Britain by
Richard Clay (The Chaucer Press) Ltd, Bungay, Suffolk

For Toby Kavanaugh
who taught me how to shoot pool.

Annihilating all that's made
To a green thought, in a green shade.

Andrew Marvell

Chapter One

Where it faced the highway, the Sunburst was just another motel, but behind the main building sat a cluster of a half-dozen concrete cottages with tiny rock gardens. Condominiums. It was on one of the Keys, the one just below Largo. Driving down from the Miami airport, Ed had pictured a resort hotel with terraces and tennis courts, but this was old-fashioned. He parked beside a crimson hibiscus and got out into the Florida heat. Number 4 was the one across the gravel road, with a clear view of the ocean. It was late in the afternoon and the light from the sky was intense.

Just as he came up, the screen door opened and a hugely fat man stepped out. The man wore Bermuda shorts and carried a wet bathing suit; he walked to the edge of the little porch and began wringing the suit into the bushes, scowling. It was him. Old as hell and even fatter, but there was no mistaking the man. Ed walked up to the foot of the steps, shading his eyes from the sun. 'You're George Hegerman,' he said, pleasantly.

The fat man grunted and went on with his suit.

'We used to know each other, in Chicago....'

The man turned and looked at him. 'I remember.'

'I'd like to talk business,' Ed said, squinting up. He was beginning to feel uncomfortable. It was extremely hot. 'I could use a drink.'

The fat man turned and finished with the bathing suit. There was a wood banister at one end of the porch and he hung it over that, spreading it out to dry. The suit was enormous. He turned back to Ed. 'I'm going out in the bay. You can come along.'

Ed stared at him for a moment. 'In a boat?'

'That's right.'

Hegerman stood at the wheel, wearing only the Bermuda

shorts and dark glasses; he piloted the small boat expertly toward the low sun. The water was flat and shallow and as blue as any water Ed had ever seen; the motor behind him made conversation impossible except for an occasional shout.

After a while Hegerman pushed the throttle forward and the boat jolted ahead, skipping over the surface of the water like a flat rock and bouncing Ed hard against the seat. He stood up like the other man and held a rail in front of him. The spray hit against his face and drenched his dark glasses. They began to pass small, humped islands made of some kind of tangled plant. 'What's that?' he shouted as they passed one, and the fat man boomed out, 'Mangrove.' Ed said nothing, feeling stupid for not knowing. His shirt was soaked now and there was water in his shoes. He seated himself and tried to get the shoes off, but the boat was bouncing too hard and he couldn't manage it. The water's color had changed to a startling aquamarine. The deep, unclouded blue of the sky was dazzling.

Abruptly Hegerman cut the throttle back and the banging stopped. The motor sound changed to a purr. Ed got his shoes off. Ahead of them was a real island with a narrow beach; they were moving toward it.

Behind the beach stood a mass of trees, through which the sun filtered toward them. When they were a few hundred yards out, the fat man cut off the motor and they drifted. Then he opened a storage compartment in the seat beside him and carefully pulled out something black. It was a camera. He tood a tubular black case from the same place, zipped it open and removed a lens that was over a foot long. He fastened it to the camera body. Ed set his shoes beside him on the seat, watching the fat man who had now erected a tripod on the deck by his seat and was screwing the camera to the top of it. Ed knew better than to ask questions; he kept silent and watched. The cigarette pack in his shirt pocket was unopened and had stayed dry. He opened it now and lit up, then peeled the wet shirt off, wrung it out over the gunwale and spread it out on the empty seat beside him. The fat man had his camera ready now, pointed toward the trees. His enormous bottom filled the back of the boat seat; he had only to lean sideways to have his eye at the viewfinder. Ed leaned back and smoked, waiting. There were ripples on the surface of the water and they glowed above their troughs with iridescence. Water lapped quietly against the side of the boat.

Abruptly there was a movement at the edge of the trees and three tall, pink birds came walking toward them like apparitions. The fat man leaned over and his camera began to click. The birds were astonishing; Ed had never seen anything like them. They walked gravely to the water's edge, looked to the right and the left. The one in the middle took a few silent steps, its knees bending backward, raised its pink-edged wings, held its long neck straight out and fanned itself into the air. Its ghostly awkwardness gone, it was flying. The other two followed. As the third took off, Ed could see that its long bill was strangely wide at the tip, as though there were a bulb growing there. It gave the big creature a lugubrious, comical look, but when it was aloft like the others it flew like a dream. The birds circled the island once and then flew away to the left, lazily and silently, their necks extended straight out from their bodies like experimental aircraft. Ed felt goose bumps. The fat man kept taking pictures, following them until they were out of sight. When they were gone he leaned against his seat, laying a huge arm across the back of it. 'That's it,' he said in a gravelly voice.

'It was something.' Eddie said. He felt a lot better. Before the birds had appeared he was beginning to feel hustled; the whole thing was like a wild-goose chase. But they hadn't been wild geese. 'Herons?' he said.

'Roseates.' The fat man was dismantling his camera. When he got it stowed back in the compartment, he reached down to the deck beside him, lifted a cover and pulled out a bottle with tinfoil around its neck; he opened it and handed it back to Ed. The label read 'Dos Equis'; it was Mexican beer.

‘Thanks,’ Eddie said, and the man grunted. ‘Roseate spoonbills.’ He reached down to a small green bottle and opened it. Perrier.

Ed grinned. ‘I remember you always drank imported beer.’

‘I have a persuasive doctor nowadays.’

Ed took a long swallow from his beer. ‘What I want to talk about is a tour,’ he said.

The fat man sipped his Perrier and said nothing.

‘There’s a man with a cable TV company and he wants to put us on cable.’

‘I don’t know what you’re talking about,’ the fat man said.

‘He wants us to go around the country playing each other while he films it for cable TV. It might go on ‘Wide World of Sports.’’

‘ESPN? Home Box Office?’

‘Mid-American.’

‘What’s Mid-American? Where’s the main office?’

Ed took another swallow of his beer. ‘Lexington, Kentucky. It’s where I live now.’

Fats said nothing. He began dismantling his tripod. ‘I want to get back before dark.’

Going back, he went more slowly, seated behind the wheel. The water had turned dark and was as smooth as gelatin; it look as if you could walk on it. The sun was behind them now. Ed took off his dark glasses. They moved toward shore, passing the mangrove islands, for several minutes before the fat man spoke. ‘I haven’t heard your name for fifteen years,’ he said.

‘I’ve been running a poolroom.’

‘A waste,’ the fat man said.

‘It looked good at first. What do you think about this TV thing?’

‘Tell me about it.’

‘The contract gives us six hundred dollars each for an appearance, and twenty-five percent of residuals. That’s if ABC or somebody picks it up. And expenses.’

'Straights?'

'Yes.'

'How many cities?'

'Seven. We could start with Miami, in two months.'

The fat man finished his Perrier and put the bottle back in the deck well. 'I don't need it,' he said. 'I've been retired six years.'

They were approaching a clump of mangroves that was larger than the others, and he cut the boat toward it. There was a narrow opening in the plants, like a tunnel. Ed ducked and they went through. Now they were going down an alley of black water, with branches overhead and the sounds of insects. Wet mangrove roots, interlacing and darkly tangled, rose above them to an impenetrable cover of leaves. It was primeval, like something on a TV show about the dawn of man. It was the kind of place that had snakes.

Just as Ed was beginning to feel uncomfortable, the alleyway opened up and they were in a broad, dark lake surrounded by mangroves, lit dimly and without shadows by the darkening sky. It felt like church. The fat man had a pair of spinning rods and reels clipped under the gunwale at his left. 'You want to fish?'

'Why not?'

'Open that well in front of you. There's shrimp for bait.'

Ed pulled up the ring and looked inside. There was barely enough light to see the small shrimp darting around. He had done river fishing with worms and grasshoppers a few years before, when he was trying to find ways of just getting out of the apartment, but he had never fished in salt water or used shrimp. The other man handed him back a light spinning rod, saying, 'Careful with the hook'; and Ed gritted his teeth, reached into the well and managed to snag a shrimp. It tickled the palm of his hand. He handed it up to the fat man. 'Where does the hook go?'

'Through the tail. Cast near the roots, but don't snag it.'

Ed got another shrimp and put his hook through its tail. 'What are we fishing for?'

'Mangrove snapper.' The fat man's arm moved out lazily, his rod swung in a graceful arc; there was a plop and then ripples about a foot out from shore, off to the left. A perfect cast, which was what you would expect. Ed cast his own off to the right, also perfectly. The old arm.

Almost immediately they both had fish bending the rods. When they reeled in, the snappers were no bigger than his hand, but fat.

After twenty minutes it was too dark but they had accumulated a string of more than a dozen. When the fat man was putting the rods away, he said, 'Where would we play in Miami?'

'Benson's Department Store. At a new shopping center.'

'And after that?'

'Cincinnati, Chicago, Rochester and Denver.'

'At department stores?'

'One's a new movie theater. And there's a fair, near Albuquerque.'

The fat man flipped on his running lights and started the motor. He swung the boat around and headed toward the cut they had entered by.

'I hope there aren't snakes,' Ed said.

'No snakes, Fast Eddie,' the fat man said. He guided them through the dark tunnel and back out into the nearly dark bay. Then he pointed the boat toward shore and pushed the accelerator forward. The boat began to skip. Ed stood and held the rail again, feeling the spray on his bare chest now. Through the dusk he could see lights from Islamorada. They raced forward for about five minutes and then the fat man cut the motor back and they moved slowly in toward the dock, where gnats buzzed around a mercury vapor lamp. 'I don't like it,' the fat man said. 'It's cheap.'

'I can't quarrel with you.'

'Then why come down here to see me?'

They were a few yards from the dock now, drifting toward it. 'Well, Fats,' Ed said, 'I didn't have anything better to do.'

*

Fats' condominium cottage had three large rooms, with expensive-looking furniture. He played classical music on his stereo while he cleaned the fish. Eddie sat on the sofa and had another beer. It was dark outside now and a warm breeze came through the big screens. After putting the filets into the broiler, Fats came into the living room, still wearing only shorts, and said, 'How would we travel?'

'Rent a car or fly. Both.'

'First class?'

'Coach.'

'How much for hotel rooms?'

'Sixty a night.'

Fats shook his head. 'Cheap.'

'Forty a day for meals.'

Fats scowled. 'Do you like capers?'

'Capers?'

'On your fish.'

He had no idea what a caper was. 'I'll try it.'

Fats when back into the kitchen and worked for a few minutes. When he came out he had a large plate in each hand. He set them on the table. Eddie walked over and seated himself. It looked professional, with the browned filets of mangrove snapper at one side and green beans and some kind of noodles with pepper. Fats got him another beer and a Perrier for himself and sat down. 'I haven't shot a game of pool in six years,' he said.

'They'll never know,' Eddie said, grinning.

'My health is terrible.'

'It might do you good.'

Fats lifted a forkful of fish. 'Shooting straight pool in shopping centers? Staying at Ramada Inns?'

'We used to live better.'

'Don't talk about it,' Fats said. He ate the forkful of fish and then set his fork down. 'I'll do it for a thousand a game and a hundred for the hotel.'

'No way,' Eddie said. 'Not unless we hook into ABC.'

'Then hook into ABC and ask me again.'

'This guy tried, Fats. They told him they wanted to see footage first.'

'What's the front money?'

'Five hundred each, on signing. It comes out of the travel.'

'Get me a thousand a game and we'll talk. You can use my phone.'

'Fats....'

'Finish your supper, Fast Eddie.'

They had something called Key lime pie for dessert. Fats ate two pieces and then made small dark cups of coffee. It was like eating in the kind of restaurant Eddie liked back in the days when he had money.

'After you beat me in Chicago,' Fats said, 'I thought you'd be back.'

'Bert Gordon was crowding me.'

'He's been dead over ten years. They don't have anything to do with pool anymore – not them, anyway.'

'I know. But I never got back into it.'

'Why don't you do this tour by yourself? I'm an old man.'

Eddie finished his coffee. 'They want us both. The man with cable TV says we're a legend.'

Fats got up, went to the refrigerator, got himself a third dessert and brought it back together with a pill bottle from the top of the dishwasher. 'They wrote me,' he said.

'Enoch told me. You didn't answer.'

'I don't like TV. I read books and I work in my darkroom.'

There was a big case along one wall, packed with hard-cover books. On the coffee table were copies of *Audubon* magazines and *The New Republic*, along with a heavy, dark volume. Eddie had picked it up while Fats was cooking. *The Encyclopedia of Philosophy*. Fats finished his third dessert and took some the pills, chasing them with sips of coffee.

'What about those department stores and that fair? Aren't they paying for it?'

'I think that's where the expense money comes from.'

'Then get the cable man to pay more.'

'He hasn't got it. It's a new business.'

'Ridiculous,' Fats said. 'If we're a legend, we're worth more than that.'

'It's been over twenty years,' Eddie said. 'The kids never heard of us. All the big old places are torn down and they play eight-ball on coin tables in bars. It's all different.'

'Don't tell me about it.'

'How do you make it now?'

'Investments. Money-market funds and double-A bonds.'

'You've got room in here for a pool table.'

'I don't want a pool table,' Fats said. 'Walking around a pool table hurts my feet.'

'You shot the best straights I ever saw,' Eddie said.

'You beat me.'

'I should have stayed with Bert Gordon, even if he wanted half the money.' Eddie looked away toward the wall where a half-dozen large photographs of shore birds hung. 'I scuffed in the little places for a few years and then I bought the poolroom and got married. It was stupid. But they'd have broken my arms if I'd played anything important, and I wasn't going to give them half my money.'

'It's drugs and prostitution now,' Fats said, 'and the Teamsters.'

Eddie leaned forward. 'I want to do this, Fats. I want to get back in it again.'

Fats looked at him a moment and then spoke. 'I'll do it for eight hundred a game and ten dollars more on the meals.'

'It would have to come out of my share.'

'That's right.'

Chapter Two

It was so hot when he unlocked the front door and walked in that he had to go back out to the parking lot after turning on the air conditioner. He waited in Freddie's Card Shop next door for ten minutes and then went back into the poolroom. The twelve tables were covered with gray plastic. The ad would be in the paper tomorrow. The fat son of a bitch was going to get two hundred dollars of his money for every game of straight pool they played. And these good Brunswick tables with green wool baize on them were going to be sold. He had brushed the surface of each one carefully every morning for years; now they would wind up in the basements of doctors' houses or in fraternity game rooms at the university. Nobody would ever tip the cues properly again and sandpaper the edges of the tips and then rub them with leather to keep them from spreading out. People didn't know how to do that kind of thing anymore. He had been forced to put the last new baize on the tables himself with a tack hammer and a cloth stretcher, because the old man who did it before had died and there was no one to replace him. A damned shame. And now it was half Martha's, along with the apartment and the car. But no alimony; she had known him too well to go for that. First Martha, then Minnesota Fats; he could not seem to keep a grip on what was his. Bert had called him a born loser twenty years ago, and Bert as usual was right. For all he knew he was the best pool player ever to pick up a cue, and here he was at fifty, nearly broke.

He stood for a long moment looking around at the heavy tables, the cue racks on the walls, the metal talcum dispensers, the brown Olefin carpeting bought when half-drunk and never installed right, the Coke machine, cigarette machine, a stain on the green of Number Three, worn pockets on Seven, a loose cushion on Four, the table where a long roll on the right always had the ball curving off toward the rail. Behind the desk were a cash register; a Metropolitan Museum of Art calendar bought by mail by Martha and displaying a masterpiece on every page; four unread paperbacks, one by Graham Greene. On the desk sat an electronic time clock with a digital readout for each table and a by-the-hour setting that had gone up steadily for a dozen years; it was set now for two dollars an hour. The whole room was a rectangular box, its walls of yellow concrete block, its floor brown, its ceiling made of smokestained Celotex squares – all of it as familiar as the palm of Eddie's right hand, as familiar as a divorced wife.

He lifted the hinged part of the desk by the cash register and went back to the near-empty rack of private cues along the back wall above the radio. He got the key from his pocket and unlocked the middle one. It was a nine-hundred-dollar Balabushka with a linen-wrapped butt and a flawless maple front end. Its long ivory point was perfectly tipped in French leather; its center joint was polished steel. The cue felt good in his hand. It strengthened him. He unscrewed it carefully, found its snakeskin case under the desk, slid the two pieces in and strapped the cover down with its brass buckle. He turned off the air conditioner and the lights, and left carrying his cue. He did not look back.

His plane was late and he had to go directly to the shopping center, with the cue case and nylon bag beside him in the cab. The air conditioner didn't work properly; by the time the driver pulled into the huge parking lot, Eddie's shirt was stuck to his back with sweat and he was coughing from too many cigarettes. It was one forty-five; they would begin at two. Above the entrance to a huge Sears store hung a banner reading GRAND OPENING. Below it was a smaller banner; FAST EDDIE MEETS MINNESOTA FATS! And under this, TWO P.M. THURSDAY. ADMISSION FREE.

The table sat right out on the parking lot, on a wooden platform a foot high. It was surrounded by temporary bleachers with a few people in them. Four small black girls sat on the platform looking somber. In the bleachers were more kids, mostly black, climbing around and shouting. Eddie's stomach sank. There was a canvas canopy over the table to protect from rain or direct sun, but there was no protection from kids, from the sounds of traffic, from the unsettling oddness of daylight. The table was like a toy in the bright light. A little four-by-eight with a stupid red cloth. A woman's table.

A television camera on a rubber-tired dolly sat at the side of the table, and another at the end. The contract had said three but there was no third in view. Eddie looked at his watch. Five till two. Fats was nowhere in sight. He walked up to the platform. The black girls stared up at him, their eyes wide. There was a man standing there wearing a brown suit and a sports shirt. 'I'm Felson,' Eddie said.

'Fast Eddie?' The man looked at his watch.

'Where's your partner?'

'He'll be here.' Eddie set his cue case on the table and then felt the cloth with fingertips. It was slick and thin, at least fifty-percent synthetic. But he'd played on worse. The wooden platform was wide enough to hold the cameras and keep them out of the players' way, but there were heavy black cables. They ran across a few feet of asphalt to a green panel truck parked at a corner where the bleachers met. The truck had big letters reading WKAB – MIAMI. A man sitting in the cab waved at him and smiled, Eddie had seen none of these people before and had no wish to talk to them. People had been drifting in ever since his arrival, but the bleachers were still mostly empty. He glanced at his watch. Two o'clock. He looked past the panel truck at the shopping-mall lot. A long gray limousine had just pulled in from the highway and was coming toward them. There was another open space between sets of bleachers on the other side; the limousine drove through this and pulled up in front of the platform. A chauffeur in gray uniform got out, walked around and opened the door. A beautifully dressed, enormously fat man stepped out. It was Fats. He wore a dark blue cotton suit that fit him perfectly, a white shirt and a red tie. There was applause from the stands. With his cue case under his arm in the way a British banker might carry a rolled newspaper, Fats stepped nimbly up on the platform, nodded pleasantly to Eddie. He held his hand out to the man in the brown suit and the man shook it. The limousine pulled away slowly. Fats opened his case and took out the two pieces of his cue. 'Let's shoot pool, Fast Eddie,' he said.

The man in the brown suit was clearly some kind of manager, but he merely stepped off the platform when Fats spoke. He crossed the empty space of asphalt and seated himself in the second row of bleachers. The stands were about a third full now, and everyone was quiet – even the children. The black girls had moved from the platform and were sitting in a row on the second bleacher seat. They wore pinafores and had bright ribbons in their hair; they looked absorbed in what was about to happen.

The TV men, two kids in T-shirts and jeans, had positioned themselves behind their cameras. 'Keep the cables away from us,' Fats said to them. He was screwing his cue together, its butt was silver and the joint white. What was disorganized and confusing before, here around this red pool table in a parking lot, was now orderly. Fats tightened his cue, took a piece of pool chalk from his coat pocket and began chalking up.

A crowd of teenage boys began scrambling into the bleachers, lining themselves up in the fourth row. Out in the parking lot a dog barked. Two balls sat on the balkline. Eddie tightened his cue, slid the case under the table and took his position behind one; Fats stood behind the other. They bent and lagged. The balls rolled down, rebounded, rolled back up. Eddie's stopped an inch from the cushion, but Fats' ball was perfect – touching it. 'Your break, Fast Eddie,' Fats said. There was a director's chair at one corner of the platform. Fats racked the balls at the foot of the table, walked over to the corner and seated himself. Eddie stepped up to the head of the table, bent down, made his bridge and broke the balls safe. The cue ball hit the corner ball, jarred it loose, bounced off the two bottom rails and rolled back up the table. The two colored balls hit their cushions and returned to the triangle. It was a perfect break. A few people in the stands applauded. At least there were some who knew what was going on.

Fats walked up to the table and without even looking it over played safe, leaving Eddie much the same shot. They played it back and forth like that for a while until Eddie, squinting down the table at a blurred seven ball, missed the safety and left Fats open. He seated himself in the director's chair and watched.

At the place in the Keys, Fats looked old and wary; Eddie had guessed him at seventy, at least. But here, with his impeccable suit and his quick movements, he seemed far younger than that. And his stroke was beautiful as ever – smooth, controlled and relaxed. He circled the table as he had in Chicago twenty years ago when Eddie himself was young and hungry and had wanted to beat this enormous man more than he had wanted anything before in his life. Eddie watched him now as he might have watched the performance of a gymnast or a magician.

Most of the people in the stands would not know a thing about straight pool, and the safeties would be incomprehensible to them; but they were watching intently. Fats moved at an even, graceful pace, bending for his shots and pocketing them without fuss. There should have been a referee, but it didn't matter; Fats had the stage to himself and took it effortlessly. When he had pocketed fourteen balls, leaving himself a perfect break shot off the fifteenth, Eddie stepped up, racked the fourteen and sat down. Fats chalked his cue and went on shooting. More people came into the bleachers, silently. The TV cameramen dollied their cameras on rubber tires, pressed their faces against the viewers, walked quietly on their sneakers. Out on the parking lot, sunlight reflected from a car bumper would occasionally flash and dazzle; sometimes a person at a distance would shout to someone else; cars moved in and out. For a few moments a radio blared. Fats went on shooting and Eddie kept racking the balls and sitting again. It was beautiful to watch. He didn't care who won.

The limousine took them to the airport for the flight to Cincinnati. Eddie leaned back into the dark velvet upholstery, into the silence and cold air. Fats sat next to him, his eyes closed. He was still wearing the suit jacket, and the tie was still neatly tied. Finally Eddie spoke. 'I don't see how you do it,' he said. 'I was lucky to get sixty balls.'

Fats said nothing.

'In Cincinnati we'll be in an auditorium,' Eddie said. 'It should be air-conditioned.'

Fats kept his eyes closed, clearly resting. As they pulled into the Miami International Airport he turned over toward Eddie and said, 'You need glasses.'

For a moment Eddie was furious. The fat man had spoken as though he were a child.

'Eddie,' Fats said later, on the plane, 'you weren't hitting them like you used to.'

'I was a kid then. Now I'm middle-aged.'

'Middle age doesn't exist, Fast Eddie. It's an invention of the media, like halitosis. It's something they tame people with.'

'Maybe you're right.' But Eddie didn't feel convinced. The stewardess came with their drinks – a Manhattan for him and Perrier for Fats, and he busied himself with arranging his seat tray and then getting the cap off the little bottle and pouring the drink on top of the cherry in the plastic glass.

'I'm over sixty,' Fats said, drinking his Perrier. 'When I was supposed to be middle-aged I ignored it and it went away. You slow down a little. You get smarter. That's all there is.'

It wasn't true. Not for him. He didn't feel the way he had felt as a young man. He felt washed out, and frightened. 'My pool game isn't what it was.'

'Then practice.'

'I do practice.'

'How often?'

It was less than once a week. In his own poolroom, shooting pool bored him. He only shot balls around when there was nothing else to do with himself. He shrugged but didn't answer the fat man.

Fats folded his hands across his enormous lap and closed his eyes. Eddie looked out the window, at the gray mass of clouds below them, and finished his drink. Pool did bore him. There was no excitement in it anymore. And the sharp young kids – kids who played nine-ball and one-pocket – annoyed him. Just their need to win radiated a chill into him. But what else was there? He had tried selling real estate, a field where his charm and looks might have helped him, and it had been terrible. You had to kiss the asses of people you didn't even want to look at. The same with insurance. He had thought he was a hustler, and a good one, until he had tried the ordinary world of American business. It had turned his stomach and had frightened him. In five weeks of showing apartments and rental houses in Lexington, smiling and nodding and lying, taking inconvenient phone calls and answering querulous or bullying or misleading questions, showing places to people who he knew were only fooling around, he had made seven hundred dollars. Seven hundred lousy dollars, before taxes. It was no good and he quit it. But what else was there? These were hard times. International Harvester, the paper on his lap said, had closed down in Fort Wayne. People waited in line from before dawn for jobs Eddie felt he wouldn't last at for a week. Machine-tool operator. Pressman. Sanitation worker. And he hadn't finished high school. There was thirteen thousand in his bank account, and that was it. He would have to stop this drift in his soul or he would be unloading cabbages at the A&P.

On the other hand, here was Fats. Sixty-five, probably. He had no job, lived well, took pictures of birds, still shot first-class pool, ate beautifully and lived in the sun. He had probably never worked a day in his life. It could be done.

He looked over at Fats, whose eyes were open again.

'How did you do it, Fats?' he said. When Fats said nothing, Eddie finished off his drink and, feeling the alcohol now, went on. 'My life is falling apart, Fats. My wife's gone and my poolroom's gone. My pool game's down to half. Less than half. How in hell did you manage to avoid all that?

Fats looked at him and blinked. 'I went on winning, Fast Eddie,' he said.

That night in his room near Cincinnati, Eddie watched television but could not get interested. Fats was right; he needed glasses. He had been so relieved at the way things went at the shopping center after Fats showed up – so pleased that Fats didn't stalk off in fury or blame him for getting them into a rinky-dinky contract – that he hadn't cared how his own game had gone. Stupid. He got up and switched the TV off. It was nine-thirty. He undressed, put on his trunks and stepped out the door. The evening air was warm and humid. The pool was across a grassy area, and behind it the huge Quality Court cloverleaf shone in green and red over a smaller sign that read WELCOME, MINNESOTA FATS! He gritted his teeth at the absence of his own name and walked over toward the pool. It was good to feel warm air on his skin. He would get his name on the sign at the next place. And he would shoot a better stick here tomorrow than he had done in Florida. Fats was good, but he wasn't impossible. Eddie had beaten him before. And Fats was gross and old; and he, Eddie, was as lean and flat in the stomach as he had ever been.

The pool was empty and well-lighted. He dove into the

shockingly warm water and began swimming across and back, not stopping between laps. He did twenty and then swam to the ladder and got his breath, then he climbed slowly out.

Fats was sitting in a poolside chair, wearing his bathing suit.

Eddie had brought a towel. He dried his hair and face with it and then looked at the other man, who was regarding him impassively. 'You're right about the glasses,' he said.

Fats said nothing. Eddie dried himself and sat down. They were not far from the highway and he could hear traffic. 'That was my first game of straight pool in years,' he said.

Fats did not reply. They sat together for about five minutes and then Fats got up, walked ponderously to the latter and climbed into the pool. He treaded water for a moment and then began to swim, slowly and lazily. He was not a particularly good swimmer but he moved along. Eddie watched him and wondered again how a person so huge could handle himself so well. After a while Fats stopped and climbed out. Sheets of water fell from his chest and belly as he came up the ladder. He stopped halfway up, resting his arms on the ladder's banisters. 'Fast Eddie,' he said, 'you're going to have to do better. It won't work unless you shoot better pool.'

'Sixty balls is pretty good,' Eddie said.

Fats shook his head, and water sprayed from his dark hair. 'I missed deliberately to give you a chance,' he said.

Eddie said nothing and stared at the water. It was probably true. He had not cared enough about the game. Finally he said, 'Maybe we should play for money.'

Fats was seating himself in a deck chair. 'I don't want complications.' Fats had brought a towel; he began drying his hair with it. 'You said you wanted to get back in it, Fast Eddie. Why is that?'

'I need the money.'

'You won't make much.'

'If ABC picks it up, I will.'

'What if they don't?'

'Then it's a start,' Eddie said.

'How much money do you need, Fast Eddie?'

Eddie looked at him. 'Sixty. To buy a poolroom.'

'You can't buy a poolroom for sixty.'

'My old one was sold and I got half.'

'Maybe you're better off out of it.'

'I don't know anything else, Fats. I can't sell cars or insurance. I quit school after the eleventh grade.'

They were quiet for a long time. Then Fats stood up, picked up his towel and looked back to Eddie. 'You've got a long way to go, Fast Eddie,' he said.

The game was in a proper auditorium downtown. The first six rows of seats had been taken out and a four-and-a-half-by-nine Brunswick table put there below the stage. Shaded incandescent bulbs hung over the green wool cloth. Admission was four dollars a seat and the auditorium was almost full. Two cameras from the local TV station sat on the floor near the table, and another was on the stage. It was a professional setup, and Eddie felt relieved to see it. There was even a referee.

Fats sat in the high leather chair at the end of the table. Eddie pocketed a half-dozen balls and then walked over to him. People were still coming into the auditorium. 'I need to start hustling pool again,' he said.

Fats looked at him. 'You're not good enough, Fast Eddie.'

After a few minutes the referee came over to brush the table down for the game. The manager, who had met them earlier at the door, walked out onto the stage. 'Ladies and gentleman,' he said, 'there are legends in the game of pocket billiards, and we have two of them with us this evening. Mr Ed Felson, known as Fast Eddie. And the incomparable Minnesota Fats.' There was loud applause. The referee, finished with the brushing, placed two white balls on the balkline. He spoke softly, like a headwaiter in a pretentious restaurant. 'The gentlemen will lag for break.'

Fats stepped up to the table with composure; Eddie was thinking of what Fats had said and did poorly on the lag. He left the cue ball six inches from the rail while Fats' stopped a quarter inch from it. He would have to break them.

This table was a foot longer than the one in Miami; the distance made a difference. He had to squint to see the edge of the corner ball.

He managed a decent break but left the cue ball a foot away from the end rail. When Fats stepped up and shot, the cue ball came out of the bottom corner and rolled back up to freeze itself. Eddie concentrated on trying to return the safety, squinting hard and stroking with care, but he hit the corner ball wrong and spread the rack open. The audience was silent. It was a bad shot – embarrassingly bad.

Fats began to make balls. He ran out the fourteen on the table, breaking apart clusters with caroms from the white ball, and left himself in perfect position for the break shot, with the fifteenth ball near the rack and the angle perfect. Eddie looked down at his hands holding the Balabushka while the referee racked and then Fats broke, smashing the rack apart. Eddie tried to tell himself that it didn't mean anything, but it wasn't true. He felt each ball Fats pocketed as though it were a rude finger poking him in the chest. Fats' position play was flawless and he moved nimbly around the table, calling out to the referee softly. 'Seven ball, corner pocket,' and 'Thirteen ball, side pocket,' and so on, until fourteen balls were gone and the only colored ball left on the table was the one he had chosen a dozen shots back to leave for the break. And when he broke them open this time, sending balls spinning across the table with a solid, sharp stoke, there was loud applause.

Fats kept it up for another rack, and another and then another. It didn't happen often, but sometimes a player ran the whole hundred and fifty balls; it seemed now that Fats was headed that way. He had been good in the parking lot at

Miami, but in here he was superb. And Eddie felt he was going crazy waiting to shoot.

Finally, after running eighty-six, Fats got a bad roll and was forced to bank on the three ball. He aimed carefully and shot; the ball rolled across the table, hit the rail and came back to miss the pocket by a fraction of an inch. The table was wide open.

When Eddie stepped up he could see there were shots all over and a ball well-positioned for the upcoming break. It was a splendid lie, but he felt awkward looking at it. Had Fats missed on purpose? He tried to dismiss the idea, concentrating on the order the balls should be made in. A part of his mind did that automatically, the way a bank teller counted money. The twelve would go in the corner, with the cue following down for the nine, there on the bottom rail. Then the three, fourteen and six. Finally the eleven, so the cue would sit a foot below the side pocket on the break. He would break from the pale blue two ball near the rack. He did not look at Fats but bent to the table, drew back his stick and shot the twelve in. It fell neatly, but the cue didn't follow it far enough; he had to cut the nine a little more than was comfortable. This left him a bad angle on the three and he had to change his plan, shooting the six in first. He managed to recover and get the three in next. That was better. He ran the rest out and left the two, with his cue ball exactly where he wanted it.

While the referee was racking, Eddie walked to the corner of the stage where Fats was sitting. 'Did you mean to miss that bank shot?' he said softly. He had intended his voice to be friendly; it surprised him with its tightness.

Fats stared at him a moment. Then he said, 'Why should you care?' and looked away. Eddie stood there feeling foolish for a moment, and went back to the table. He felt impotent and angry. He wanted to hit someone.

The lie was perfect. The two was easy, and the natural angle of the cue ball would take it into the side of the rack to break them open for the next shot. Eddie tightened his jaw, bent down slowly, pulled the butt of the Balabushka back farther than usual and slammed into the cue ball. The cue ball smashed into the two, and the two whacked into the corner pocket, vibrated back and forth and came back out onto the table. He had shot too hard. The cue ball buried itself in the rack like a small, furious animal and spread the balls wide.

It was horrible. He stared for a moment and then turned away. He walked over to the corner, not looking at Fats as they passed each other. He seated himself, holding the stick loosely at its joint with its butt on the floor beside him. Fats began running the balls.

Eddie tried to look away a few times but it was no good; his eyes were drawn back to the table in front of him where the fat man kept moving crisply from one side to the other, barely straightening up between shots, making them one after another, clicking them into the pockets and always, always playing perfect dead-ball position.

In a monotone, the referee kept counting: 'ninety-eight, ninety-nine, one hundred, one-oh-one...' And then it became 'one forty-nine' and, on a simple pocketing of the seven ball in the side, 'One fifty.' Suddenly there was loud applause. The score was one fifty to nine. Eddie began unscrewing his cue.

Chapter Three

When he came into the kitchen, Jean was at the sink putting vitamin pills into little egg cups, and she didn't turn around. 'I'm giving you four C's, Eddie, because you smoked so much last night.' Jean was big on health. On the counter by the blender sat jars of lecithin granules, brewer's yeast and desiccated liver, together with a large bottle of safflower oil. During their first month together, it was croissants and scrambled eggs with chives; now it was vitamin pills and instant coffee.

He walked into the little living room with its rock maple furniture, and raised the Venetial blinds. The morning sun was already ferociously bright on the suburban lawns; it would be another hot day. Across the street their Pakistani neighbor came striding from the front porch of his brick ranch house to the Toyota at the curb, on his way to the laundromat he managed. Before the poolroom closed, Eddie and he would sometimes nod amiably to each other in the mornings – neighbors off to work at the same time. Now that was over; Eddie's working day would consist of one phone call. The Pakistani started his car and drove off. Eddie stood at the window, thinking now of Minnesota Fats. One fifty to nine.

Jean came in with the vitamin pills and a plastic mug of Folger's Instant. 'Maybe you'll beat him in Chicago next week,' she said.

Eddie took the vitamins and said nothing.

'You looked terrible last night.' she said. 'You shouldn't have stayed up so late.'

'I couldn't sleep. It hurts like hell to lose like that.'

'It isn't that important, Eddie.'

'If it isn't,' Eddie said, 'what is?'

'I've got to go to work. I'm already late.'

Donahue had another sex-book author – a woman who talked about freeing yourself up and discarding the old tapes. When Donahue began working the audience with his coy smiles and earnestness, Eddie turned it off and called Enoch's office. Enoch Wax ran Mid-American Cable TV from an office downtown. He never returned calls.

'Mr Wax isn't in right now,' the secretary said.

'What about my check?' Eddie said.

'Mr Wax didn't say anything about a check, Mr Felson. But he did say that Chicago has cancelled. They decided to use Rich Little for the program, instead. The impersonator.'

'I know who Rich Little is. Have you called Fats?'

'I left a message on his answering machine. If you'll come in Monday afternoon, we'll be running the tapes from Miami. Mr Wax will be in then.'

'I'll be there,' Eddie said.

Without Chicago, there would be ten days until the next match in Denver. Eddie found the Yellow Pages, looked up 'Eye Doctors' and was referred to 'Opthalmologists.' He picked one on Main Street, and called.

The doctor put drops in his eyes that made him squint and, evenutally, see watery haloes tinged with iridescence. In the trick chair that was uncomfortably like a dentist's, Eddie peered through eyecups at black letters on the far wall while the doctor clicked circles of glass into slots, making the letters go from black to gray and back again, making them elongate or compress, blur or sharpen. He chatted of the upcoming racing session at Keeneland as he slipped disks in and out of the machine, interrupting himself with questions about the clarity of what Eddie saw. There was some randomness to the progression, but gradually the white square with its letters became sharper, until the black edges had a delineation that was remarkable. In Eddie's stomach was a sudden hope: he had forgotten how clearly a man could *see*.

'That'll do it,' the doctor said.

'When do I get the glasses?' Eddie said.

'Eight days.' The doctor swung the machine away from Eddie's face and Eddie blinked.

'Can't I get them sooner?'

'Come in Monday.'

The red cloth on the table was even redder on the TV monitor, but you could see the balls well enough. Fats was shooting, and for a while his large body blocked the view of the balls – until the picture switched to the other camera. Eddie lit a cigarette, leaned back and tried to relax. It was the first he'd seen of the tapes.

'I'm really sorry about the money, Eddie,' Enoch said. 'Wednesday for sure.'

Eddie said nothing. He caught a quick shot of himself sitting and felt a strange embarrassment. There he sat, doing nothing, not even at the moment watching Fats shoot pool. It was the first time he had ever seen himself on television.

Fats kept shooting for what seemed an intolerable length of time. In the TV office, Eddie sipped coffee from a Styrofoam cup, smoked cigarettes and waited to see himself. He remembered the shot Fats would miss on – the three ball, a long cut into the bottom corner. The office was small and disorderly. There was no sound yet on the videotape, and the only noise was from the air conditioner in the window.

He got his glasses out and tried them carefully. They felt strange sitting on his nose and digging slightly into his ears, but the picture on the screen became clearer when he put them on.

Then Fats stepped up to the three ball and Eddie leaned forward in his chair to watch. Fats missed, but barely. It did not look as though he was doing it deliberately.

On the screen Fast Eddie stepped up. Looking at himself on television, Eddie was shocked at his inelegance, compared to Fats. He could have been the older man. The TV Eddie, holding the Balabushka, hesitated over the position for a long time before bending to shoot. And when he bent, he looked stiff.

'Well now!' Enoch said from his seat next to Eddie's. 'There you are.'

Eddie said nothing, watching himself with dismay.

He went directly from Enoch's little suite of offices to the shopping center and parked where he had always parked when the place was open for business. The big sign was down now, leaving rough holes in the concrete-block facade, and there was a card reading THIS SPACE FOR RENT on one window. The door key was still on the ring with his car keys. He opened up and flipped on the lights. It was a shock. There were only seven tables. Numbers Five and Nine had red tags with the word Sold. The water cooler was still there; after turning on the air conditioner he took a long drink. Then he folded the dust cloth off Number Four, got a box of balls and spread them out on the green surface. He took the Balabushka from its case, screwed the two pieces together and set the assembled cue on the table. He slipped his glasses from his pocket and held them up to the light; they seemed clean enough. He put them on and picked up his cue. It was three o'clock in the afternoon.

At first it was exasperating, and he thought it might be impossible. He kept looking over the frames as he shot. He tried holding his head higher, but then the frames split his vision. But he had seen other players shoot with glasses on; it could be done.

He held his head even higher, not bending down as far over the table as he was used to, and tried stroking that way. He made a few easy shots, but his neck felt stiff from it. And everything looked strange – the table seemed shorter. But the balls at the far end had a sharpness he hadn't seen for years. He kept at it, and by four o'clock he was getting the feel. It was a matter of the way he held his head and his body.

He remembered how awkward he had looked on television, and that had been without the glasses. He could feel the awkwardness in himself now and he hated it – he hated wearing these damned things on his face, hated the way his body felt as he bent over the table. He kept at it for the rest of the afternoon and eventually began making longer and longer runs of balls. He ended by pocketing nearly fifty without missing, cutting in several difficult ones across the entire length of the table. By that time, it was seven o'clock. Jean would be wondering where he was. He put the balls away, brushed the table, took his cue apart, turned off the air conditioner, and left.

Six years before, to celebrate paying off the mortgage on the poolroom, Eddie and Martha went to Northern California. It was Martha's idea; she wanted them to have the nude massage at a place she had heard of. 'You're naked,' she said, 'and all you can hear is the sound of the surf.' Eddie was willing to go along. He needed a vacation from fluorescent lights and the clatter of pool balls; and he hadn't been back to California in the twenty years since he had left, with Charlie, to try his skill on the road. They flew Supersaver to San Francisco, rented a Ford from Avis, and drove. But by that time Martha had a cold and she spent the time fussing with Kleenex and checking her watch while Eddie drove silently. He tried to ignore her. It was good to be back in California.

His masseuse was naked too. He hadn't expected that. They had told him to strip and then to lie on the padded bench on the wooden deck below. He was alone there on his stomach, looking out at the water, for ten minutes before she showed up. The surf was loud, and he didn't hear her come up but only saw, sleepily, her deeply tanned body. Her hair was brown and gold and she had freckles like smashed raisins on her neck and her breasts. She was about thirty.

'I'm Milly,' she said. 'Sorry I'm late.'

'I've been enjoying the sun.'

'Do you want oil?'

'Oil?' It sounded like a gas station.

'Some people like to be rubbed with oil. We use Chinese sesame.'

'Sure,' he said. 'I want the whole thing.'

She said nothing, but poured pale oil from a jar into the palm of her hand and rubbed it between her palms. Then she said, 'Relax now,' and began rubbing his back.

He closed his eyes and began to relax. It felt good. The woman's hands were firm and practiced in what they did. She rubbed his calves in long strokes, ending with a firm squeeze at the ankles. When she bent down, he could feel the heat from her breasts at the backs of his knees. The oil felt wonderful on his skin; in direct sunlight he was feeling baked and basted. The woman was humming something softly; he could hear her between the crashings of the waves below. Martha was back at the hotel watching TV and filling herself with Dristan. It was good to be away from her for a while. Milly began squeezing his ankles harder, around the Achilles tendon; it was painful in a way, and sent little sparks into his head; but there was something remarkable about it – as though his feet were being liberated. He began to get hard.

Milly was massaging the soles of his feet now, still humming. 'Your body's in good shape,' she said, 'for a man of your age. Do you work out?'

'Three times a week.'

'It shows. Do you eat meat?'

'Sure. Are you a vegetarian?'

'I'm supposed to be. But I had salami for lunch.'

She might fuck. But where would they go? No one else was on the little deck with them, but it was still public, and someone could come in. She was oiling his toes individually now, and running her fingers between them. He opened his eyes for a minute and looked back at her. She was facing him with her head down. Between his feet he could see the dark of her pubic hair.

'You're getting turned on, aren't you?' Her voice was matter-of-fact.

The bright sun seemed to burn away the need for indirection. 'What about you?'

'No,' she said, finishing with his toes. A moment later she

added, 'I like women.'

'That's a shame.'

'No it isn't. There's nothing wrong with it.' She began patting his feet. 'Let's talk about something else. Are you an athlete?'

'I run a poolroom in Kentucky.'

'Oh,' she said. 'My dad has a pool table in the basement. I used to play eight-ball. It was awfully competitive. Do you play pool?'

'Sure.'

'Isn't it very competitive?'

'It's better to win than lose.'

'Why?'

He didn't answer. He had heard that question before. She came alongside him now and began putting oil on the small of his back. 'Who cares whether you win or lose?' she said. 'What difference does it make?'

'If you're playing for fifty dollars a game, it makes fifty dollars' difference.'

'A hundred,' she said. 'The difference between plus fifty and minus fifty.'

'Be my manager,' Eddie said.

She leaned over and began pressing hard into the muscles of his back on either side of his spine, using more oil. Several times her breasts brushed against his side. 'It's the way men want to win just to be winning,' she said. 'It's a sexual thing – like war – and there's no end of it.'

'Is that why you like women?'

She laughed and rested for a minute. 'No.'

'You were being competitive when you said the difference was a hundred dollars.'

'You're right.' She began to knead around his spine. Her pubic hair pressed against his hip like warm bristles.

'You like winning arguments.'

'I don't bet money on them.'

That wasn't what we were talking about. Nobody bets money on wars either.'

'My dad did. He bet the Germans would win.'

'How'd he do?'

'Don't be facetious.' She began rubbing his ass, gently, using more oil.

'My my!' he said.

'Enjoy,' she said.

'Let's fuck.'

'Come on,' she said. 'Take it easy.'

He rolled over on his back, carefully so as not to fall off the bench. 'Come on, Milly,' he said, 'you can bar that door.'

'I told you,' she said, 'I like women.' She looked thoughtful.

'Give me a break,' Eddie said. 'Let's don't compete about this.'

'Well,' she said and smiled slightly. She reached out and took it in her hand. He had to hold himself back. 'That's the ticket,' he said. 'Climb on.'

'I don't even know your name.'

'Eddie Felson,' he said quickly. 'They call me Fast Eddie.'

'*Fast Eddie*!' she said. 'My God, Daddy used to talk about you.'

'Come *on*,' he said. 'Don't just stand there.'

'Fast Eddie,' she said. 'Jesus Christ!' And then, 'I don't have my diaphragm.'

'Then use your goddamned hand,' he said. 'Use the Chinese oil.'

Suddenly she laughed and squeezed him. 'I can do better than that.' She bent down to him.

'There you go,' he said. She put her free hand under him, moving her head up and down slowly, more or less in rhythm with the sound of the surf below them.

It was wonderful, and he took her address and phone number afterward, but he never called. It was the last time sex had been really good. On the way home from California he decided he needed a mistress, but it was years before he found one. And nothing with Jean ever turned out as simple and pleasant as it had been that day at Esalen with Milly. Nothing.

He had not realized before that day at Esalen how middle-class he had become, how his life had consisted of the business and the apartment and the marriage and the slow moving toward the grave. Cigarettes, Manhattans before bedtime, art posters on the family-room walls, *Time* magazine, anger buried so deeply that it seemed more a part of the rooms he lived in than in himself; television. Martha wanted a Mr Coffee and he wanted something from her, something sexual but more lasting than sex; and he swore at her that they had two coffee makers already and what they drank was instant. There were two toasters. The freezer was full of hard blocks of meat wrapped in Reynolds Wrap. To the front door came magazines that were never read, along with offers of bargain rates for new magazines, discounts on photo developing, discounts on travel. There were telephones in every room, even in the bathroom by the toilet, and there was no one he wanted to call.

When he found Jean after twenty years of marriage, he thought he had found a way out of the boredom and drift. But he was wrong. The affair was tepid from the start; Jean's life was, if anything, narrower and less interesting than his. The principal effect of the relationship resulted when Martha found out about it. When she said, 'I want a divorce,' he hardly blinked; his soul yielded Martha her point without protest. At the moment, the only difficulty he foresaw was in disentangling with Jean, who bored him by now as much as Martha did. It was only the next day, when Martha told him she had seen a lawyer and intended to keep their apartment for herself, that he realized he needed Jean. At least until he could find a place to stay.

He had lived a life without drama for twenty years, remembering from time to time the games of straight pool he had played as a young hustler – some of them filling the entire night until sunlight came shockingly through poolroom blinds and lay unwanted on the chalk-smeared green of the table. Urbana, Illinois. Fresno and Stockton in California. Johnson City. Valley Falls. Carson. Poolrooms with eight-by-ten tables and men holding bottles in paper sacks – men lined up to watch him as he played the local poolroom shark through the night. One pocket at forty a game. Fourteen-and-one straight pool for a hundred. Two hundred. Sometimes a thousand. A cone of yellow light hung above the table and the colored balls rolled harshly on the worn green, plopping into leather pockets. Paper money. Wrinkled old tens and hardedged new twenties, jammed into the table's side or corner pocket and tamped down by the heavy balls dropping on it. After he ran the final rack of straight pool or drilled in the winning ball in one-pocket or stiffened the final ball up the rail in a game of banks, he walked to where the money was, taking out the bills a few at a time and smoothing them. Then he folded and pushed them down in the front pocket of his pants, feeling the pressure against the top of his leg while he watched someone racking the balls up for the next game. A night in some small town could pass like that and seem a matter of minutes. Or in the bigger places there might be a crowd with college students in it – girls sometimes, trying to look knowing despite the innocent makeup they wore, girls in tweed skirts and angora sweaters. That would be 1960. Sometimes the man he played – in Columbus, Ohio, or Lexington, Kentucky, or in Chicago – would carry a name Eddie had heard for years but never before attached to a face: Shotgun Harry, Flyboy, Machine Gun Lou, Detroit Whitey, Cornbread Red. And then, in Chicago, at Bennington's in 1961, Minnesota Fats. They had played for over thirty hours, and for the first time Eddie lost. Up to then he had beat them all – all the local favorites, all the resonant old names heard in the poolroom in his teens where he had played five or six hours a day during his last years of school. He had beaten them all and earned his own name doing it: Fast Eddie. Because he liked raising the bet. He had come back and beaten Fats – beaten him until Fats quit with a shrug of the shoulders and with words that Eddie would never forget, no matter what else he might forget in the life that kept passing less and less intelligibly before him: 'I can't beat you, Fast Eddie.'

And then Bert had told him he was no longer on his own. From now on, if he played he would be backed by Bert's people and would share what he won with them.

That was the end of it, of the all-night pool with strangers, the travelling, the hotels and the sleeping all day. He never saw Bert again. He dropped him from his life as he had dropped the crippled Sarah in that same summer of his twenty-eighth year, in Chicago. Somebody had spoken of a poolroom for sale in Kentucky, and borrowing from Martha, he made a down payment, changing his life with a signature and the seal of a notary in a bright suburban bank. The lease on the apartment, and the marriage, followed like the sequence of shots, unquestioned, in a game of nine-ball.

Sometimes it all came back and he would feel again the late-night vigor from the old poolrooms and the bedazzled love for his old skill at the table. His win over Fats had become known around the country and, a few years after it, some fat pool player whom Eddie had never heard of started appearing on television. Watching the man shoot, Eddie was reminded of Fats and of the night he played him. It came back to him with a tightness in his stomach and a prickling of the hairs on the back of his neck. It was a Sunday afternoon and the poolroom was closed. When the television show ended with trick shots, Eddie went to the poolroom to play straight pool alone for hours, missing supper doing it, playing at first with the old excitement, remembering players like One-Eyed Tony and Wimpy Lassiter and Weenie Beenie; and then picturing Fats, silent and heavy and nimble, pocketing balls like a gross dancer. After hours of making shots in the closed poolroom, on the center table, alone, Eddie finally permitted the sensation that had nagged him since watching the stupid show on television. It was a feeling he could not bring himself to name. It was grief. The best part of him had died and he grieved for it.

Chapter Four

He had seen the woman before, in a situation much like this one. Both of them were waiting for something, and he could remember thinking how aristocratic she looked. She was about forty and had curly silver hair. She had been sitting in the tiny waiting room of Enoch's office when he came in. He took the only other chair, put his glasses on and began reading from a magazine called *Entertainment Monthly*. It was full of pictures of child actors, each giving the kid's credits in TV commercials. He glanced over at the woman from time to time. She could be a TV actress herself; she was strikingly good looking.

At a small desk, Enoch's secretary, Alice, was reading too. It was like a library. Eddie would have gotten up and walked out if he had anywhere to go. He didn't need the money right away, but it would make him feel better to collect something. So far the advance was all he'd been given, and most of that had gone to Fats.

After a while the phone on Alice's desk rang. She picked it up and spoke softly for a minute. Then she looked at the two of them apologetically and said, 'That was Mr Wax. I'm sorry, but he's tied up and won't be in until tomorrow.' Eddie looked at the woman sitting across from him. She was furious.

I've been here forty minutes,' she said, 'and I was here an hour yesterday.' Her voice wasn't bitchy; it was strong, clearly angry and had an accent. British.

'I'm really sorry, Miss Weems,' Alice said. 'It's this thing with the demolition derby Saturday....'

'I'll call tomorrow before I come in,' the woman said. She turned and walked out of the office. Eddie watched her leave. Her figure was terrific.

He stood up and stretched. 'Who's the British lady, Alice?'

'Arabella Weems. She's looking for work.'

'She looks like a movie star.'

'Come on, Mr Felson. She's a local woman.'

'I know. I've seen her someplace.'

'I promise we'll have your check tomorrow, Mr Felson.'

'I'll hold you to that,' Eddie said, leaving. He should have started a conversation with Arabella Weems. She was the most interesting woman he'd seen in a long time.

Alice had the envelope the next day at noon. The check was for the fee and expenses to Miami only: six hundred thirty-two dollars and change, after witholding. It was supposed to be over a thousand. 'I'd like to see Enoch,' he said.

'Mr Wax is busy,' Alice said. 'Why don't you have a seat?'

'I'm getting tired of this,' Eddie said, and looked up to see Arabella Weems coming out of the office with Enoch.

'Maybe in a week or two,' Enoch was saying. 'We'll give you a call if we need you.' And then, 'Hello, Eddie. I'm sorry about the check. Cincinnati hasn't come through yet. All I can do is call you when they do.'

'You have a contract with them,' Eddie said, looking at Enoch levelly. He hated the bags under Enoch's eyes, the way his tan suit and striped shirt gave him the look of an aging tout.

'I have indeed,' Enoch said, smiling sadly at Miss Weems as though she were his daughter. 'But what can I do? It's hardly occasion for a lawsuit.'

Eddie stared at him a moment and then turned and left. As he was going down the stairs to the street, he heard a woman's footsteps behind him. Outside in the sun, he stopped to light up a cigarette. When Arabella Weems came out the door, he nodded to her and said, 'Slippery, isn't he?'

She looked at him straight. 'I had an uncle like him. He was a revolving son of a bitch.'

'Any way you turn him?'

'You have it.' She was still angry but not so much so. He liked her way of talking, liked her accent.

'I'm Ed Felson,' he said. 'I think I've seen you before.'

'Fayette County District Court. June fourteenth.'

'That's right,' Eddie said. 'You were the one whose husband didn't show up.' They had been waiting together – like today – in divorce court.

'He was late for the wedding too.'

'Did he ever show?'

'Eventually.'

'And did it go all right?'

'Swimmingly.'

For some reason her toughness did not bother him. Her hair looked even better in natural light. 'Let's have lunch together,' he said.

She looked up at him. 'I don't know you,' she said carefully.

'Levas's makes a good Greek salad.'

She frowned. 'I've eaten Levas's Greek salad. Have you tried Japanese?'

'Japanese?'

'We fought a war with them. There's a new place on Upper Street.'

He had seen the ads, but never thought of going there. It was the sort of place chic people went, and Eddie did not consider himself chic. 'I don't understand chopsticks.'

'I'll teach you.'

The chopsticks were a nuisance, but he could eat some of the things with his fingers. She ordered sashimi for herself – raw fish that looked like Christmas candy – and negamaki for him. It was thin slices of beef wrapped around green onions.

'Are you English?' he said, picking up one of the little beef rolls with his fingers.

'I was born in Devonshire but I've lived in Kentucky fourteen years.'

She wore no makeup and her eyes were very dark. She had a book beside her on the table. The title was in a foreign language.

'The university?' he said.

'My former husband is a professor.'

That explained it – the book and the fact that he'd never seen her around. The university was something you read about in the paper. 'Are you an actress?'

She laughed. 'I want a job in television, but I'm no actress. I'm a typist – or was before I married.'

'What about the university?'

'I don't want to work at the university,' she said, sipping tea and looking up over her cup at him. 'I have spent the last twelve years of my life being a professor's wife. I would rather be a script girl for a sleazy TV company – ' She stopped herself. 'Perhaps I shouldn't say "sleazy." You have a connection with them.'

'They're sleazy. How do you like being divorced?'

'I left him six months ago.' She picked up a piece of sashimi deftly with her chopsticks. 'He may not have noticed yet.'

'I would notice,' Eddie said.

She looked at him but said nothing. They ate in silence awhile and then he said, 'I haven't got used to it yet. Starting over.'

'It's difficult.'

'Mine got most of what we had.'

'What was that?'

'Not much. A small business.' He did not want to say 'poolroom.' 'I'm scuffling now – like you.'

She raised her eyebrows. 'Scuffling?'

'Doing a show with Mid-Atlantic. A sports program.' He was willing to talk about himself with this woman, but he didn't want to tell her he was a pool player or that he had, until recently, owned a poolroom. 'It's not much money. I've got to find something better.'

'Me too.'

She appeared well off, even if she was looking for a job. Her hair was expensively cut, and the light jacket she wore fit her beautifully. She had education and looks and poise. She probably could do a lot better running Mid-Atlantic than Wax did.

'Can't you do better than typing?'

'I don't mind typing?' she said. She had finished her lunch and she pushed the wooden tray away now, along with the untouched rice. 'Right now I want to find work that doesn't require thought.'

'You look like you could do almost anything,' Eddie said.

'I don't feel that way.'

'Do you want dessert?'

She looked at him. 'I live a few blocks from here. Let's go to my place and have a drink together.'

Eddie blinked at her, shocked.

Her apartment was one large room on the fourth floor, with high windows overlooking Main Street. The walls, the ceiling and even the floor were painted white. When they came in, she went to the windows, pushed them open on their hinges, and the enormous white curtains at each side billowed out into the room like parachutes. There was a white sofa and two white chairs; one wall was covered with a white bookcase. From the center of the high ceiling hung a glass chandelier; it was shaped like an inverted bell, and etched. Over the sofa was a huge painting of a car driving through a field of yellow wheat. It was amateurishly painted – as though by a child – but bright and lively.

He turned from the picture and looked at her. She had taken off her jacket, and the T-shirt she wore showed her breasts were high, even though she was not wearing a bra. 'You're the first person from the university I've met,' he said.

She frowned. 'I'll fix drinks.'

The wall by the door held a unit with stove, refrigerator and sink. On a shelf over this were some bottles. 'Is Scotch all right?' she said.

'I'd rather have bourbon.'

'Okay.' She got a bottle down and a shot glass. She set two

tumblers on the sink and poured a shot and a little extra in each.

He took the drink and walked over to the window, ducking around the billowing curtains. He looked down at the street, full of traffic. He had never thought of living like this – right downtown. Across the street were Bradley's Drug and Arthur Treacher's and a clothing store. The sidewalks were full of people. He like it, liked the noise from it. He drank his drink, not looking back to see what she was doing. It was ten till two. He turned and saw her seated on the couch with her legs under her, looking up at him. She was holding her glass and it was still full. 'Nice apartment,' he said.

'Thanks. Shouldn't we make love?'

He looked at her. 'Don't be like that,' he said.

She looked as though she were going to say something, but she was silent, still looking up at him. Her nipples were evident under the white T-shirt. Her figure was fine and she had a beautiful face and voice and he liked her accent. But she did not arouse him.

'I'm not ready to make love,' he said. 'This is all new to me. This place...' he gestured back toward the windows '...and you. I don't feel at home yet.'

'I'll fix you another drink.'

'What for?'

'Maybe you'll feel more like it.'

Suddenly he was annoyed. 'Don't give me that,' he said. 'I don't think you're in the mood either.'

She looked at him.

'You just want to put the ball in my court.'

She hesitated. 'Maybe you're right.

'I am right. You're not the only sex that gets exploited.'

She frowned and took a long swallow from her drink. 'You're so good looking,' she said. 'I didn't think you'd be smart.'

He walked back to the window and looked out again. Far to the right, on the next block downtown, was a theater. He could just read the marquee.

He turned back to her. She had moved her legs out from under her and was now sitting on the sofa in the regular way, with her feet crossed at the ankles. She had nice feet, with pale blue shoes that fit her well. In the light from the window her complexion glowed. 'Have you seen *Reds*?' he said.

'Reds?'

'The movie. With Warren Beatty.'

'No.'

'Let's go see it.'

She looked astonished. 'At two o'clock in the afternoon?'

'They wouldn't play all afternoon if people didn't go.'

'People who have nothing better to do.'

'Do you have something better to do?'

She looked at him and then shrugged. 'Let's go,' she said.

It was a long movie, with an intermission in the middle, and they didn't get out until after five. Arabella was a lot more at ease when they came out. While they stood blinking in the bright afternoon light – startling after the dark theater – she said, 'I used to be a Socialist. My grandmother wanted me to work for the Party, but I never did.'

'Why did you come to America?'

'I don't like English men.'

'Laurence Olivier?' he said. 'Mountbatten?'

'They never asked me out.'

'I could have been a Socialist,' he said. 'Some people say it's subversive. What goes on in daily business is what's subversive.'

'Daily business?'

'Real estate. Insurance. Mid-American Cable TV.'

'I wish you could have met my grandmother.'

'Let's go back to your apartment.'

'Don't you have to be anywhere?'

'No. Do you?'

'I don't want to make love.'

'That's a relief,' Eddie said. 'I want to see your place again. I like all the white.'

'Eddie,' she said, 'you are a prince. What do you do for a living?'

He was silent awhile before he spoke. 'I don't want to tell you yet,' he said.

Eddie knocked, and then opened the door to Fats' room. Fats was in a Danish Modern chair by the window, almost completely obscuring the chair, his enormous bottom stuffed into it and hanging over. The plastic swag lamp above the table by him shone theatrically on boxes of junk desserts: King Dongs, Devil Dogs, Twinkies. He held a Ring Ding Junior – a kind of chocolate hockey puck – in his hand and was chewing on another. The television was off. Nothing else was going on in the room. Eddie felt for a moment as though he'd found him masturbating. He stood with his hand on the doorknob, silent, while Fats finished chewing.

'Come in, Fast Eddie,' Fats said.

Eddie walked in. 'I thought you were more of a gourmet than that.'

'Don't gourmet me,' Fats said. 'Do you think they sell French desserts in the Rochester Holiday Inn? Eclairs? *Mousse au chocolate*?'

Eddie shrugged and seated himself on the bed. 'That's quite a few of them.'

Fats looked at the Ring Ding in his hand with distaste. 'I am not overweight for nothing.' He took a bite, chewed, swallowed. 'What do you want, Eddie?'

'I was thinking,' Eddie said. 'Maybe we shouldn't finish the tour.'

Fats looked at him and said nothing.

'If "Wide World of Sports" isn't going to pick us up . . . '

'You've heard something?'

'If they haven't done it by now they probably won't.'

Fats finished his Ring Ding and picked up a package of Twinkies. 'Well,' he said, 'I've been enjoying myself. Relatively speaking.'

Eddie frowned. 'You're being paid more than I am.'

'And I'm winning.' He pinched the top of the Twinkie pack and zipped it open expertly – the way a wino opens a bottle of muscatel, Eddie thought. He slipped out a Twinkie, held it between finger and thumb. 'My game has been good and I enjoy the applause. Now that you've got glasses, you should practice.'

'It bores me, Fats.' He leaned forward. 'I mean it seriously bores me.'

'Then something's wrong with your head.' Fats popped the Twinkie into his mouth and picked up his glass of Perrier.

'There's nothing wrong with my head. I've just been away from serious pool too long. I'm too old to play for money.'

'Fats swallowed, drank some more Perrier and looked at him. 'Fast Eddie,' he said, 'if you don't shoot pool, you're nothing.'

'Come on, Fats. Life is full of things.'

'Name three.'

'Don't be dumb.'

'I'm not being dumb. How good is sex when you're half a man?'

'I'm not half a man.'

'I don't believe you,' Fats said. 'I can tell by the way you shoot pool.' He took another Twinkie out of its wrapper. 'Money comes after sex. Maybe before. I already know you don't have money.'

Eddie tried to be cool, but he wasn't able to smile. 'That's sex and money. Two things.'

'Self-respect,' Fats said.

'I can have self-respect doing something besides shooting pool.'

'No you can't,' Fats said. 'Not you.'

'Why not? I didn't sign a contract that says I shoot pool for life.'

'It's been signed for you.' Fats finished his glass of Perrier. 'I played all of them, forty years. You were the best I ever saw.'

Eddie stared at him. 'If that's true,' he said, 'it was twenty years ago. This is nineteen eighty-three.'

'August,' Fats said.

'I don't see so well. I'm not young anymore.'

'August fourteenth, Nineteen eight-three.'

'What are you, a calendar?'

'I'm a pool player, Fast Eddie. If I wasn't, I wouldn't be anything at all.'

Eddie looked at him in silence. Then, not ready to let it go, he said, 'What about the photographs? The roseate spoon-bills?'

'Roseate spoolbills?' Fats said. 'I am what I am because I shoot pool.'

'Maybe you're right,' Eddie said.

'I am right. Practice eight hours a day. Play people for money.'

'I don't know. . . .' Eddie said.

'I know,' Fats said. 'If you don't practice, your balls will shrivel and you won't sleep at night. You're Fast Eddie Felson, for Christ's sake. You ought to be winning when you play me. Don't be a goddamned fool.'

'You make it sound like life and death.'

'Because that's what it is.'

Back in Lexington, he tried it the first morning. Out to the closed poolroom at nine for eight hours of practice. When he unlocked the door he was shocked. There were only three tables in the room. He tried to shake off the dismay and began to shoot. It made him dizzy, walking around the table for hours in the near-empty room, bending, making a ball and going on to the next one. But he stayed with it doggedly, leaving for a few minutes at noon to get two hot dogs and a cup of coffee at Woolworth's. He shifted from straight pool to banks but got bored with that and started practicing long cut shots, slicing the colored balls parallel with the rail and into the corner pockets. His stroke began to feel smoother but his shoulder was tired. Was Fats right? Had his balls been shrivelling. He started shooting harder, making them slap against the backs of the pockets, rifling them in. Fats knew a lot. Loaded on junk food, his belly and ass enormous, over sixty years old, Fats shot pool beautifully; he had balls. Balls was what he, Eddie, had started playing pool for in the first place – that was what they all did. Mother's boys, some of them. He had been shy when he was twelve and thirteen, before he first picked up a pool stick. When he found out about pool and how well he could play it, it had changed him. He could not remember all of it, but it had even changed the way he walked. He smashed the orange five ball down the rail and into the pocket. Then the three, the fourteen, twelve, hitting them perfectly. He went on blasting at them, but missed the final ball. It came off the edge of the pocket, caromed its way around the table, bouncing off five cushions, and then rolled slowly to a stop. His back was hurting and he had a headache.

It was almost five o'clock. The phone at the room had been cut off for weeks. He went outside to the pay phone in the parking lot and called Arabella.

'I'd like to come over for a drink,' he said.

'I'm going to a play at eight. You can come for a while.'

'I'll bring wine,' he said, and hung up.

'Tell me about your husband,' Eddie said. He was seated in one of the white armchairs. 'Is his name Weems?'

'Harrison Frame.'

'Haven't I heard of him?'

'It would be hard not to,' Arabella said. 'He used to do a television show on the university channel.'

'You sound like you hate him.'

'Do I?'

'Yes.'

She took a thoughtful swallow from her wine-glass. 'I suppose you're right. Let's not talk about him. What have you been doing today?'

'Catching up on my homework.'

'Did you?'

'Did I what?'

'Catch up?'

'I only started.' He got up and went to the window, looking at the traffic in the street and the buildings across the street. 'I like this apartment a lot,' he said.

'Eddie,' she said from the sofa, 'I've been living in this one room for two months and I'm going crazy.'

'It'll be better when you find a job.'

'I'm not going to find a job. There's a recession going on. President Reagan speaks of recovery, but he's another one.'

'Another what?'

'Another goddamned performer, like my former husband. He's only working the room, our president. Counting the house and working the room. The son of a bitch.'

'*Hey*,' Eddie said, laughing. 'You sound terrible. Are you drunk?'

'If three glasses of wine makes you drunk, I'm drunk.'

'I'll get you something to eat.' He left the window and went to the refrigerator. There was a wedge of Brie and four eggs. Nothing else. 'What about a soft-boiled egg?'

'If you say so.'

He boiled her two of them and, since there was no butter, merely put them in a bowl with salt and pepper and handed it to her. He heated some coffee and gave her a cup of it black.

She was a real cutie, eating her eggs on the sofa. She hunched over them with her silver hair glowing in the late afternoon light from the big window, spooning them in small bites. He sat across from her and watched, sipping his own coffee.

'Thanks, Eddie,' she said when she finished. She held the bowl in her lap and smiled. 'Why don't you tell me what you do for a living?'

He hesitated. 'I was a poolroom operator until a few months ago. A long time ago I was a player.' He felt relieved; it was time he told her about pool.

'A poolroom?' She didn't seem to understand.

'Yes.'

'But what has that to do with Enoch Wax?'

'I'm doing exhibition games for Mid-Atlantic.'

'Then you must be good.'

'I lost the first two matches.'

She didn't seem to notice what he said. She just kept looking at him. Finally she said, 'Holy cow. A pool player.' She sounded excited by the idea.

'My game isn't what it was. I practiced all day today and it bored the hell out of me.'

She bit her lip a moment, then reached forward and set her empty bowl on the glass coffee table, next to a vase of orange gladiolas. 'It must be better than sitting around an apartment.'

'Not by much.'

She stretched and yawned. 'My God, Eddie! First you cheer me up, now I'm cheering you up. It could go on forever. Why don't you go to the play with us tonight? I can inveigle a ticket.'

'I've never seen a play.'

'All the more reason to go.'

'Maybe you're right. What's the name of it?'

'A *Streetcar Named Desire*. At the university theater. The principal character bears some resemblance to you.'

He looked at her. 'Stanley Kowalski or Blanche DuBois?'

'*Well*,' she said, 'a closet intellectual.'

'I saw the movie.'

'You didn't say Marlon Brando or Vivien Leigh.'

'Look,' he said, irritated, 'I'll go to the play with you. But I'm tired of being figured out. I'm not a rube. I know who Tennessee Williams was. I just don't go to plays. Nobody asked me to before.'

They had dinner at the Japanese place, and this time Eddie ordered Sushi. He had practiced with pair of pencils at Jean's apartment, picking up cigarettes. The trick was to hold the bottom one steady and use the top one like the jaw of a clamp.

The Sushi was easy. Arabella watched him for a moment but made no comment.

They met the other couple outside the theater, in the Fine Arts Building. The Skammers, both of them professors. He was history and she was math. They were both thin people, both in running shoes and bright cotton sweaters, both easy going and cordial. She had reddish hair and was pretty in an unexciting way. Eddie noticed the man was wearing a gold Rolex. The four of them had only a few minutes to go before curtain time.

He had never seen even a high-school play and was uncertain what to expect. The actors were college students, and from his third-row seat he could see their makeup. It took him awhile, feeling selfconscious with real people on the stage in front of him, but after a few minutes he got into it. He liked Stanley; the student playing the part had the right swagger. And Blanche was a genuine loser – the real thing – with her talk and her posing. Arabella, sitting by him, laughed aloud at some of Blanche's lines, but he didn't find her funny. It would be frightening to be like that, in that kind of a fog. It was fascinating to listen to her talk, to hear her construct her version of her past and Stella's, and to watch her come apart. He had seen pool players come apart like that. 'I have always depended on the kindness of strangers.' You didn't have to be taken off by men in white suits to fail like that. You could stay home, drink beer, watch TV. There was a lot of it going around.

That was what he said when Skammer asked him, afterward, how he like it. 'There's a lot of that going around.' They all stared at him and then laughed loudly.

'Eddie,' Arabella said, 'will you teach me to shoot pool?'

He was feeling good. 'Right now?'

'Why not? Do you know a place?'

'Shoot pool?' Roy Skammer said. 'That's a stunning idea.'

'Oh boy!' Pat said. She had been crying at the play and her face was streaked from it. They were walking along the campus on their way to the car.

'Don't knock it,' Roy said. 'In my sophomore year I did little else. I was a veritable Fast Eddie.'

Arabella looked at him. 'A Fast Eddie?'

'Of the Princeton Student Union.'

'There's a table at the Faculty Club,' Pat said. 'Roy is the eight-ball terror of arts and sciences.'

'My my,' Arabella said. And then to Eddie, 'Will you teach me?'

Eddie shrugged. He was still feeling high from the play. It was a warm night and the light from mercury lamps was filtered through tall trees along the campus walk. He was not really interested in shooting pool. His right shoulder was sore from the eight hours at the room that day and he was not interested in seeing how well Roy Skammer shot eight-ball. Roy Skammer seemed amiable and smiled a lot, but Eddie did not like him. He did not like the man's glib way of talking.

'I'd like to learn,' Arabella said.

'Okay, I'll show you how.'

'If you'd like,' Roy said, 'I'll help.'

There was a little bar when you came in the front door. A group of men were sitting there at a table drinking beer. A couple of them waved to Roy. 'There he is,' one of them said to Skammer; and another said to Arabella and Eddie, 'Don't play him for money.' There were dark oil portraits above the bar, probably of former professors.

The pool table was in a big upstairs room with an Oriental rug on the floor and more paintings of scholarly-looking men on the dark walls. It was an old Brunswick table with fringed pockets and a cloth with brownish stains on it. Skammer flipped a switch and yellowish lights over the table came on. 'Go ahead,' he said to Eddie. 'I'll go down and get some beer.'

Since they walked in the door, Eddie had felt a little stiff. He had never been around professors before, had not even been on campus in his years in Lexington. The Skammers made no attempt to impress with their education, but he felt inhibited. They were the kind of couple you sometimes saw on the street or read about in magazines. But when he got a pair of cue sticks out of the wall rack and gave one to Arabella, he began to loosen up. He showed her how to hold the cue at the balance and to keep her left arm straight. He had her stand sideways at the table and bend at the waist, letting the stick slide across her open-hand bridge. She concentrated and did it surprisingly well. Pat had played before and didn't require instruction. Watehing Arabella shoot the white ball around, she said, 'You're pretty damned apt, Weems'; and Arabella, bending to shoot at the seven ball, said, 'You don't type a hundred forty words a minute without being apt.'

'Come on,' Pat said, nobody types one forty. The ribbon would disintegrate.'

Arabella frowned harder at the seven ball, then bit her lip. She pumped her right arm and hit the cue ball surprisingly hard. The seven rolled across the table and into the side pocket. Eddie could have hugged her. She looked up at Pat and said, 'On a good day I do one fifty. Haven't lost a ribbon yet.'

Roy came in with four cans of beer and handed them out. 'Let's play some eight-ball,' he said impatiently. 'I want to show my trick shots.'

'I'll rack,' Eddie said.

'Wait a minute!' It was Arabella. 'I don't know the rules.'

There had been some two-piece cues locked at one end of the wall rack. Roy went over and unlocked one of them. 'We'll explain it as we go along.' He came back with his cue. It was an old Wille Hoppe, with a brass joint. 'Pat and I will be partners, and Arabella and Ed. The losing team buys the next round.'

'You're on,' Arabella said, looking at Eddie.

'Two out of three games,' Pat said.

'Sure.' Arabella began chalking her cue the way Eddie had showed her. 'That'll give me time to get in stroke.'

The women went first. Pat broke weakly and missed an

easy shot on the four ball. That gave the Skammers the solids. Eddie explained to Arabella that they had to shoot the striped balls in; he showed her how to make the thirteen in the corner. She was still awkward with her cue, but she concentrated and shot it in. But her position was terrible and she miscued on the next one. Roy went to the chalk dispenser and banged powder into his left hand. Too much of it, making a little cloud. 'I want everyone to pay complete attention,' he said. He didn't seem entirely to be kidding. 'You are about to see eight-ball shot the way it was intended to be shot.' He walked to the table and pointed at the two ball with his stick. 'I am going to bank this blue ball into the side pocket right here' – he pointed to the pocket – 'and the cue ball will roll into position for the six afterward. Very few white people understand this kind of playing.'

'Quit grandstanding, Roy,' Pat said. 'Make the shot.'

'Certainly,' Roy said. He bent down, stroked, then stood up again. It was not a difficult bank, but Eddie felt he would miss it; it needed inside English to avoid kissing the cue ball. Roy bent down again, and to Eddie's surprise used the inside and English and made the two. The cue ball rolled over to the six.

Pat applauded. Looking at Eddie, Roy said, 'Would you like to double the bet?'

'Sure,' Eddie said.

'That's *two* rounds,' Roy said. He bent and shot the six ball in, and then the one. But after he made the one, his cue ball rolled too far, giving a bad lie on the three. He tried another bank, missed it, but the cue ball rolled by luck to the top rail. The striped balls were clustered at the other end of the table and it didn't look as though anything could be made. '*Well,*' Roy said, 'anybody want to bet a few dollars on the side?'

Eddie looked at him and said softly, 'You don't want to do that.'

There was an embarrassed silence for a moment, and then Arabella spoke up crisply. 'I'll bet you twenty dollars we win.'

'So that's it,' Roy said. 'Those instructions Ed gave you were a front. In fact you're the the United Kingdom pocket billiards champion.'

'You'll find out,' Arabella said. 'Put your money where your mouth is.'

Roy laid his cue stick on the table and slipped his wallet out of his jeans pocket. He took out two tens. Arabella was carrying a leather purse. She took out a twenty. 'I'll hold the stakes,' Pat said and took the money.

Eddie stepped up to the table. The only shot on was the eleven and it was a killer: it sat a few inches from the bottom rail and a long way from either corner pocket. The cue ball was nearly frozen to the top rail. Eddie leaned his stick against the table and put on his glasses. He picked up the cue and said, 'I'll go for the eleven,' and bent down.

'If you make it, I'll eat it,' Roy said, kidding and not kidding.

'Fine,' Eddie said and drew back. Through his glasses the red stripe on the eleven was as sharp as the edge of a crystal wineglass. He stroked the cue hard and loose, smacking powerfully into the cue ball. The cue ball hurtled down the table, sliced the eleven paper-thin and bounded off the bottom rail, its path barely altered by contact with the eleven. As the cue ball came flying back up toward Eddie, the eleven rolled slowly, its red stripe turning over and over like a hoop. The white ball sped around the table, crashed into a cluster of balls and stopped. The eleven ball, still moving in its unhurried way, arrived at the mouth of the corner pocket, hesitated a moment at the edge, and fell in.

'Jesus Christ,' Roy said.

Eddie ran the rest and banked the eight into the side. Nobody said anything while he did it. Then he handed the rack to Roy. The thing about eight-ball was that you only needed to make eight of the fifteen. When the balls were ready. Eddie slammed the cue ball into them, pocketed two and proceeded to run out the solids. He played it like straight pool and nudged the eight into an easy lie while making one of the earlier balls, and then pocketed it on a simple shot. During all this his cue ball never touched a rail. His position on every ball was perfect.

'Jesus Christ,' Roy said when it was over. 'Do you need a manager?'

Arabella spoke up. 'He's Fast Eddie, Roy.'

'Come on. . . .' Roy said.

'He's Fast Eddie. You've been hustled.'

Afterward, when he was taking her home, Eddie said, 'There are thousands of guys like him. They all play eight-ball.'

'How many are there like you?'

He hesitated. 'Not many.'

'I should think not.' She stopped at the door of her building. 'You looked anything but bored.'

'I wanted to beat him.'

'Maybe that's the secret.'

He spent the next day practicing. His shoulder ached from the day before and by noon his feet were tired, but he took an hour break before lunch to work out in the gym and that made his shoulder and feet feel better. He drove directly back to the poolroom afterward and banked balls up and down the long rails for several hours. It was only when he stopped for a break at three-thirty that he realized the glasses were no longer a problem. He could see clearly and he no longer had to tilt his head in an uncomfortable way to use them.

He had not spoken to Martha for weeks and had no idea how long the last tables would be there before being sold. The Coke machine and the cigarette machine were gone. The telephone had been taken out. On the faded brown carpet with its cigarette burns and dust were large dark rectangles where the other tables had sat for fifteen years. It would be at least a month before the pasta-and-croissant place moved into the room; he knew they were having trouble financing. Martha's lawyer's ad, offering pool tables for sale, still appeared daily in the classifieds. He always checked it in the morning paper and it always tightened his stomach to see it: FIRST QUALITY POOL TABLES, IN EXCELLENT CONDITION.

There wasn't any point in thinking about it. It had wiped him out for a week after the settlement, and that was enough. There was a certain pleasure in getting it done with, and another kind of pleasure in being out here himself with the blinds drawn and a Closed sign in the window, shooting balls into pockets. He kept it up until the pain in his shoulder came back and got worse than ever. But he felt better leaving the room than he had the day before. His game was sharper. The day had gone by quicker, even if he allowed for the workout at the gym. He would be playing Fats on Saturday in Denver. Maybe things would go differently.

It was another supermarket opening, outdoors like the first had been, but this time they played in front of packed stands and with three TV cameras. During the middle of the game, Eddie broke loose after a string of safeties and ran sixty before being forced to play safe again. When Fats stepped up to shoot, he said to Eddie, 'You're hitting them better,' and Eddie said wryly, 'Practice.'

But Fats had already scored over ninety balls – fifteen or twenty at a time – before this, and when he stepped up he ran the rest of them out. The score was 150-112. There was no time for talk afterward; Eddie's flight to Lexington via Chicago was leaving in an hour. Fats would be going to Miami a few hours later.

He planned to practice the next day in Lexington but woke with a sore throat and a tenderness in his joints that meant fever. It turned out he had the flu and was sick for three days. He called Arabella on the second morning, after Jean was out of the apartment. 'I get over things like this pretty quick,' he said.

'It's a nuisance anyway,' she said. 'Can I bring you something?'

'Arabella,' he said, 'I should have told you. 'I'm living with somebody.'

'That's another nuisance.'

'It's not a permanent thing, with Jean. I should have told you.'

'Eddie,' Arabella said, 'I don't have time to talk.' Her voice was like ice. 'I'll see you around,' Eddie said, and hung up.

On the fourth day he was still weak, but he took his Balabushka and drove out to the poolroom. Nothing was changed on the outside, but when he unlocked and went in, there were no more pool tables. Not one. He stood there with his stomach knotted for a minute before closing the door and locking it. It was all over. He walked along the mall, past the A&P and Freddie's Card Shop, and into the little bar-and-grill. They had just opened up and he was the only customer. 'Give me a Manhattan, Ben,' he said to the bartender, seating himself. He still had the Balabushka in the case with him; he set it in front of him on the bar.

He was hung over the next morning and did not want to be devious with Jean. He came into the kitchen and said, 'I think it's time I moved out.'

She was rinsing a plate and she went on rinsing for a minute. 'Where, Eddie?'

'The Evarts Hotel. I can get a room for twenty-eight dollars a night.'

'And when?' They could have been talking about mowing the lawn.

'This afternoon.'

She put the plate in the dish drainer and looked at him coldly. 'I'll fix you a supply of vitamins.'

Before he unpacked, he found the history department number in the directory and called Roy Skammer. Professor Skammer was just back from class, the secretary said. Could she say who was calling?

'It's Ed Felson.'

There was a wait and then Skammer came on the phone. 'Fast Eddie,' he said.

'I have a favor to ask. I'd like to use the table at the Faculty Club for practice.'

'You aren't good enough already?'

'The table I was using is gone.'

'Gone?'

'My ex-wife sold it.'

'Jesus!' Skammer said. 'Put not your faith in things of this world.'

'How about it – the club?'

'The table isn't played on much, but the committee takes a dim view of outsiders.'

'What about in the morning?'

'That might work. They open at seven for breakfast. Nobody shoots pool that early.'

'How do I get in?' He might sound pushy, but it was necessary to be pushy. If Skammer wanted so badly to be thought a nice guy, then let him worry about it.

'Well...' Skammer's voice sounded doubtful. 'Why don't you come by early tomorrow and tell Mr Gandolf you're a guest of Professor Skammer. I'll give him a call when we finish.'

'Where do I find him?'

'In the club library. All the way back on the first floor.'

His room faced a back alley; he was awakened at five by a garbage truck and couldn't get back to sleep. He had lain awake for hours the night before, looking at the dumb wallpaper and the little sink in the corner of the room and thinking of Arabella. He should have told her from the beginning that he was a pool player. He should have told her about Jean. It was stupid.

He lay in bed now, waiting for daylight, and thought about her. It had never occurred to him that he could have that kind of woman, with her high-toned good looks – the clear jawline, the look of amused inteligence. He was crazy about her voice, her accent, the words she chose in the sentences she made. And she liked him. She even admired his pool game. He had almost blown it, but it wasn't blown yet. He began to want her strongly, more that he had ever wanted Martha or Jean, more than anyone since that afternoon at Esalen when Milly – overtanned and sweaty in the sun – had bent down and taken him in her mouth. He felt like a teenager in the first throes of lust; he couldn't get the thought of her out of his head. He got up, washed his face in the sink, and shaved. He rinsed the lather off in the shower, and by the time he had dried off and was getting his clothes on, there was gray light at the window and his desire was gone.

He left the room at six-thirty and was at the door of the Faculty Club, carrying his cue case, when the old man opened it up.

After such little sleep, his energy at the table was surprising. He had the room to himself, hearing only the occasional clink of dishes from the dining room below; and he shot the balls with concentration and force, hardly missing at all for hours. The pockets were a shade too easy – wider open than they should have been, and a bit filed down so that doubtful shots would fall in. But he didn't mind that; it might help his confidence, and his confidence needed help. He kept making balls, setting up difficult shots for himself and pocketing them remorselessly. He felt sharp and clear, and the fact that he wore glasses seemed now to mean nothing.

For the rest of the week he came in every morning, after walking across the campus at dawn. He would drive out South Broadway, the wide avenue nearly devoid of traffic that early, and leave his car in the university lot marked for visitors. Then he would walk across the campus to the Faculty Club, following a long, curved concrete pathway under high dark trees, crunching underfoot the leaves from overnight. It was too early for students, but he would pass glum maintenance men in dark uniforms, puffing on cigarettes, or nurses on their way to the university hospital with white uniforms half covered by jackets. Few people talked at that time of day; something deep in Eddie responded to the silence. He liked the early-morning life of this big place, with its brick classroom buildings, the new high-rise dormitories off to the east, the solid old library that he walked by every morning. He wore his leather bomber jacket with the collar turned up against the chill, carried his cue case under his arm and walked briskly. It felt like a new life.

By Wednesday he had developed a routine. He would spread the fifteen colored balls out at the foot of the table, place the cue at the other end, pick the ball he would break the next rack from, and then try to run the other fourteen. He gave himself a difficult shot to begin with so the exhilaration from making it would carry him on through the rest of the rack. If he made it. When he missed, he set it up again and kept trying until he got it. It was painful at times to miss repeatedly, since the opening shots he set for himself were tough ones, but he needed that too. His game might look good to a person like Skammer, as the punches of a professional fighter would feel devastating to a street punk; but he wasn't preparing himself for street punks. He would be playing Fats again in a week. It was time he started beating him. He could run a rack of balls easily enough, if he made the first one. But that wasn't enough. This was an easy table and there was no pressure; he should be running in the seventies and eighties. As a young man he would never have missed on a table like this.

Every now and then people would come in to watch him shoot. Young professors, sometimes carrying their coffee cups from breakfast. They would stand around quietly for a half hour or so and then leave. No one asked to play and he was glad of that. He did not feel like an interloper at the Faculty Club after the first week; he felt he belonged there. Increasing the length of his runs was uphill labor, and there was a suspicion it might be hopeless, that whatever fire he once possessed had been extinguished; but he kept shooting pool. The difference between now and the way it had been before the tour with Fats was that now he could see the alternative more clearly.

At their next match, in St. Louis, he did better but Fats still beat him. One fifty to one forty-two.

'I don't know what the hell to do,' Eddie said afterward. 'There's no money in this tour. When it's over I'll have less than I started with.'

'People won't pay to watch pool games. We're not rock singers.'

'That's the fucking truth.' Eddie lit a cigarette. 'I don't know how to make a living, Fats. I have to get another poolroom.'

'I've already told you all I have to tell.' Fats stood up from his bleacher seat and walked over to the table where the game had just finished. They were waiting for a car to take them to the airport and the car was late.

'I remember what you told me,' Eddie said. He got up and came over. There were still a dozen or so people in the bleachers, but they were not watching Fats and Eddie anymore. 'You told me I need balls. There's truth in that, Fats, but no money.'

'That's debatable.' Fats picked up the three ball and sent it spinning around the table. It went three rails and fell in the corner pocket. In the parking lot a car began honking in short bursts, then stopped. 'I also told you to play in tournaments.'

'That's ridiculous,' Eddie said. 'The World Open is in New York this winter and first prize is eight thousand. The entry fee is five hundred, and you have to stay in New York for two weeks. There's only money in that if you come in first.'

'Then come in first,' Fats said.

'Against Seeley and Dorfmeyer? *You* couldn't beat them, and I can't beat you.'

'Don't tell me who I can't beat, Fast Eddie.' Fats took the

seven ball and did the same three-rail toss, this time plunking it into the corner pocket on top of three.

'Then you play the World Open.' Eddie looked up into the stands a moment, where a group of people was finally getting up to leave. It had been a dull crowd and their applause had been light, even for Fats' final run of forty and out.

'I don't need to play the World Open. When I finish this tour next month, it'll be the last game of pool I'll play. I don't need it anymore. You're the one who needs it.'

'I've never played tournaments, Fats. A hustler didn't do that. You didn't want to come out of the closet.'

'The times have changed, Eddie. Straight pool is out of style. You could stay in that closet and starve.'

'Or sell real estate.'

Fats looked at him thoughtfully. 'The money's in nine-ball.'

'I don't play nine-ball.'

'You can learn.'

'Nine-ball is a kid's game. It's what they play in those bars where you put a quarter in the table and another in the jukebox.'

'They play for a lot of money in some of those bars.'

'In Cincinnati you said I wasn't good enough.'

'You got better.' Fats looked at him. 'Do you know what Earl Borchard made last year in nine-ball tournaments?'

'No.'

'Sixty thousand. And I don't know what he made hustling on the side. They say he plays the bar tables.'

'How would you know how much money he makes?'

'In *Billiards Monthly*.'

Eddie got the magazine at the poolroom but never did more than flip through it. It was mostly ads for pool-table and cue-stick manufacturers, or books on trick shots. There were 'profiles' of young players – usually a few lines of praise under a glossy photograph of somebody holding a pool cue. It made him vaguely sick to look at it. There were also ads for nine-ball tournaments, in places like Asheville and Chattanooga and Lake Tahoe. 'Sixty thousand?'

'That's in seven tournaments. About ten weeks' work.'

He'd had no idea there was that much money it it. 'He's got to pay expenses.'

'You paid expenses when you were on the road. Did you ever make sixty thousand?'

'Borchard's the best. What does the second-best make?'

'Don't ask.' Fats turned back to the table. 'If you don't trust your eyesight, those bar tables are better. Smaller.' He looked at Eddie. 'They play eight-ball on them too. A man can make a good living at eight-ball in bars.'

'Eight-ball is stupid. There's nothing to it but slopping around.'

Fats looked at him silently a minute. Then he went to the place at the end of the table where the balls were kept, squatted down and took them out. He racked them into a triangle, with the black ball in the center. 'Let's play a game of eight-ball,' he said. He got his cue case from the bleacher and took his silver-wrapped Joss from it. Eddie watched him in disbelief. You did not think of a player like Minnesota Fats playing eight-ball. Fats tightened his cue, went to the head of the table, took his stance and blasted the balls apart. The weight behind his stroke was impressive. Balls went everywhere and two of them fell in. 'In the first place,' he said, 'you have to make one on the break.'

'You can't be sure of that.'

'On a bar table you can,' Fats said. 'I'm going to take the stripes.' A striped ball and a solid one had fallen in on the break, giving Fats his choice. 'Do you know why?' He was like a schoolteacher at the blackboard.

Eddie looked over the table. 'Those four stripes in the open.'

'Not at all,' Fats said. 'In eight-ball the main thing is not to leave a shot. Not in the important games. Sometimes you let him have a few balls when it's time to. You have to control it. I'm shooting the stripes to control the solids.' He bent down and made the thirteen ball. There was movement in the bleachers. Eddie looked up to see the half-dozen remaining people coming down to the front row to watch.

'I'm going to shoot the nine now,' Fats said, 'and I'm going to make my position a few inches off, for the twelve. The kind of thing that happens now and then.' He bent, shot the nine ball in. His cue ball rolled too far, leaving a difficult shot on the twelve. It would have to be banked. 'Now, the thing about the twelve,' Fats said, 'is that I don't have to make it. Watch.' He banked the ball across the side and missed it. The cue ball rolled to one side of a cluster of balls, where the only shot was on the fourteen ball. 'If I'd made it, I'm fine. If I miss it, he has nothing.'

'I know how to play safe,' Eddie said.

'I'm talking eight-ball safe,' Fats said. 'I'm trying to tell you that if you learn how to control this game you can make a living at it.'

'In bars?'

'In bars, Fast Eddie.'

Eddie thought about it, about the games of eight-ball he had played with Skammer. 'In the South?'

Fats looked at him. 'Winter's coming on.'

'You've been talking nine-ball tournaments,' Eddie said. 'Now it's eight-ball.'

'You have to crawl before you can walk.'

'What does that mean?'

'You're not ready for nine-ball, Fast Eddie. Borchard would walk right over you, and so would a half-dozen others. You can play eight-ball on brains and experience, and you've got those.'

'Thanks.'

Fats started taking his cue apart again. The people behind him in the stands were watching him, fascinated. 'If you do it for six months, it might put you back where you were. Then you can take up nine-ball.'

'I hate the punks who play nine-ball.'

'It's that or real estate,' Fats said.

'Where would I play eight-ball for money?'

'When we get to the airport I'll give you a list. Our car's coming.' Fats pointed to the parking lot. A blue car was driving up. It had a sign on its side reading Airport Service.

'Where would you get a list of places to play eight-ball?'

Fats put his cue in its case. 'How do you think I made the money to retire on? While you were racking balls in Kentucky, I was putting quarters in slots in North Carolina.'

Eddie stared at him. 'Wearing that suit?'

'They make blue jeans in my size. It costs twelve dollars extra.'

Chapter Five

When he was a kid in Ohio, you never broke the balls with a jointed cue or with the white ball; you used a house cue stick and a special dull brown cue ball. Charlie taught him that, and it was Charlie who bought him his first Willie Hoppe cue, with the black leather wrappings on its butt and the brass joint. 'You don't *slug* them with this, Eddie,' Charlie said. 'The joint can't take it.' In those days Eddie would pick out a club of a cue – twenty-two or twenty-three ounces – and smash the rack open with it before using the Willie Hoppe. It was all different now. The balls were made of something called phenolic resin, and their colors were brighter: the old dark green stipe on the fourteen was now a bright emerald with a glow to it, and the nine was canary yellow, like something in Walt Disney. You broke the rack with the white ball now and, with a handmade Balabushka cue, slammed them as hard as you could. You couldn't ruin the steel joint.

Eddie took a deep swing and blew the eight-ball rack open. The three and the seven fell in, but the cue ball stopped near the foot spot and didn't follow through to rebreak the balls the way he intended. He looked over the spread, checking out the five other solids and then the eight ball, which had to be made last. There was no problem with any of them; on a table this small, they were all simple enough. He concentrated, took care, and ran them out.

'You shoot a good stick.' It was a different bartender from the one yesterday – a blond kid in a white apron. At four in the afternoon, two old men were huddled over boilermakers at the far end of the bar; Eddie was the only other customer.

'Thanks.' Eddie laid his cue stick on the table and walked over. 'Let me have a draft.' He tried to be pleasant and casual, although he did not feel that way.

The kid drew one and set it on the bar. 'I haven't seen you here before, have I?'

'I came in yesterday.'

The kid nodded and began drawing a beer for himself. 'You shoot eight-ball like a pro.'

Fats had told him not to hold back, to play his best stick, or nearly. Hold back ten or fifteen percent if it seemed smart. He had been practicing for an hour without holding back at all, as he had the day before. No one had shown any interest. The only problem was the oversize cue ball; you couldn't draw it back right, and sometimes he snookered himself and missed the next shot. Otherwise it was like child's pool. He fed quarters into the slot, retrieved the balls, racked them up, broke, and shot them in. The main thing was the sluggish cue ball; it took getting used to.

Eddie sipped his beer and then looked at the kid. 'I understand you have some good players around.'

The kid grinned. He was about twenty-five and had a pleasant face. 'I thought you might have that understanding. When I saw your cue stick.'

'I like to play for money.' It had been true once, anyway.

'There's a guy called Boomer.'

'Boomer?'

'His real name, I think. Dave or Dwight or something Boomer. He'll play you.'

'Would he play for a hundred dollars a game?'

The kid blinked. 'If he's got it.'

'Does he have a backer?'

'A stakehorse?'

'Yes. A stakehorse.'

'There's a man with him sometimes who only watches.'

'Is he likely to come in soon? I mean tonight?'

'I don't know.' The kid set his beer down and walked to the pass-through that let back to the kitchen. '*Arnie*,' he said.

A thin black face appeared at the opening.

'This guy wants to play pool with Boomer.'

The head nodded and glanced briefly at Eddie. 'Isn't there a number to call?'

'In the register. Under the checks.'

'Okay.' The kid went to the register, opened it, lifted the bill compartment with one hand and shuffled through papers with the other. He found a folded sheet of notepaper and turned to Eddie. 'Do I call him?'

Eddie felt a tightness in his stomach. 'I'd appreciate it.'

'Son of a bitch!' Boomer said when he saw Eddie's Balabushka. 'I was dragged from the comfort of my home to play a man with a stick like that. May the Lord deliver me!' He took a red bandanna handkerchief from his back pocket and blew his nose loudly. 'Protect me from men with Balabushka cue sticks.' He looked at Eddie's face for the first time, squinting at him. 'I bet you do trick shots.' His face was broad and red and heavily lined; he looked like some kind of wild-eyed field hand. A drug-crazed sharecropper. He wore a faded tan military shirt with epaulettes, and baggy corduroys that fell over the creased insteps of cowboy boots. It was hard to tell what his age was – anywhere from thirty to fifty – but he had a potbelly and wrinkles around his eyes. The eyes were a pale, unreal blue, and cold as ice. 'I bet that Balabushka makes them balls dance around like agitated molecules.'

'It's no better than the man behind it,' Eddie said.

'Jesus Christ,' Boomer said, 'you look serious.' A few people in the crowd laughed. In the hour since the bartender called, fifteen or twenty people had gathered.

'Why don't you get your stick out,' Eddie nodded toward the leather case Boomer was carrying, 'and we can shoot pool.' He held his cue in one hand and had the other in his pocket; he hoped fervently that his nervousness didn't show. He had forgotten how it was to play a man on his home table with his home crowd around him. And Boomer had taken possession of the tavern the moment he came in, with his loud voice and his boot heels clacking on the Kentile floor.

'If this stick don't wilt for shame when it sees yours,' Boomer said. He opened the top of the case and slid out a two-piece cue. It looked plenty good enough – a Huebler or a Meucci. Probably a three-hundred-dollar cue. When he screwed it together he did so deftly, with a light and accurate touch that contradicted the roughness of his appearance. Eddie had seen that before in the old days. Rough-looking country men with soft hands and, when they bent over a pool table, the light touch of a jeweler.

'Eight-ball is what we play here,' Boomer said.

'A hundred dollars a game.'

'Oh my god,' Boomer said, 'I am lying in my king-sized bed watching a rerun of 'Magnum PI' and the telephone rings and now here I am talking to a stranger with an upscale cue stick who wants to play pool for a hundred dollars. There's no comfort in life.'

'Do you want to play?' Eddie said quietly. The man was getting what he wanted; Eddie was beginning to feel rattled.

'Wayland,' Boomer said to the bartender, who had been watching all this attentively, as had everyone else in the place. 'Let me have a Drambuie on the rocks and a dish of potato salad.' Then, to Eddie: 'Put a quarter in the table.'

They flipped a coin for the break and Boomer won it. He used a heavy house cue to smash the balls open, the way Charlie had taught Eddie to when he was a kid, and pocketed three of them. Then he switched to the jointed and ran the balls out. Eddie handed him two fifties. It was six o'clock. The crowd was getting larger; they leaned against the rails of the tavern's other two tables and stood in the space behind them. The bar stools had filled with men who were now turned toward them, watching.

Boomer shot quietly, as Eddie expected he would, and almost as gracefully as Fats. His stroke was eccentric, swooping the cue stick over a long, wavering bridge, but he hit them solidly. And he was used to the heavy cue ball; on one shot he drew it back lightly by three feet.

'Winner breaks,' Boomer said, and went to the bar for a mouthful of potato salad and a drink. He came back wiping his mouth with a paper napkin, jammed the napkin into his hip pocket, took his cue and broke the balls. The table was three and a half by seven; after a solid break shot, the balls were distributed evenly all over it. Eddie had never played on a table like this before; he wasn't sure how many games a man could run on it.

Boomer bent and sank his first ball, and then looked at the crowd around him. 'I got to keep making these little fuckers,' he said. 'If I give that Balabushka a chance, it'll put me in the County Home.'

'It's only a pool cue, Boomer,' somebody in the crowd said.

'Don't sweet-talk *me*,' Boomer said. 'That cue has radar and microcircuits in its tip. With a cue like that a man can stay in bed and send the cue stick out on Saturday nights. "Bring in five hundred, Balabushka" is what you say. I know about them high-technology pool cues, come from Silicon Valley with a college degree.' He shook his head, bent and shot, cutting the seven ball into the side. His cue ball rolled a few feet for perfect position.

Eddie remained silent. He had seen routines like this before. The best thing to do was stay loose and not try to enter the spirit of it or make a fool out of yourself. So far, it was impossible to tell just how good Boomer was. Fats had said there were three or four professionals in this town – men who made their livings entirely by hustling on bar tables – and apparently Boomer was the best among them. Eddie leaned against the empty table a few feet from the one Boomer and he were playing on, and tried to relax. Boomer was funny; but there was threat in the way he talked, and in the cold-eyed look he flicked toward Eddie from time to time. Eddie watched, and kept quiet, and waited for him to miss.

When Boomer had two more balls to make, he overshot a

long cut and his cue ball rolled too far, leaving him out of position. He shrugged, banked at one of the remaining balls, missed it and rolled the white ball into a perfect safety. It was an 'if-I-miss' shot of the kind Fats had demonstrated back in Denver.

Eddie tightened his cue stick and looked at Boomer. 'What's the house rule if I don't hit one?'

'I get the cue behind the line,' Boomer said. 'Same as a scratch.'

That was a pisser. If Eddie didn't hit one of the stripes, Boomer would have an easy run out. And the cue was snookered behind the six. He studied it a moment. The thing to do was bank off the near rail and try to tap into the eleven ball and hope for a safety. It was the only smart thing to do.

But the twelve, down at the far end of the table, was a few inches from the corner pocket. The cue ball could be banked two cushions out of the corner, down the long diagonal. A very difficult shot. If he missed it, Boomer would own the table. It was a one-in-ten shot, a two-rail kick-in. Eddie looked at the bartender. 'Let me have a Manhattan, on the rocks,' he said. He stepped up to the table, adjusted his glasses, carefully spread the fingers of his left hand in a high bridge over the snookering six ball, elevated the back of his cue, looked once behind him at the twelve ball and shot, hard, smooth, and angry.

The cue ball bounced out of the corner, rolled the diagonal of the table and clipped the twelve ball sharply. The twelve rolled briskly into the pocket. 'Son of a bitch!' Boomer said. 'Goddamned microchips.'

'Printed circuits,' Eddie said, going to the bar for his drink. The men on the bar stools stared at him silently. He waited while the bartender put the cherry in, took a long swallow and came back to the table feeling, at last, relaxed.

Boomer was good, but nowhere as good as Fats. He couldn't bank well, and his main strength was in easy runs. He would have been a good straight-pool player if hustlers played straight pool anymore, and he was certainly good enough to make a living at eight-ball in barrooms. Eddie held himself steady, and by ten o'clock he was seven hundred dollars ahead.

When Boomer gave him the last pair of fifties, he looked at Eddie coldly and said, 'If you want to play me anymore, my friend, you're going to have to give me some weight.' He had dropped the wild-country-boy act and spoke quietly.

Eddie was finishing his supper – a bacon and tomato sandwich. He took the paper plate over and set it on the bar and then came back. The crowd silently made way for him. 'What do you need?'

'I'll take the break,' Boomer said.

Eddie looked at him, at his strange face with the look of crazy, mean intelligence; the veiled threat in his cool eyes; the small hands now holding his thin, delicate cue. 'I won't give you the break but I'll bank the eight ball. If we play for five hundred a game.'

'I've heard of guys like you,' Boomer said.

'I bet you have, Boomer.'

Boomer stared at him a moment and then gave a small grin. 'I've got to make a phone call.'

'Go ahead.'

He went to the pay phone at the end of the bar while Eddie got himself a cup of coffee. His shoulder had begun to ache, and now that Boomer was calling his backer or whatever, he felt the tightness in his stomach again. That was something else he had forgotten over the years: the goddamned *fear*.

The backer showed up surprisingly soon. He was a small man in a tight gray suit and dark necktie. The men leaning against one of the empty tables made room for him and he stood there, not leaning, and watched while Eddie racked up the balls and Boomer broke them. He made one on the break. It was going to be touch. For a moment Eddie felt like a fool giving such odds. Banking the eight could be ruinous. You couldn't afford to miss against a player like Boomer and on tables like this. Boomer ran three of the stripes and then played safe. Eddie did not try anything fancy this time but played a safety back. It went back and forth like that for several shots, but then on a draw shot, Eddie did not pull the heavy cue ball back as far as he had meant to and he left Boomer a piece of the eleven. Boomer said nothing, but zeroed in and cut it into the side. He ran out. Eddie took five hundred out of his wallet. Boomer nodded over toward the man in the suit and said, 'Just pay my friend.' Eddie walked over and handed the little man the bills. He took them silently, smoothed them out and began counting. Eddie walked back over to the table and racked the balls. Then he went to the bar and finished his coffee, watching the table as he drank. Boomer swung his bat of a cue into the break ball and spread the rack. A stripe and a solid dropped in. He began running the solids. Eddie walked back over to the table. His feet and his shoulder were hurting, and the coffee hadn't really helped. What was he doing, saying he would bank the eight on this man's own table, with his own crowd, here in some town in North Carolina whose name he had already forgotten? Haneyville. That was it – the first name on the list from Fats. 'Some high rollers there,' Fats had said. Well, there one of them was, making balls like a machine. *Plop, plop* they went, into the big pockets of the little table. *Plop*. The last was the eight ball. Eddie got another five hundred and gave it to the dapper little man. He was now, after four hours of pool, three hundred dollars behind. And quite a few quarters. He put another quarter in, telling himself he had better bear down; when the balls came rolling through the chute he took them out and racked them, eight ball in the center, for Boomer.

And Boomer boomed them open, dropping three. He was getting hot now. Maybe he had been holding back before. Eddie watched him, for a moment feeling some of the helplessness he had felt against Fats in Miami and Cincinnati, with a tight, painful sensation in his stomach. Boomer was moving around the little table faster now, sliding balls into pockets quietly while the whole crowded barroom full of men in working clothes watched him, fascinated. The gray smoke above the cone of light over the table was nearly solid; men sipped their drinks silently; no one played the jukebox or talked. The sound of Boomer's boot heels when he moved from shot to shot was like footsteps in a library. He made all the striped balls, shot the eight in the side, and Eddie paid the man in the suit.

'I may never find out if you can bank that eight ball,' Boomer said as Eddie was bent near him, getting the balls from the rack.

Eddie froze and stared at him a moment. 'Let's play for a thousand,' he said. He had twelve hundred dollars with him.

'You're on,' Boomer said.

He finished racking them, surprised at his own steadiness. He had not planned to play for that much money. Boomer might run out without giving him a shot. Boomer had gone over to the nearby table and was whispering with his backer, whose face was impassive. Eddie looked at him and immediately knew he would miss soon.

Boomer stepped up to the table, drew back his cue and slammed into the rack of balls. They spread out, but nothing fell in. 'Son of a bitch!' he said, this time meaning it.

The balls were wide, and the eight was an inch from the side pocket. After making the others, Eddie could bring the cue ball near it for a simple cross-side bank. First, he would have to cut the seven thin, slip it into the bottom corner, and let his cue ball roll the length of the table to sit down by the three. It wasn't easy. He glanced up at Boomer, who was standing a few feet from the table.

'Don't miss,' Boomer said.

Eddie stared at him a moment. 'Boomer,' he said, 'you're scared of me.'

He bent down, stroked smoothly, and cut the seven ball in. The cue ball rolled up the table and sat down sweetly behind the three. He shot it in, and then the four ball and the two and the others, finally giving himself position for the bank on the eight ball. He stopped a second to chalk his cue and then bent, stroked, shot. The eight ball struck the cushion smartly, rolled across the table and fell into the pocket.

Boomer got the money from his backer, handed it to Eddie. This time Eddie did not take out his wallet. He folded the bills and pushed them down into his pants pocket while Boomer stood watching. 'You're not quitting, are you?' Eddie said pleasantly. He liked the way his voice sounded.

Boomer shook his head.

'Then rack the balls,' Eddie said.

He got her number from long-distance information and dialed from the phone by his bed. It was a little before one. He had woken up at noon, showered, and ordered coffee from room service.

'Pat told me you were living alone,' she said. Her voice did not sound friendly, but at least she was willing to talk.

'I sure am.'

'Where are you?'

'In the Holiday Inn in Haneyville, North Carolina.'

'What in god's name are you doing in North Carolina?'

'Playing pool for money.'

'I thought you didn't do that anymore.'

'Sometimes I even surprise myself.'

'Is that what you called to tell me?'

'I'll be at Bluegrass Airport at six. If you'll pick me up, I'll take you to the Japanese place for dinner.'

'Eddie,' she said, 'I don't know. . . .'

'I know,' he said, looking at the stack of over four thousand dollars, he had won from Boomer. 'Pick me up at the airport. We ought to be together.'

She was there waiting for him, looking terrific in a black wool sweater and blue jeans, her gray hair freshly washed and fluffy around her face, like a movie star on her day off. He was carrying his cue and nylon bag, and they didn't kiss. She shook his hand, looking him over. Neither of them spoke.

Finally she said, 'We don't know each other very well at all.'
'Like hell we don't,' he said.

She hadn't found herself a job yet and was getting tired of looking. She would have given up weeks before and settled for living on alimony if it weren't that staying in the apartment was driving her crazy. They had a long quiet supper while she told him these things; afterward they went back to her apartment and, for the first time, made love. They were like old friends, old lovers. The week apart and the trip and the money had changed everything for him and they could both feel it. He knew what to do and so did she. They lay on her sofa bed afterward and talked. He would look for a while at the lights of downtown outside her windows, closed now against a September chill, and then turn back to her smooth white body beside him in the bed. They smoked his cigarettes and stubbed them out in a coffee saucer between them.

'You're playing pool for money again?' she said, breaking the silence.

'It's been a long time.'

'You mean gambling, don't you? Not just giving an exhibition.'

'That's right. Gambling.'

'In England people spoke of billiards sharks. You call them hustlers, I think. Is that what you are?'

He looked at her a moment. 'I'm not a pool shark.'

'I'm sorry. What *do* I call you – a hustler?'

'Call me Eddie and hand me a cigarette.'

She frowned and gave him one. 'Whatever you are, you aren't a professor.'

He took the cigarette and lit it. 'I fly to Albuquerque in a month to do an exhibition. Before that I'm going to Memphis to play eight-ball at a roadhouse called Thelma's. How would you like to come along?'

'You want me to travel with you? Like a gun moll or something?'

'There you go again.'

'As the consort of a pool player.'

'Do you have anything better to do?'

She rolled over and kissed him on the neck. 'No, I haven't,' she said.

'You'd like it if I played tennis.'

'Or bridge?' Arabella, dressed only in pale blue panties, was pulling something big out of the closet. Another painting, apparently, wrapped in brown paper. She laid it flat in the center of the living room and, while Eddie watched from the bed, seated herself cross-legged on the rug and began to remove masking tape from the paper. 'Or the French horn?'

'Something like that. Shooting pool sounds like shooting craps.'

'It does?' She got one end of the wrapping free and began slipping the framed picture out of it. Eddie leaned up on his elbow to see it better but could not make it out. Her small breasts as she bent over were wonderful, and so was the curved ridge of her backbone. 'What happened to nightgowns?' he asked.

'It's a warm apartment.' She began folding the paper neatly into a square, pressing the wrinkles out of it. He had already noticed the towels in the bathroom closet, folded and stacked as though displayed in an expensive store. Everything about her apartment was orderly. When she finished, she got up from the floor and carried the paper to the green oriental chest at the far wall and set it neatly in a drawer. From the drawer she took out a hammer and brought it over to the bed. 'Here,' she said. 'You can drive the nail.'

'Toss it on the bed. I'll get it in a minute.'

'Come on, Eddie. I want to hang this picture.'

He reached over and got a cigarette. 'Not without coffee.'

'I'll make some instant.'

'Instant coffee leads to divorce.'

'Maybe so,' she said. 'I'll use the Vesuviana. It would be simpler if you'd take tea in the morning.'

'Arabella,' Eddie said, 'it would be simpler if the world was flat.'

'I'll make the coffee.' She tossed the hammer beside him on the bed and went to the stove. 'Why should I want you to play tennis, Eddie?'

'It has class.'

She turned to him from the stove with the coffee can in her hand. 'I hate that word. My grandmother used it all the time. It was working class or leisure class.'

'That's not what I meant. You're an aristocrat.'

'Come on, Eddie,' she said. 'It's my accent. You Americans are all alike when it comes to British accents.'

'I mean the way you look. The way your apartment looks, with the white floor and oil paintings.'

'It's called *taste*, Eddie.'

'What does your taste say about hustling pool?'

'My taste doesn't say a fucking thing about it.' She turned, carried the coffee can back to the stove and took its top off. She began spooning coffee into the basket of the little machine.

He hesitated a moment and then said, 'I think Martha was ashamed of it.'

'Was Martha your wife?'

'Thoroughly.'

'That's a funny thing to say.'

'I'm learning to talk like you.'

'You're an Anglophile.'

'There's a lot of that going around.'

She got the coffee machine back together and put it on the burner in front of the stove. 'Well I'm not Martha. When I saw you playing pool with Roy I was thrilled.'

He looked at her back for a moment as she adjusted the flame. Then he stood up barefoot and took the hammer. 'Where do you want to hang this?'

'I admire skill,' Arabella said, coming over to him, 'and I respect people who live by their wits.' She handed him a brass picture-hanger. 'Center the painting above the chest.

The trees in it will look good over the green.'

He held up the framed canvas for a moment. Like the painting over the sofa, it was crude and bright, as though done by a skilled child. There were two figures and a horse standing under trees; everything was as simply drawn as in a child's painting, but each leaf of the trees had been individually painted.

'It's what some people call naive art,' Arabella said. 'It was done by a woman without formal training.'

'It would make a good jigsaw puzzle. Sharp lines.'

'These two pictures are all I got from the divorce, if you don't count the alimony. Harrison kept the furniture – even the sheets and towels.'

'Why did you get the paintings?'

'Because they're mine. A friend bought me the other one and I bought this myself.'

'Harrison likes naive art?'

'He hates it. It was the friend who taught me about naive art. Contemporary folk art.'

'Okay.' He went over to the chest and held the painting up. 'I'm pretty good with a hammer, too.'

'It's what attracted me to you in the first place.'

On his fourth night in Arabella's apartment he lay awake in bed next to her for over an hour. It was late, but there were still sounds of traffic from Main Street through the closed windows. He wore shorts in bed and she was naked, covered by the sheet and a silvery down comforter. She slept facing him, the sheet and comforter huddled under her left arm, which was bare and white with light freckles toward the shoulder. Even in sleep her face looked smart. What was he doing in bed with a woman like this? The lashes on her closed eyes were perfect, curling slightly upward above unblemished cheeks. Her small hand lay on his arm.

She was on the rebound from a genteel life and she liked him. She was interested in what he knew about running a small business, had asked him solid questions about it over dinner that evening, wanting to know how he had figured his operating expenses and what the problems were with taxes. She liked the idea of hustling pool; it excited her to be with a gambler. She liked his looks.

He liked her air of competence and ambition, the clarity of what she said, the authority her voice had on the telephone, the way she disdained makeup, did not talk down to him, slept naked, swore, and never wavered in matters of taste. When she made love she did it without the encumbrance of modesty or indirection, although her passion was restrained and her orgasms silent. But they did not know each other very well yet. He had his own restraints too and was afraid sometimes to let go, but he felt he could talk about that with her when the time came.

One thing that disturbed him was the newspaper in the desk drawer. Unpacking three days before while Arabella was out, he had checked the desk for an empty drawer, sliding out the bottom one first. A newspaper sat on top of a pile of newspapers. He took it out idly and saw that the paper under it was another copy. Below that were others – at least a dozen, all the same. There were two photographs on the front page; one was of Nancy Reagan and the other was of a smiling young man with light, curly hair. Above this a headline read: ART EXPERT KILLED IN CYCLE CRASH. The word *art* caught his attention; Arabella knew a lot about art. The article identified the man as Gregory Welles, assistant professor at the university and editor of the *Journal of Kentucky Arts and Crafts*. Arabella wrote articles from time to time for the journal. He looked at the date at the top of the page; it was a little over a year old. Welles had swerved on a country road to avoid being hit, had gone over into the ditch, had died. With him at the time was Mrs Harrison Frame, who escaped serious injury. Welles and Mrs Frame had been visiting the shop of a craftsman in Estill County. Eddie had noticed two moon-shaped scars on Arabella's knees; when he asked about them she said, 'I was in a wreck,' and changed the subject.

Twelve copies of the same paper. He looked closely at the

young man's face. It was a plain, American face, but Eddie felt his stomach tighten as he looked at it. Of course she would have had other lovers. It shouldn't bother him. What did he want – a forty-year-old virgin? And the man was dead. Still, he did not like it. He hated it. He hated the young man, the man Arabella had gone off with, riding country roads behind him on his motorcycle, the man she had been able to talk art with, had probably slept with as she was now sleeping with him. Eddie finished the article. Greg Welles had died at twenty-six.

Thelma's parking lot was half full when they drove up at nine-thirty. He had wanted to get there before any serious games would start and was afraid he might be too late. Fats said this was the hottest place in the whole South. Eddie's stomach was tight and his mouth dry. He was ready to play.

The bar was packed and noisy, with a Loretta Lynn recording from the jukebox – loud as it was – only barely discernible against the talking and shouting of the people jammed at the bar and filling the small tables. There were a half-dozen illuminated beer signs over the bar itself; a sequined globe hung from the center of the ceiling, with colored lights sparkling on it. There were no pool tables in sight. Arabella looked around as though she were at a circus, her eyes wide.

He spotted a doorway with a sign over it reading GAME ROOM, he took her by the elbow and led her past the crowded tables. The dance floor was filled with couples in bright silky shirts and jeans, with young men wearing big mustaches, and long-haired women. Arabella seemed astonished by it all, and when he got her into the relative quiet of the other room, she said, 'It's just like the movies.'

There were five tables of the same small size as Haneyville's, and games were in progress on three of them. One of the others had a plastic cover over it, and on the fifth a foursome of silent children were poking cue sticks at balls. Arabella looked at them for a minute; none was over ten years old. Then she whispered, 'Is that the junior division?'

For some reason he felt irritated at the joke. 'The parents are probably back there dancing.'

'With one another?'

'Honey,' he said coolly, 'I don't understand these places any better than you do. I'm just learning my way around.'

'I thought you made your living in places like this.'

'In poolrooms. Not barrooms.'

She got quiet then, and he began watching the three games. The ones on the first two tables were not much; none of the players had a decent stroke or knew what to shoot at, but what was happening on the middle table was something different. It was a cool, quiet game of serious nine-ball. One player was oriental. Japanese, with delicate features, narrow eyes and brown skin. He wore a blue velvet jacket that fit perfectly across his narrow shoulders, and a silvery open-collared shirt underneath, matching his silver trousers. The man he was playing was thirtyish, with a heavy beard and workingman's clothes.

Two high director's chairs sat against the back wall. Eddie took Arabella by the arm, led her over to them and seated himself with his cue case across his lap.

The Japanese was impeccably dressed. His hair, his nails and his shave were perfect. Eddie liked the quiet way he concentrated on his shots. The other player was quiet too, but sloppy in appearance, at least compared to the Japanese. He looked like Lon Chaney in the werewolf movies, at about the middle of the transformation, with bushy hair coming down over his forehead and the full beard.

They watched for about a half hour, and then Arabella leaned over and said, 'When are you going to play?'

'If somebody comes in. Or if one of them quits.'

Just as he said this the bearded man, who had lost four games since they started watching, lost another. He handed the Japanese some money, unscrewed his cue, and left.

Eddie looked at the Japanese and grinned. 'Do you want to play some more?'

'Eight-ball?'

'What about straight pool?'

The little man smiled. 'We usually play eight-ball here.'

'All right.' Eddie stood and unfastened the clasp on his cue case. 'What were you two playing for?'

The man continued smiling. 'Twenty dollars.'

'How about fifty?'

'Sure.' Eddie could hear Arabella draw in her breath behind him.

The Japanese was easy to play but difficult to beat. There was no belligerence or muscling to him, but he shot a thoroughly professional game. He ran the balls out when he had an open table to work with and played simple, effective safeties when he didn't. When Eddie made a good shot he would say, 'Good shot!' He made a great many of them himself. Eddie had difficulty with the heavy cue ball. All bar tables used them, so the ball would bypass the chute when you scratched; and he knew he would have to get accustomed to the sluggishness. It caused him to misjudge his position a few critical times. After an hour had passed, he was down by a hundred dollars. He was racking the balls and considering raising the bet when the other man spoke. 'Would you like to double the bet?'

Eddie finished racking, hung the wooden triangle at the foot of the table and said, 'Why don't we play for two hundred a game?'

The Japanese looked at him calmly. 'Okay.'

But at two hundred Eddie went on losing. On some shots the cue ball seemed to be made of lead and would not pull backward when he needed it to. During the third game at two hundred, Eddie ran all of the stripes without difficulty but failed to make the eight ball because the weight of the cue ball threw his position off. There was no life to the damned thing; it was maddening.

The Japanese seemed unconcerned with the problem, making balls steadily, clicking them in like a tap dancer. They hardly spoke to each other. Eddie kept paying, racking the balls, and watching the other man shoot. Being short, he bent only slightly from the waist; his long cue stick seemed more intimate with the table, more neatly parallel to it, than Eddie's. Eddie felt that pool tables were too low for a man of average height, and he himself was taller than average. When the Japanese stepped up to a shot, the way he bent his waist and extended his left arm, the way his right arm cocked itself for the stroke, and the way his quiet eyes zeroed in on the cue ball and then on the line extending from the cue ball to the ball he was going to pocket were perfect. The open front of his powder-blue jacket hung straight down, missing the side of the table by an inch; the crease at the bottoms of his silver trousers broke neatly above the tops of his polished shoes; and his brown, unlined face showed a hint of exquisite sadness. When Eddie stepped up to shoot now he felt, compared with the other man, big and clumsy, like the big, clumsy barroom cue ball he had to hit.

When Eddie was nine hundred dollars down, the man excused himself to go to the bathroom. Eddie walked over to Arabella. 'I hope you're not bored.' he said.

'It's really a thrill,' she said. 'I wish you'd teach me more, Eddie, so I could understand it better.'

'Sure.'

She looked behind her to see if the other player was still gone from the room. Then she leaned forward. 'When are you going to start beating him, Eddie?'

'As soon as I can.'

'Aren't you losing on purpose? Isn't that the way you do it?'

'I told you,' Eddie said, frowning, 'I'm not a pool shark. I'm trying to beat the man.'

'Oh,' she said, clearly disappointed.

'I'm having trouble with the cue ball. . . .'

She just looked at him.

Just then a waitress came in. 'Anybody here want something from the bar?'

'Sure,' Eddie said, and then to Arabella, 'What would you

like?' He realized that his voice was cold.

Arabella spoke to the waitress. 'Do you have white wine?'

'Sure, honey,' the waitress said brightly. 'You want dry or extra dry? We've got a nice dry Chablis.'

'I'll have a glass of that.'

'Bring me a Manhattan on the rocks.' Eddie was feeling uncomfortable. The man on the far table ordered beer.

Just then the Japanese came walking back into the room. 'Do you want a drink?' Eddie asked.

'Bourbon and soda.' He smiled at Eddie. 'Tough work, shooting eight-ball.'

There was something about him. Eddie could not help liking him. A lot of hustlers were that way, since their livelihoods depended partly on charm; but the feeling for this little man was stronger than that.

The Japanese picked up his cue, set its butt on the floor between his feet and held it so its tip was level with his chin. Then he slipped a small metal rasp from his coat pocket and began tapping the cue tip with it. It was something Eddie hadn't seen for so long that he had forgotten: the man was dressing the tip to make it hold chalk better.

When he finished, Eddie said, 'Could I use that a minute?'

He nodded and handed it to him. Eddie stood his cue in front of him and gave it a few taps.

'That's a very pretty stick,' the Japanese said.

'Thanks.' Eddie scuffed the center of the tip where there was a hard spot, and then began chalking it heavily. The other man took a square of chalk and did the same thing. He looked at Eddie and said, 'I'm Billy Usho.'

'Ed Felson. This is Arabella.'

'I've enjoyed watching you play.' Arabella twirled her wineglass by the stem.

'That's nice.' Usho smiled. 'My wife says it bores her. Out of her skull.'

'That's a shame,' Arabella said. 'I think it's a beautiful game. Very intricate and bright.'

Eddie began racking the balls. He felt, as he had before in

his life, that if he didn't do something his money would drift away from him and he would go on losing. He did not like Arabella's sympathy with the little man. He did not like his own. The Japanese was like Fats: another cool man who dressed impeccably. Another star. Eddie was better than this dapper Japanese, better maybe than Fats.

'Let's play for five hundred,' Eddie said.

'That's a lot of money for eight-ball.'

Eddie straightened up from racking and shrugged. At the table across the room, the men who had ordered beers were staring at him. They must have heard him say five hundred dollars. He noticed for the first time that the kids had left the other table, had apparently been gone for some time. He looked over at Arabella briefly; her face was expressionless. He turned back to Billy Usho. 'What have you got to lose?'

'Okay.' Billy picked up the chalk again, ran it lightly over the tip of his cue, bent to the table and smashed the rack of balls open.

Eddie took a deep breath and watched, not sitting, keeping his back to Arabella. The five ball fell in; that gave Billy the solids. Eddie kept his eyes on the table and not on Usho's clothes or his smooth, youthful face.

None of the solids was in an easy position, and the cue ball was frozen to a side rail. Billy studied the lie for a long time before he played safe. The cue ball stopped between the eight and the four, out of line with all the striped balls. Eddie would have to keep his nerves steady and his balls tight just to get a decent safety out of it. The cue ball would have to be banked rail-first into the eleven. It was a pisser.

Just then the waitress came in with their drinks. Eddie gave her a ten, took his Manhattan and turned back to the table. If he shot it hard, the eleven might go in the side; it was a foot and a half away from the pocket and in a direct line with it. But, Jesus, to thump that big cue ball off the cushion and try for a perfect hit on the eleven was a killer. He looked at Billy's Japanese face, his almost pretty face, for a moment and thought, *To hell with him*. He took a long swallow from the sweet drink, set it down, not looking at Arabella, and walked over to the table. He could make the eleven ball.

He did it quickly, spreading his fingers of his left hand over the eight, elevating the cue stick, stroking once and then tapping the cue ball. He could feel the purchase on the big, chunky ball that roughing the leather of the tip had given him. He watched the white ball pop off the rail and hit the eleven dead center, watched the eleven roll into the side pocket. The cue ball stopped in position for the thirteen. Eddie chalked, took three steps over and pocketed the thirteen. Then the nine, the fifteen, the fourteen and the twelve. The black eight sat four inches from the lower corner and his cue ball ten inches from the eight. He plunked the eight ball into the pocket and went back to his Manhattan. Billy paid him silently and racked the balls.

At midnight Eddie raised the bet to a thousand and Billy brought in two backers. One wore a dark suit and looked like a banker. The other could have been a rodeo cowboy. He chewed tobacco, drank Rolling Rock beer, and paid Eddie in worn-looking hundred-dollar bills from what seemed an inexhaustable supply.

At one in the morning, Eddie put Arabella in a taxi and sent her back to the Holiday Inn. She kissed him sleepily before getting in the cab. 'I'm glad you started beating him.'

'You know what I'm going to do tomorrow?' Eddie said to her. 'I'm going to buy some new clothes.'

After they closed the bar at two-thirty, a crowd of a dozen diehards stayed to watch. Someone kept feeding quarters into the jukebox in the other room; the muted voices of Conway Twitty and Merle Haggard came through the open doorway. Billy's face was no longer unlined, and his hair no longer neatly combed. There was a smear of talcum powder near the lapel of his blue jacket, and his narrow eyes were narrower.

Eddie was reaching a place he had almost forgotten, where the nerves of his arms and fingertips seemed to extend through the length of the Balabushka to the glossy surfaces of the balls themselves, to the napped green of the table. There were no aches in his feet or shoulders, and his stroke was unruffled, pistonlike, and dead-accurate. He could not miss. There was no way he could miss. The whole fatty accumulation of his middle-class life had fallen away from him, and his movements at the table were both fully awake and dreamlike. The visual clarity was astounding. The click of his cue tip against the cue ball, the click of the cue ball against the ball he was tapping in or easing in or nudging in or powering in was like the click of oiled machinery. He was silent and loose; in some newly awakened reach of his mind he was dazzled by himself.

Billy did not quit for a long time. It was amazing that he didn't quit. He shot fine pool, even better than he had played at the beginning, and he even won games. There was no way to prevent him from winning games. But he had no real chance. By three o'clock in the morning it must have been clear to everyone in the room, as it was to Eddie, that he had no chance; but he kept on playing and his backers kept handing money to Eddie.

With the rail-first bank on the eleven ball, he had lost his clumsiness with the cue ball; and now he made it dance for him, still sluggish though it was. He had found the string for it and his control was flawless. He even felt a certain fondness for the big white ball, like the fondness he had felt for Billy Usho; but now he was in command of both. There was nothing in life like this. Nothing. To stroke and hit the cue ball, to watch the colored ball roll with the certitude that he himself imposed on it, to see and hear the colored ball fall into the pocket he had chosen, was exquisite.

Coming into the room, he tried not to wake her, but she stirred when he closed the door. A moment later she turned the bedside light on. She was squinting at the clock radio, her hair disheveled and her breasts bare. She didn't look at him. 'Dear God!' she said. 'Its five o'fucking clock.'

'A quarter after,' Eddie said.

'Maybe you *should* play tennis.'

'No I shouldn't.' He set the cue stick in the closet and began unbuttoning his shirt. He took it off and laid it across the back of a chair. 'I'm going to take a shower.'

'Come on to bed.'

'After the shower.'

'All right,' she said, sitting up and rubbing her eyes. 'I missed you last night. How much did you take him for?'

'Take him for?'

'Isn't that what you say?'

He grinned at her, a bit dreamily. He felt thoroughly tired. His arms and legs, his chest and back, felt warm and relaxed, and the dull ache in his insteps and in his right arm – his stroking arm – was more a comfort than a pain. He reached into his right pocket and pulled out a handful of bills. He dropped it on the bed at her side and then pulled out another handful. Hundreds had a special shade of green on their backs, and the numbering that read '100' was curved pleasantly at the corners, the engraving baroque and substantial. He had always loved them. He dropped the second beside the first, then pulled out more, along with a fistful of loose bills. Arabella had become wide-eyed. She stared at the money and then up at his face. He felt deeply relaxed and yet alert; if someone attacked him he would respond like a drowsy leopard, like a great white shark, lazy and deadly.

'Good god in heaven!' Arabella said softly, looking at the money beside her.

He dug deeper and found another dozen of them in that pocket. Then he shifted to the other pocket, where there was a roll, pulling it out with thumb and forefinger. On the bed the roll uncoiled itself like a living thing, to become a sheaf. More bills were beneath it. He slipped them out a few at a time. The pile of green bills next to Arabella now filled up the space from her knees to her elbows, covering about a foot's width of the bed. She reached down, scooped up a double handful and held them against her cheeks as a child might hold a beloved doll. 'Where have you been all my life, Eddie?' she said.

'Who cares?' Eddie said. 'I'm here now.'

The next day Arabella drove to Thelma's with him at noon and played a pinball machine while he waited around for someone to come in. He got a handful of quarters at the bar and practiced, but none of the people who walked into the bar for an afternoon beer came back to the room where Eddie, feeling like a house hustler, was banking balls up the rails. By late afternoon it had gotten to him. During his years in Lexington he had come to hate these long days with pool tables and the endless, desultory shooting. There were games going on at the other tables now, but not for money. The excitement of the night before was gone. By the time they had their supper at the bar his arm was tired and his feet ached.

After supper Arabella sat in the canvas director's chair she had watched from the night before, reading a book. At nine he went out to the bar, got two bottles of beer and poured hers into a glass.

'Well,' she said, 'think of how you did last night.'

'Do you want to play?'

'All right.' She closed her book and set it on the table by the beer.

He showed her how to draw the cue ball by putting bottom English on it and how to make a proper bridge with her thumb and forefinger. Her concentration was impressive. He set up balls for her and watched her tap them in, and for a while, it was a pleasure. She liked getting things right. He took the seat she had been in, drank his beer slowly from the bottle and watched her. After a while he was reading from *The Collected Stories of V. S. Pritchett* while she shot the balls around on the table. They were strange little stories, about Englishmen; he read three. When he looked up from the third, Arabella was standing in front of him, her arms crossed over the top of the Balabushka.

'It does get boring after a while,' she said.

Eddie stretched and yawned. 'Not at five hundred a game.'

'Let's go to the room, Eddie. 'I'm tired.'

The next evening around eight o'clock, Billy Usho came in. This time he was wearing a chocolate-brown velvet jacket and tan slacks over light Italian shoes. He was carrying his cue case and he smiled ruefully when he saw Eddie sitting in the director's chair.

'What if I bank the eight?' Eddie said.

'Blindfold, maybe,' Usho said.

'Have a seat,' Eddie said. 'Where can I get a game?'

'Next to impossible.'

'A friend told me there were money players around here.'

'Not anymore. Who's your friend?'

'Fats, from Chicago.'

'Oh yes,' Billy Usho said, looking very Japanese. He could have said, 'Ah so!' He opened his case and took out a cue that was different from the one he had used before. Its butt was wrapped in brown linen that matched his jacket. 'I hear Fats came through here six years ago and cleaned them all out. But there was money in those days. It's not like that now.'

'You're just passing through too, aren't you?'

'I've been here a week. You have to work at it.'

Eddie fell silent for a while. Then Eddie said, 'Did you ever play the nine-ball tournament at Lake Tahoe?'

'Those tournaments are a bitch. You got to come in first or second, or the hotel bill eats you alive.'

'I hear Earl Borchard makes a good living at tournaments.'

'He's a genius. So's Babes Cooley.'

Eddie got down from his chair, put a quarter in the table and began shooting banks. Usho came over and watched.

Eddie tapped the five ball cross-side, freezing the cue ball. 'I haven't seen anybody play serious nine-ball for twenty years.'

Billy looked at him speculatively. 'Where've you *been*?'

Eddie slammed a long cross-corner bank on the twelve

ball. 'In a fog, Billy. I've been in a goddamned fog for twenty years.'

'Good bank on the twelve,' Billy said.

As they walked out onto the parking lot at one, a carload of teenagers drove up, screeching to a stop in the space next to Eddie's car. Six of them got out, the boys staggering and laughing, the girls squealing. Eddie and Billy watched as they went under the big red neon sign into Thelma's. As Eddie was unlocking his car he turned to Billy and said, 'Do you think I could beat Earl Borchard at nine-ball? Or Babes Cooley?'

'No,' Billy said, 'I don't think you could.'

'Why not?'

'This eight-ball in bars is nothing but a scuffle. The best players are in nine-ball.'

'What about straight pool?'

'Nine-ball. That's where the money is.'

There was no way not to leave Arabella stuck in motels over the next two weeks. She read books, spent some time on the telephone, and they went to matinees of movies together, saving the night for pool-shooting. She would go to whatever bar he was working and stay an hour or so, but it was tedious for him and more so for her; there wasn't anything for her to do.

Worse, he wasn't making any money. The best game he found was for twenty dollars, and the man quit him after a few hours of it, leaving Eddie with a profit of a hundred eighty. That was in the first week, and even it was not repeated.

After three days in a Holiday Inn in Beaufort, North Carolina, Arabella's boredom was beginning to show. She tried to be cheerful, but there were long silences between them at breakfast – or at what was lunch for her and breakfast for him. One day at noon, when he had just gotten up from a long, unsuccessful night at a downtown bar, several things went wrong. The hotel laundry service had lost two blouses, the television set had lost its ability to make a coherent picture, they went to lunch and the waitress brought her the wrong sandwich. She had ordered the Big Chuck hamburger; the waitress brought her liverwurst. Arabella stared furiously at the glossy white bread. Eddie tried to hail the waitress as she disappeared into the kitchen.

'Eddie,' Arabella said, 'I want to go home.'

'There's an afternoon flight from Raleigh. I'll go with you.'

It was colder in Lexington now, and he wore a scarf and gloves on his way to the Faculty Club in the mornings. The leaves had all fallen from the trees and been raked from the neatly cropped grass of the campus; there were still rake marks like the lines in the fine gravel of a Japanese garden. Eddie walked briskly from the parking lot to the club, chin down against the morning cold, cue case tucked under his arm. He liked it. After the raw towns in the South, with their neon and poverty, the university – with its substantial old brick buildings, its neatly kept walks, its sense of order and security – was a profound relief. He would walk into the anteroom of the Faculty Club, past the wooden tables where breakfast was being set up by students in white jackets, up the wooden stairs to the second floor and down the hallway to the game room, to uncover the big mahogany table and begin his morning's work. He knew he did not belong here either by education, social class or any right other than Roy Skammer's invitation; yet, he felt far more at home than by the bar tables near tavern dance floors or in the rough, smoke-stained rooms of North Carolina roadhouses. He felt at ease in the faded genteel quiet of an upstairs room with oil portraits of professors on the walls and chamber music sometimes drifting up from the lounge below. A faded oriental rug sat under the pool table, extending out a few feet from its periphery; Eddie's leather jacket and scarf hung from the brass hook of a mahogany coatrack; the rotund face of an emeritus professor of history looked sternly down on the table; Eddie thought of him as Lexington Fats. Sometimes after pocketing a particularly difficult shot he would look up confidently at the old man's face.

He had hoped his game was improved from the weeks of eight-ball, and it was. He was now making runs in the seventies and missing less. The glasses were a godsend. Whatever muscles of back and shoulder and arm it took to play pool for hour after hour had toughened; nothing in his body hurt anymore. He was still not as good as he once had been, when he could make a hundred balls without missing, but he felt he was getting there. In Albuquerque he would give it his best shot, and if he was hitting, would beat Fats. It was about time.

Arabella spent her days at home working on articles for the folk-art journal or typing papers for professors, sometimes complaining about the bad prose and footnotes she had to rattle her way through at her Selectric, but she seemed content to be working. The apartment was small for the two of them, and they spoke sometimes of finding a bigger one. They went out to movies some nights and spent others reading or watching television. Something in Eddie fretted at this part of his life. It was solid and easy, but he wanted something else. As his pool game came back, the old restlessness had reentered his spirit; he wanted to be playing for money, taking risks, staying at good hotels, sleeping till noon, winning money in cash, in hundred-dollar bills.

On his fourth day back from the South he went to Martha's apartment to pick up some winter clothes he had left behind. Martha was there, and as usual had a cold. She was cordial but edgy as he pulled an armload of clothes from the maple dresser – sweaters, corduroy pants and an extra scarf. Being in the old apartment made him dizzy; he found he had nothing to say. She was silent too. He got what he needed and left.

Arabella told him there was space at one side of her big

closet. He opened its sliding door to a four-foot row of dresses. There must have been forty of them, on hangers covered with quilted rayon. He ran a hand along colored silk, wool and linen. Near the closet floor a shelf held two long rows of shoes, lined up perfectly in Arabella's British way, blue and red and brown and black shoes. Each held a lavender metal tree, its color precisely matching the coat-hanger covers.

Eddie found space at the end for his clothes and he hung them there – bemused by the array of the dresses and shoes, radiating along with the smells of potpourri and moth crystals the sense of another life.

A few days later they made a stab at apartment hunting. To get a subdivision with moderately priced apartments, they drove through a fine old residential district, along a gently curving street lined with heavy elms. At a stop sign Arabella said, 'Look there,' and pointed to a house on Eddie's side. Far behind an enormous lawn sat a white-columned porch banked by shrubbery: the house itself was of gray limestone with a red tile roof and a row of dormers; it had tall, airy French windows on the first floor. 'That was my house,' Arabella said. It went with the clothes. She had lived there fifteen years, with a distinguished professor of art – a man who had his work shown in galleries in New York and who appeared often on television. Now she was the mistress of a pool hustler – a former pool hustler. Eddie said nothing and drove on.

'Don't you miss the parties?' he said to her that evening.

'What parties?' She had just finished doing a paper on hydraulic engineering and was tapping the sheaf of pages against the top of her desk. 'I need a paper clip.'

'Behind your typewriter. I mean parties at the university, when you were a faculty wife.'

'Sometimes. Not often.' She found the clip, fastened the papers together and put them in a manila folder. Then she stood up and stretched. 'At faculty parties what the women talk about is their children, and I don't have children. It was a chance to dress up every now and then, but then I had to listen to Harrison. The two cancelled out.'

'I've heard that professors need wives.'

'To do the laundry?'

'You really are pissed at him,' Eddie said. 'I meant to look good at parties, to help his career.'

'People say that, but it's not really true. Harrison is what he is because he fills out a good grant-request form and looks superb in an Irish fisherman's sweater. I don't really hate him, Eddie. Thinking about him just irks me.'

'What were you in it for?'

She looked at him a long moment, then lit a cigarette. 'I don't know. Maybe the clothes.'

'You got a lot of them.'

'Security. I wanted to be taken care of, Eddie. By somebody good-looking and with a good career.'

'There's nothing wrong with that.'

'Would you want it?'

He lit a cigarette and said, 'What in hell are you mad at?'

She walked to the desk and picked up the paper she had typed. 'I'm mad at Harrison and I'm mad at the professor who wrote this study of stress resistance in water-retaining structures.'

'I think you're mad at *me*,' Eddie said.

'I'm tired of the university. There are students who graduate from here with nothing in their heads but drugs and rock music.'

'You're forgetting sex. I think it's me you're mad at.'

She looked at him. 'Eddie, why don't you get your act together and start playing tournaments?'

'I'm not good enough yet. I may never be.' He looked at his watch. It was midnight. He walked over to the sofa and began unfolding it into a bed. 'If you lived in a house like that, why don't you have a lot of money?'

'The house belongs to Harrison's mother and didn't figure in the settlement. I get eight hundred a month in alimony.'

'You could live on that.'

Arabella was quiet while he got his shoes off. Then she said, 'Eddie. When I got upset in North Carolina and wanted to come home, it wasn't just the boredom and the bad food.'

'I thought there was something.'

'I need to do more than support a man in his career. It was beginning to feel as if I'd never left Harrison.'

'Thanks.'

'I'm sorry. You're not like Harrison, but you're another kind of star.'

That annoyed him but he said nothing.

When she spoke again her voice was resigned. 'I could do more work for the arts-and-crafts journal. They've offered me an office for reading copy.'

'Take it.'

'It's still working for professors.'

'Then don't take it.'

'I just don't know.' She looked upset. She walked to her desk and picked up the folder with the paper she had just finished typing. 'Maybe all I want is to be with a good-looking man who's good at what he does.' She tossed the folder back on the desk. 'There's a lot of pressure on women these days to be themselves. Maybe it's all a mean joke.'

Eddie looked at her. 'No it isn't,' he said.

'But what can I *do*?'

He stood up barefoot and stretched. 'I know that one. 'It's a real son of a bitch.'

Chapter Six

The game was at a fairground outside Albuquerque; from the parking lot came the smell of horses and straw, even on a cold November day. When Eddie got out of the taxi, Fats was at a hot-dog stand, eating a Coney Island piled with chili. In the autumnal sunlight his face had a distinct pallor.

Fats chewed and swallowed before he spoke. 'I've seen the table,' he said. 'A four-and-a-half-by-nine Gandy. It looks all right.'

'You look pale, Fats,' Eddie said.

'I was sick two weeks ago.' Fats held his cue case under his arm and finished the hot dog. He wiped his fingers and chin with a paper napkin, wadded it, dropped it in a trash bin nearby.

'Maybe you shouldn't be here.'

'Being here is no problem. The chili dog is the problem.'

'Then stop eating chili dogs.'

'Let's play pool, Fast Eddie.' Fats turned and started walking toward the open-air arena with a banner reading THE GREAT MINNESOTA FATS AND FAST EDDIE SHOOT OUT. He was, as always, light on his feet.

In the taxi afterward, Eddie stared out the window at the distant Rockies. He had concentrated, shot well, seen the balls clearly and lost by seven points. One fifty to one forty-three.

Fats was leaning back in his seat, his black cue case across his lap. Finally he spoke. 'That was a good run.' Eddie had scored over eighty balls before missing a difficult bank shot.

Eddie said nothing. It made five matches in a row that Fats had beaten him. There would be only one more – at Indianapolis in early December. If he couldn't beat a seventy-year old man one game out of six, he was hopeless. He had no business trying to play pool for a living.

'Did you use the list?' Fats said.

'Most of it.' He had not tried the two towns at the bottom, although one was in driving distance of Lexington.

'It's a good list,' Fats said. 'I won money in every place on it.'

'It worked at first. I beat Billy Usho in Memphis for seven thousand. A few thousand from a man named Booker.'

'After that?'

As the road curved, Eddie could see the eminence of Scandia Peak, snow-capped, from between two lesser mountains. 'Nothing. Maybe enough to pay the hotel bill.'

'Did you find Ousley in Connors?'

'I hear it's a terrible place.'

'Ousley has money. He owns coal mines.'

'Maybe I'll go next week.' He looked at Fats. 'Tell me something. Have you ever had a job?'

'No.'

'Have you ever played nine-ball tournaments?'

'I don't like the kids who play them.' Nine-ball had always been a different world from the one Eddie knew, even though he had played it from time to time.

'If I don't take a job,' Eddie said, 'I've got to do something. There's more money in nine-ball than there is in bars.'

Fats pursed his lips. 'You might win the small ones.'

'There's a big one in Chicago next month. And then, in the spring, there's Lake Tahoe.'

'You won't win those. How much nine-ball have you played?'

'Not a lot.'

'Earl Borchard could beat you at straight pool, and he plays nine-ball better. You need more experience.'

'Fats, I *have* experience. I was beating every player in the country when those kids were in kindergarten.'

'This is nineteen eight-three,' Fats said.

'November.'

'That's right. I was looking in *Billiards Digest*. There's a tournament in Connecticut the day after we play in Indianapolis. It goes three days, and first prize is twenty-five hundred. You can practice nine-ball a few weeks and then get in.'

'I've *been* practicing.'

'That's right,' Fats said, 'but I just beat you.'

They drove the rest of the way to the airport in silence. When the driver slowed to get in line at the Eastern Airlines terminal, Fats said, 'It's mainly a matter of growing up.'

Eddie looked at him but said nothing.

Arabella was out when he let himself into the apartment. A note by the telephone read, 'Roy Skammer called twice,' and gave the number. He opened a beer and dialed.

'Fast Eddie,' Skammer said, 'how would you like a job?'

'You're full of surprises.'

'The man who runs the billiard room at the College Union is retiring, and I talked to the dean about hiring you.'

'How many tables?'

'Eight or ten. There's Ping-Pong, and some other things. Do you know where the building is?'

'Yes.' It was the only modern building he walked by on the way to the Faculty Club.

'Why don't you drop in tomorrow morning and look it over? The old man's name is Mayhew.'

'I will,' Eddie said.

Arabella had been serving wine and cheese at a student art show in the university gallery; she didn't get home until midnight. Eddie didn't mention the job. When she asked him about Fats he said, 'I still can't beat him.'

'Maybe next time.' She had gone into the bathroom to soak her feet. 'I don't know why I agreed to run those openings. Thelma's was more interesting.' She began filling the tub.

'Fats says I need to grow up if I want to beat the kids who play nine-ball.'

'That sounds like Heraclitus. The way up is the way down. The way forward is the way back.'

'I don't like riddles.

'Sorry,' Arabella said. She splashed water on her ankles and then bent to begin soaping her feet. 'I don't think I've ever understood growing up.'

'I was more of an adult at thirty than I am now.'

'You have to be grown-up to see that.'

'You have to be grown-up to do something about it,' Eddie said.

The first thing he saw when he came in the double doors was the row of machines: PacMan, Donkey Kong and Asteroids. They were in a basement anteroom, with a Pepsi dispenser and a row of pay phones. It was nine-thirty in the morning and no one was playing. Eddie walked past the machines, pushed open another pair of double doors and found himself in a poolroom of sorts. There were eight four-by-eight Brunswick tables in front and four Ping-Pong tables in back. Behind them was a row of a half-dozen pinball machines. To his right toward the far end of the room was a counter; behind it stood a sour-looking old man with dirty-looking white hair. He wore a striped shirt and a necktie, and he scowled at Eddie. From the ceiling hung long rows of fluorescent-light fixtures, several of which were flickering. The floor was covered with pale green plastic tile. From a radio on the desk beside the old man came the voice of the morning talk-show host Eddie had listened to, while opening up his own poolroom, for years.

After a minute the man looked in Eddie's direction and raised his eyebrows. Eddie turned and walked out. He would rather sell used cars than work in a place like that.

The sign said FOLK ART MUSEUM, but the place he parked by looked like a junkyard. There was a fence made of rusted bedsprings, each separate frame decorated with a painted metal cutout in the middle. The one nearest the car showed a man in a sombrero holding a red guitar; next to it was a giant daisy, its yellow center sun-faded and with rust at the edges of the white petals. The entrance, Arabella said, was around at the side. She led him past more cutouts – a top hat, Popeye, a crouched tiger – to a wide gap in the bedsprings, with a giant rabbit head at each side. Eddie looked at these a moment as they went through and saw they were made from the hoods of junked Volkswagens painted pink, with the big ears cut from fenders and welded on. They were not cute rabbit heads; they had wicked grins.

Eddie and Arabella were on the road to Connors, Kentucky, where he hoped to find and play pool with the man called Ousley. This junkyard that Arabella wanted to write about was on the way there.

The area inside the fence was the size of a football field. Filling it like a mad cocktail party were dozens of metal figures, most of them life-size and quasihuman. Near him was a steel woman with an enameled face and enormous breasts; it took Eddie a moment to realize the breasts, painted flesh color, had been made from automobile headlights. The body was car bumpers, the arms were exhaust pipes, the head was a piece of a muffler, and the beehive hairdo was of wires and springs, with sequins glued to the metal. The face had a horrible grin, a grin that was both come-on and deathly. She was dressed in a black rayon slip and stood on a small pedestal made of two-by-fours. On this sat a neatly lettered card reading NEW YORK MODEL.

'What do you think?' Arabella said. There was no shade in the yard, and she squinted up at him amusedly.

'It gets your attention,' Eddie said.

At the far end was a kind of shed with an enormous amount of clutter, mostly of rusted metal car parts. Arabella led Eddie that way, past figures of brightly painted women made from manifolds or exhaust systems or fenders or what appeared to be small boilers. Each had a pedestal and a card, with names like EVERYBODY'S AUNT HILDA or KINDERGARTEN TEACHER. Some of the women had the heads of animals. One of these chillingly bore the face of a praying mantis.

As they approached the shed a shirtless man emerged from the shadowy piles of junk that filled it. He was short and squat and heavily muscled. When he came out into the light, Eddie could see that his forearms were covered with tattoos. He looked to be in his sixties and angry.

'Hello, Mr Marcum,' Arabella said. 'I've brought a friend.'

The man squinted at him suspiciously and then at her. 'You're the Weems lady. Did you find me a Heliarc?'

'No,' Arabella said, 'I told you I couldn't afford it. This is Ed Felson.'

Marcum, who was even shorter than Arabella, peered up at him. Then he held out a stubby and scarred hand. 'She's a good lady,' he said, nodding toward Arabella. 'I can't get nothing out of her, but she's a good lady.'

'You make all these yourself?' Eddie looked back at the field full of metal women.

'Every goddamned one of them. You wouldn't have a beer in that car of yours?'

'No.'

'Maybe you could get us some.'

'After a bit, Mr Marcum,' Arabella said. 'I want to show Eddie your sculptures.'

'What happened to that young man? I thought he was going to sell my things in Lexington.'

Arabella looked at him a moment and then spoke carefully. 'You were asking for more money than Greg could pay. He said there would be no deal.'

'We were just haggling,' Marcum said. 'He could have called me back.'

'Greg wasn't able to invest anything near what you were asking. What I want to do, Mr Marcum,' Arabella said clearly, 'is interview you. I've brought a tape recorder.'

'The said I was going to be on television over a year ago but nobody came by. Maybe I wasn't pretty enough.'

'This isn't television. I want to do an article for *Kentucky Arts* magazine.'

'Is there money in it?'

'It might get some attention for you.'

'Shit,' Marcum said. 'My neighbors give me all the attention I want. Money's what I could use.' He turned to Eddie. 'You can buy us some beer at the A&P. Just take a left and go two blocks.'

'Okay,' Eddie said. 'What about Miller's?'

'Get Molson's, if they got it,' Marcum said. 'Heineiken's is all right too.'

'I'll get the recorder out of the car,' Arabella said.

As Eddie handed her the little Sony from the backseat, he said, 'Who's Greg?'

'An art dealer.'

Eddie put the key into the ignition. 'He's dead isn't he?'

'That's right,' Arabella said. She put the strap, over her shoulder and walked back into the junkyard. Eddie drove off, remembering the youthful face of the man in the newspaper. He could visualize the two of them – Arabella and the artistic young man – fussing over Marcum's crazy cartoon 'sculptures.' He got a six-pack of Molson's and a bag of Cheetos at the supermarket and then drove away.

Eddie walked around the yard in sunshine, drinking a beer from the bottle and looking at the statues as though they were people at a party. The materials they were made of were appropriate to the looks on their faces, to the insolent way they stood and stared forward. He felt an affinity for the anger of the old bastard, banging and welding his gallery of bitches in this dead-end coal-mining town. Arabella was back in the shade sitting on a rusted boiler interviewing Marcum. It was one of those surprisingly warm November days when the odd gust of wind could chill you while the open sun made you perspire. Eddie finished his beer, stared for a while at a chromium woman with a chromium dog on a real leash, and then walked back to the shed.

Arabella stood up as he came near. Apparently she had finished. Marcum was opening another beer for himself. 'I saw you looking at the woman with a dog,' Arabella said. 'I'm trying to buy it from Deeley.'

For some reason this irritated him. 'Where would you put it?'

'By the door to the bathroom. I like the New York Model, but she's awfully heavy and big. What do you think?'

'Buy what you want,' Eddie said. 'We can carry it in the backseat.' He walked over and got the last beer.

'I'm going to take another look,' Arabella said.

When she had left, Marcum spoke to him. 'How do you like my girls?'

'I like mine better.'

The old man laughed. 'She's a peach, all right. She your wife?'

'I don't have a wife.'

'That's the best way. Why buy a cow when you can get milk free?'

'I don't know anything about cows,' Eddie said. 'It looks like you don't care much for women.'

'People say that. I just call 'em the way I see 'em.'

'You must have seen some mean ones.'

The old man shrugged. 'If I could get the right kind of welding equipment. A Heliarc.' He looked at Eddie thoughtfully. 'That young man she was here with before you, when they came in on a motorcycle. He said you could buy a used Heliarc in Lexington.

'I don't know anything about welding either,' Eddie said. 'What kind of man was that young man?'

Arabella was out in the yard, bending over to look at the legs of the chromium woman.

Marcum peered up at him thoughtfully. 'I didn't like him.' He indicated Arabella – now standing with her hands on her hips – with a forward motion of his bald head. 'She liked him plenty, though.'

Eddie said nothing. He took a long drink from the beer bottle. Arabella came back over to them. 'Look,' she said to

Marcum, 'I'd like to have the woman and dog, but I don't have a lot of money.'

Marcum shrugged. 'I couldn't let it go for less than four thousand.'

'I just don't have it, Deeley.'

'A fellow from Chicago offered me six.'

'You should have sold it,' Eddie said.

'It's worth ten,' Marcum said. 'That piece makes a statement and it's got good, clean welds.'

Eddie nodded. He had seen the welds, and they were irregular and gapped. There was rust on the woman's feet where they touched the ground. It would take no more than two days to make that thing, including the dog. He reached into his pocket and pulled out the cash he had brought for pool. He counted off ten fifties, holding the money so Marcum could see it, slipped the rest of the roll back in his pocket and set the five hundred on a grinder table beside them. 'I'll give you this for it,' he said.

'That's a work of genuine American folk art,' Marcum said. 'There's thousands taken pictures of the piece and tried to buy it.' Marcum's livelihood consisted of charging people a dollar to see his 'museum' and take snapshots.

'You can make another in two days,' Eddie said. He looked hard at Marcum.

'It wouldn't be the same.'

'*Eddie*,' Arabella said, 'you don't just . . .'

He kept looking at Marcum. 'Maybe better.' He looked at the piles of scrap metal that virtually surrounded them. 'You've got enough bumpers here to make forty.'

Marcum looked at him angrily. 'I couldn't take less than a thousand.'

Eddie shrugged, picked up the bills and put them in hs pocket.

'Just a minute,' Marcum said softly, 'just a goddamned minute . . .'

'I had no idea you carried so much cash,' Arabella said. She was holding the metal dog in her lap as though it were a real puppy. The chromium woman lay on the backseat.

'Cash brings things into focus.'

'It seems wicked.'

'The man's broke. Five hundred will keep him in Molson's Ale til the Fourth of July.'

'Poor Deeley,' Arabella said. 'Poor Deeley.'

It took them another hour, going eastward along Interstate 64, to reach Connors. During the election campaign there had been a flood of Democratic television commercials showing shuttered factories and dying mill towns; Connors looked like one of those commercials. Eddie turned off the four-lane, rounded the cloverleaf, pulled up at a stop sign, and there it was: tin storefronts embossed to resemble stone, Kay's Luncheonette – a converted ranchhouse with dusty African violets in its picture window; small buildings of sooty concrete block bearing neon – BURTON'S DRIVE-IN LIQUORS, BILLY'S PACKAGE STORE, IRENE AND GEORGE'S BAR AND GRILL. As seen from the highway, the town's periphery was shut-down coal tipples and gray factories with empty parking lots; its center was the four-way stop sign where Eddie's car now sat.

He pressed the accelerator and went through the intersection.

'It might be fun,' Arabella said.

Eddie said nothing, and drove along the main street until he saw the sign directing them to the motel. He followed the route grimly and found the motel at the edge of town, with a view of the interstate highway they had just left. The Bonnie Brae Inn – TV, Pool, $22.00 DBL. He pulled into the near-empty parking lot, by the sign saying 'Office.'

'This is it?' Arabella said.

'Unless we go to Huntington, West Virginia.'

'And you'd commute. Is there anything interesting in Huntington?'

'There's a Chinese restaurant.'

'Let's try it here,' Arabella said cheerfully.

The room wasn't too bad. Eddie carried her Selectric in from the car, set it on the round table by the window and plugged it in. There was a straight-back chair by the dresser, and she brought that over, put a sheet of paper in the typewriter and typed a few lines. 'It'll be fine,' she said, looking up at him.

'I'll get the other things.' He took the box from the car trunk with the Vesuviana, the can of espresso, the loaf of bakery rye, the cups and spoons and the hot plate, the half-dozen books and the big bottle of dry white wine. Then he brought in the woman and dog made from car bumpers and set it by the window. The view was of a barren field with dark hills in the distance, but the light was good. He began checking things out. The television worked; the mattress was firm; the carpet underfoot was thick. Arabella had taken off her shoes and was walking around.

'I ought to carpet my apartment, Eddie,' she said. 'It's fun to go barefoot.'

'The statue looks good,' Eddie said. 'I'll give you a call if I'm going to be late.'

The bar at the Palace had one of those big-screen projection TVs; a quiet row of men in working clothes were watching a Rock Hudson movie on it as he came in. He stood at the bar, ordered a beer and looked around. Behind him sat two coin-operated tables, with no players.

'I'm looking for a man named Ousley,' he said when the bartender gave him the bottle.

'Ousley?'

'He plays pool for money.'

The old man sitting next to Edde looked up. 'If it's Ben Ousley you want, he's gone to California. Two years back.'

'You a pool player?' the man on the other side said, reaching out shakily to touch Eddie's cue case.

'I'm looking for a game.'

'Used to be some big games in here,' the first old man said. A younger man down at the end of the bar spoke up. 'Norton Dent,' he said clearly. 'He'll play you.' Eddie did not like the tone of his voice.

'Fine,' Eddie said. 'Where is he?'

'He might be in tonight,' the young man said, looking down the bar at Eddie. 'Maybe tomorrow.'

'Can you call him?'

The young man looked away. 'No. You'll have to wait.'

Eddie shrugged. There was a quarter change from his beer. He put it in the table, racked the balls, opened his cue case and took out his cue. When he was screwing it together he looked up to see that most of the men at the bar were ignoring the movie; they had swiveled in their seats to watch him. It was somehow unnerving, being stared at by these lean old men in blue and gray shirts. They watched impassively from small eyes set in seamed faces, like a photograph from the Great Depressions.

He broke the rack and began to shoot, banking the balls. The table was easy. His stroke was smooth and certain and he made clean shots, bringing them sharply off the cushions and into the pockets. It was a matter of getting the feel of the table under pressure, and keeping it. He had almost forgotten that, over the years. He ignored the men watching him, neither grandstanding for them nor missing deliberately to devieve them; and he banked the balls in prettily with his glossy Balabushka. It was reassuring to come into a strange place like this, with its dim hostility, and fall immediately into perfect stroke.

He came to the bar and got two dollars' worth of quarters. The movie was still on, but no one was watching. They were all looking at him. He got the change and went back to the table.

By six in the evening, the bar was full of men, but no one wanted to play. There was a grubby washroom, and he cleaned the table grime from his hands as well as he could before taking his cue apart and putting it back in the case.

The young man was still at the end of the bar, still drinking Rolling Rock beer. He didn't turn around when Eddie came up to him. 'I'll be back at eight-thirty,' Eddie said. 'If your friend comes in, tell him I'm looking for him.'

'He's no friend of mine,' the man said, staring at his beer bottle.

'Eight-thirty,' Eddie said.

The young man turned around and looked up at him with a cold, inward stare. 'I'll tell him your name. If you'll tell it to me.'

'Ed Felson,' Eddie said. 'I'm called Fast Eddie.'

The young man turned back to his beer.

'I did eight pages on Deeley and watched 'Search for Tomorrow.' Or maybe it was 'Search for an Abortionist,' considering the overall tone.'

'You had a better day than I did.'

'It wasn't bad. I took a walk down the road and found a drive-in movie.'

'Maybe we can go tonight. The man I'm waiting for may not show up.'

"*Debbie Does Dallas*,' Arabella said. She was pouring them each a glass of white wine from the big bottle, using the motel's plastic glasses. 'I suspect it's about oral sex.'

'Sounds like a winner.' Eddie seated himself on the bed next to a pile of Arabella's papers and took the wine glass 'We'll stay through tomorrow. The player I was looking for, the one Fats told me about, isn't in town, but there's one other. He'll be in tonight or tomorrow.'

Dent was there when he came in. He was a huge, soft-looking man in his thirties, with sideburns and a gray T-shirt with the words EAT ME. He was shooting balls on Eddie's table, using a using a cheap jointed cue with a scarlet butt. The young man was still sitting at the bar. The TV was off. On the jukebox Bobbie Gentry sang 'Ode to Billy Joe.' A couple of the old men had their heads on folded arms at the bar. 'Here he is,' the young man said coldly to the big man at the table. 'Fast Eddie.'

The big man went on shooting. He was drilling the balls straight in, and he looked good at it. When he had finished the table, slamming the last ball the long diagonal into the far corner pocket, he looked up at Eddie. His face was pale and treacherous-looking, with a pout to the thick lips. He had the weedy beginnings of a mustache. Bobby Gentry finished and Johnny Cash started, 'Don't Think Twice, It's All Right.' Eddie did not like the looks of the man nor the feeling in the buzzed-out barroom, but decided to heed Cash's words and go with it.

'I heard of you,' Dent said.

Eddie nodded noncomittally. 'Do you want to play eight-ball?'

'I expect you mean for money,' Dent said in a drawl, 'being as they say you're a hustler.'

'I started hustling pool thirty years ago,' Eddie said. 'I'll play you eight-ball for fifty a game if you want to play.'

'Shit,' the man said, 'you sound mean as a snake, Fast Eddie. Maybe you're just too good for me.'

Eddie shrugged. 'Maybe I am.'

'I'll try you for fifty.'

'Fine,' Eddie said. He took his glasses from the pocket of his leather jacket and put them on.

They tossed a coin for the break. The other man won it, broke the balls wide and ran half the solids before dogging a thin cut into the corner. Eddie played it carefully and had him beaten in five minutes. He was nervous but he had no trouble controling the game. The room was silent when he finished. Dent reracked the balls. Then he reached up with the tip of his cue and slid a wooden bead along the string near the back wall over a big Miller's High Life poster.

Eddie looked at him.

'Break the balls,' Dent said.

'You owe me fifty dollars.'

'On the string,' Dent said, looking back over his shoulder toward it. Then he reached into his pocket and pulled out a clump of bills fastened with a money clip in the shape of a naked woman, and flashed it for Eddie, 'Okay?'

'It's the way we do it here,' the young man at the bar said.

Eddie shrugged stepped to the table and broke the balls. He ran four of the solids and then missed deliberately, leaving Dent an easy shot on two stripes. Dent ambled heavily up to the table and began shooting; he made all the stripes and then pocketed the eight. Eddie felt annoyed at himself for making it that easy. The man was good enough without help. He would play it straight and not throw off; he would beat this man, with his dangerous baby face, his hostile, shifting eyes until he quit.

It was difficult at first. Dent shot eight-ball well, but Eddie bore down and beat him, gradually adding beads to the string. His stroke was better than it had been for years, better even than during the long run against Fats at Albuquerque; he bent and shot, bent and shot, and the balls kept falling in. He won six in a row before Dent set his cue against the wall and took a huge sheepskin coat from a hook near it. He put the coat on, his back to Eddie.

Eddie looked up at the string. There were twelve beads pushed over to his side of it. He looked toward Norton Dent, even huger in his coat, and began taking his cue apart.

'You owe me six hundred dollars, Norton,' Eddie said.

Dent turned slowly. His voice was soft, almost amiable. 'You've got to collect it.'

Eddie had the cue in two pieces now. He set the smaller one, the shaft, on the table. He took off his glasses and set them beside it. 'Is that how you pay what you owe, Norton?' he said levelly. The danger was palpable, but he ignored it, did not care about it. He wanted to kill this oaf.

Dent took a step closer. Behind him, every man in the room was staring at them, waiting.

'I don't pay what I don't have to pay,' Dent said, 'you pool-shark piece of shit.'

For a moment Eddie felt a horrible weariness, heard an old voice saying *Do I have to do all this*? He gripped the small end of the cue butt, stepped forward and swung hard, going for the side of the man's head.

Dent was young, and faster than he looked. He ducked and turned; the stick fell across the collar of his coat. With his free arm Eddie rammed him in the stomach, cursing the coat that would soften the blow and knowing it wasn't going to work, that he was going to get hurt. Maybe the others at the bar would stop the man.

Immediately Dent's weight was on him, wrapping him in a bear hug, the greasy smell of the coat in his face. He dropped the cue butt and got in one solid punch against the side of the man's nose before the sheer weight on his body held him down and a blow crashed against his neck and seemed to explode intolerably in his head.

He came to as some men were putting him into the back-seat of his car. He was numb and could not see well. The men had been talking, and one of them was saying, 'You can follow us and pick me up.' It was the young man, the one who had been presiding over this whole thing, from the start. He was talking to a man in a red baseball cap. 'Where to?' the man in the cap said.

The young man seemed friendly and sympathetic now. His coldness had gone. 'You'll be all right,' he said to Eddie in a confidential tone of voice. 'Have you got a place to spend the night?'

'The Bonnie Brae.'

'Give me his pool stick and glasses,' the young man said to the one in the baseball cap. An older man was standing next to him, watching with solicitude. Eddie was sitting in the car, with the door beside him closed and the window down. The young man climbed into the driver's seat. The man in the cap put Eddie's cue case through the window and Eddie took it. He followed with the glasses. 'Let me have your keys,' the young man said. Everything seemed friendly, well-organized. It was as though they did this every day of their lives. Eddie felt his face for blood, but there wasn't any. He reached into his jacket pocket, found the keys, handed them up to the driver. 'Pump the gas pedal first,' he said.

'You got him in the eye.' the old man said. 'He's a rough son of a bitch.'

Eddie leaned back in his seat, beginning to feel the pain in his body. He worked his hands a minute. They were all right. Nothing broken.

'My god!' Arabella said. 'Did you get drunk?'

'I got beaten up.'

'I think you bloody did.'

It was after midnight, but she was able to get a first-aid kit from the motel office and put Bactine and Band-Aids on the cuts across his back, from the poolroom floor. He had bruises, but there was nothing to do about them. A blotchy place was developing on the side of his neck, and there was a smaller bruise on his forehead. He hurt badly in three places and his head throbbed. He was still dizzy. In the bathroom mirror his face looked terrible. 'That gross son of a bitch,' he said. 'I'd like to go back there and break his thumbs.'

'How horrible,' Arabella said.

'It would hurt like hell.' He came into the bedroom, limping slightly. His right leg was getting stiff. Arabella's typewriter sat on the table with a stack of paper and the coffee-maker beside it. The plastic curtain over the closed window had the same design of boomerangs that the restaurant table had. On the dresser next to the TV sat the wine bottle. He poured himself a glassful carefully, using the hand that was the least sore, and then took a long swallow. He turned to look at her sitting against the bed pillows. 'When we go back,' he said, 'I'll take the job.'

Arabella was no longer a faculty wife, but she was still invited to faculty parties. The first time she suggested he go, Eddie declined; but he was bored at the apartment watching television alone, and he went with her the next weekend. For an hour or so he felt uneasy with the professors and their talk of tenure and department cutbacks. He was painfully conscious of his own lack of education. The home he was in, with canvases on the walls painted by the professor who had invited them, with its plain, expensive furniture, represented an entirely different scale of life from the house he had lived in with Martha, with its cheery wallpaper in the kitchen. The kitchen here was white and austere; the men who stood around in it with drinks in their hands were all professors of art or English or history. Eddie read books but he knew nothing about those disciplines; nothing, from experience, about college.

But he did not live with Martha anymore. The elegant British woman in the silk dress, the woman with the curly silver hair and bright, intelligent eyes who looked right at men when she talked to them and who moved around with these people as more than an equal, was his woman. And he did not live in a suburban house with asphalt shingles on its sides; he lived in a high-ceilinged, white-walled apartment with folk-art paintings, downtown on Main Street.

Standing in the kitchen near the refrigerator, he listened to three art professors across the room. They were discussing next year's raise in salary. One of them changed the subject to the Cincinnati Bengals' chances for the Superbowl. No one was talking about art. No one had talked about art or literature or history in the hour he had been in the house. He looked at their clothes; not one of them was dressed as well as he. He took a sip from his Manhattan, walked over to the group and joined in. They talked about the scarcity of good quarterbacks. After a while, Eddie introduced himself. There was nothing to it.

The bedroom overlooked a garden that separated the building from the back of a clothing store. There was a kitchen with white countertops, a dining alcove, and a big living room overlooking Main Street. They would have to buy a dining table and bedroom furniture. It was on the second floor and the view from the living room was not as broad as the view from Arabella's other apartment, but they were still downtown. Arabella had just started her editorial job with the journal and she was too busy to take more than a quick look; but when he told her it was three sixty a month, she said, 'Take it, Eddie.' He signed the lease and gave two months' rent as a deposit. Then he called a moving company.

'Eddie,' Skammer said, 'I'd drop it all and go on the road. I don't care about tenure. If I could shoot pool like you shoot pool. . . Shit, if I could play the *oboe*, or learn to be a chef. . . .' They were in the Skammers' big kitchen.

'Roy signed up for a cooking school in France,' Pat said, 'but we backed out at the last minute.'

'Lost my nerve.' Skammer plucked the onion from his Gibson and held it between thumb and forefinger for a moment.

'Lost your deposit money too,' Pat said.

Skammer shrugged and popped the onion into his mouth.

'It's hard to make a change,' Eddie said.

'You're doing it,' Arabella said.

He looked up from the couch at her. 'It was handed to me. The judge gave the poolroom to Martha.'

'Some have greatness thrust upon them,' Skammer said.

Eddie looked back to him. Skammer wore perfectly fitting beige corduroys, beige Saucony running shoes and a white cotton boat-neck sweater that fit him loosely. 'What's wrong with teaching history?'

'Grading the papers,' Skammer said immediately.

'You complain a lot about departmental meetings,' Pat said, 'and about living in Kentucky.'

'Camouflage,' Skammer said. 'I give lecture courses in world history, and I *enthrall* students with my enlightened chatter. I point to maps and I tell anecdotes about the wives of generals. I describe political factions and frown over conditions in the cities.'

'It sounds fine to me,' Eddie said.

'You *love* it,' Pat said levelly. 'You love the sound of your own voice.'

'Maybe I do. But when I read the humbug they write in exam books with their blue Bics, I want to cut my throat.'

'You and your exquisite sensibilities,' Pat said. 'Sit down and I'll serve the salad.'

'You're changing the subject,' Roy said. 'Everytime I read their papers I want to resign.'

'Maybe it's because there's no show business in grading papers,' Pat said.

'You and your damned insights,' Roy said, cheerfully.

The Skammers lived in a farmhouse on the Old Frankfort Pike. All of the rooms were austere except for the kitchen, which had a brick fireplace and a white sofa. The high-tech table and chairs were lit by track lights, and the floor was scarred pine, varnished and bare. A big window looked on a field with patches of snow and a barn in the distance.

Arabella put the salad bowl on the table and carried the wooden fork and spoon to Roy. 'Toss the salad,' she said. 'Maybe you don't want feedback from your students.'

'That's the truth,' Roy said. He went over to the table and slipped the implements under the mound of lettuce leaves in the wooden bowl. 'Maybe I just want to show off.'

'There are worse things than that,' Eddie said.

Roy began agitating the leaves expertly. 'I'd rather shoot pool,' he said.

'In front of an audience,' Pat said.

'*Honi soit qui mal y pense*,' Roy said, lifting the leaves and letting them drop back into the bowl.

'The trouble with shooting pool,' Eddie said, 'is that it's no good if you don't win.'

'Ain't *that* the truth,' Skammer said.

'Let's eat,' Pat said. 'The roast'll be ready in ten minutes.

When they were driving home Eddie asked Arabella how much money the Skammers made.

'He's an associate professor,' she said. 'Twenty-six

thousand, probably. She's an assistant and makes about twenty.'

'They're doing all right.'

Arabella was quiet for a minute. Then she said, 'I think he really does hate it. He doesn't have the strength to leave.'

'It sounds like a good life to me.'

'He tried to kill himself. A couple of years ago.'

'Come *on*. . . .' Eddie said.

'With pills. He took a sabbatical to write a book and he didn't write anything. Just hung around the house and tinkered with the plumbing. One morning he didn't wake up and Pat took him to the hospital. They pumped him out.'

Eddie shook his head. 'I wouldn't have thought he was the type.'

'Well,' Arabella said, 'there's a lot of it going around.'

The second drugstore he tried had dental plaster. He bought two cartons of the large size, along with a deck of plastic playing cards, and put them in the backseat. The next morning he drove out to the old poolroom.

The windows were boarded up, but the key still opened the front door. There were no workmen around. He had never seen workmen, only the sporadic effects of their presence. The carpet was gone now, and the counter had been torn out and lay against the wall like a passed-out drunk. He ignored all this and walked to the back wall where the closet door stood by the men's room, still bearing its Employees Only sign. Nothing in it had been touched. He took down a large roll of cloth wrapped in clear plastic and labeled SIMONIS, easing it from the top shelf and putting it into an empty toilet-paper box. On another shelf was the tenon lathe, like an oversize pencil sharpener; he set it carefully next to the roll of cloth and then got the magnetic tack hammer, the four-foot level and a stack of roofing shingles. From a low shelf he took a small carton labeled TWEETEN ELK MASTER and a cardboard box filled with white plastic cylinders. He took those and then looked around himself. After the familiarity of the supplies closet, the devastated poolroom was a synchronistic shock, moving him instantaneously from the way things had been to the way they were now. The effect was not altogether unpleasant; there was no love in him for this place. He could have torn it apart himself. He looked at his watch. It was seven-thirty. The college Rec Room didn't open until nine.

He got there a little before eight and locked the door behind him for privacy. Mayhew's supplies closet was at the end of the room facing the pinball machines; he got from it a brace with a fork bit, a hex wrench and a screwdriver.

In ten minutes he had the rails off number eight and was removing the old cloth, using the screwdriver to pry loose the staples that held it. When he was finished he folded the faded and worn fabric and put it in the trash. The three-piece slate underneath was a mess; he cleaned out the loose plaster and then picked the rails up from the floor and set them on it. By the time he had the feather strips pulled and the old cloth off the cushions, it was nine. He stopped working, turned on the rest of the lights and opened up. Three students were at the door, all of them in down coats, waiting to play the arcade machines. He got quarters for them from the cash register and went back to work, ignoring the dim electronic threats from the machines and the voices of the students.

You had to level the table itself first; if you did it after patching the slate, the patches would crack. He used the center slate for a benchmark, setting the level across it and then tapping a shingle under one of the table legs to bring the bubble to center. He switched the level to right angles, checked it and slipped in another shingle. It took several minutes to get it right, placing the level the long way, the short way, and diagonally, choosing between thick and thin shingles. Three black students came in to play nine-ball; he gave them the balls and the diamond-shaped nine-ball rack, ticketed their table for the time. The clock punched out 11:42 on the card. The lunchtime crowd would be in at about twelve-thirty; he would be too busy to finish the table. He hurried back to it, wanting to get the three pieces of slate leveled and patched before that happened.

It went pretty fast. It was years since he had done any of this, but he had forgotten none of it. There was something deeply satisfying about doing it and doing it right. Not many people knew how. Clearly, Mayhew – or whoever did it for him – did not. Eddie got the rest of the old plaster off the slates and leveled them, sliding playing cards between the big slabs of slate and the wooden joists that held them, raising one end and then the other by the thickness of two aces or a jack, until they were all three perfectly aligned. He sighted down each end of the table and then used the level. With a whiskbroom he swept the plaster dust away; he went back to the closet, took an empty coffee can and began mixing the dental plaster.

The joints of the slates were patched in twenty minutes, along with the countersink holes for the heavy screws that held the slates in place. By the time he was finished, the lunchtime crowd began to come in and he let the plaster dry while he marked time cards and handed out balls.

He had to stay behind the counter for the next hour and a half, keeping an eye on things, making change and taking in money. During a short break he clamped the tenon machine to the countertop; then he took a few cues that were in need of repair and began replacing their ferrules. The Elk Master tips would go on later. One cue was too warped to be worth the effort; he put it in the trash with the worn-out cloth from Table Eight.

At two the crowd slacked off abruptly, leaving for classes. It would be slow until three-thirty or so, when Mayhew came in. They would work together to handle the crowd until Eddie left at five. By two-thirty, a dozen cues had new white ferrules and leather tips. He went back to Table Eight and sanded down the plaster, using progressively finer paper until the joints were silky and rock-hard. He checked the bed one final time with the level and then unrolled the Simonis cloth. At first he planned to save this one superb billiard cloth for last; now he had decided to start out with it. He had been saving it for several years, for a rainy day. His rainy days had come, and maybe gone. He got shears out and began to cut the strips for the six rails. It took him two hours to get the cloth cut, trimmed, pulled tightly over the rubber cushions and held in place with the feather strips. But the material was a pleasure to work with. It was virgin wool from Belgium – fine, smooth, tightly woven and a dazzlingly bright green. By four o'clock he had the rest of it cut, stretched across the slate table bed and fitted around the six pockets. He was kneeling beside the table putting in the last of the number-three tacks with the tack hammer when Mayhew came in.

Eddie had said to him several days before that he planned to work on the equipment; Mayhew had nodded curtly and muttered, 'Go ahead.' Now he ignored Eddie and went behind the counter and turned the radio on, to his gospel show. Eddie gritted his teeth and spit the last of the tacks out onto the peen of the hammer. The show would go for two hours, with sanctimonious music, a sermon and letters. It was infuriating, but there was nothing to do about it except wait for spring, when Mayhew would leave for good, retiring from his twenty-year job of running this half-assed poolroom. After a few minutes, during a commercial for Preparation H, Mayhew walked back to the men's room, passing Eddie but not looking at him. Eddie had the first rail in place and was fastening it to the slate bed with a hex wrench. When Mayhew came back a few minutes later, he stopped and looked over the freshly covered table. Eddie finished one of the rails and set the wrench down. 'These Gold Crowns are solid,' he said. 'Good slates and rails.'

Mayhew looked at him a moment. 'There was a lot of wear left in that old cloth.'

They had all the pictures hung, but there were still Arabella's books in boxes. They spent that evening putting them into the built-in book cases in the dining room. 'You haven't said much about your job,' Arabella said.

'There's not much to say about it.'

'How's Mayhew?'

'I can stand him till spring.'

'Do you shoot any pool?'

'I don't have the time. How do you like editing?'

She didn't answer for a moment but worked on the books, getting them alphabetized onto the shelves. 'I ought to read these Chekhov stories,' she said after a while. 'I've had the books a dozen years. Editing an academic journal's a bore.'

'Maybe you'll find something better.'

'It isn't likely.'

'What we need,' Eddie said, 'is a drink.'

Arabella put the last of the Chekhov volumes neatly on their shelf, stood back and looked at them. 'A drink,' she said, 'and then a movie.'

During the next week, he covered Tables Six and Seven, using Peerless rubber-backed cloths this time. They were less elegant then the Simonis on Number Eight, but were durable and certainly better than what they replaced. The cloths had been sitting in a stack on the top shelf of Mayhew's supply closet; Eddie saw them there on his first day. They were covered with a layer of dust.

After doing the tables he went to work in earnest on the rest of the cues, throwing out a half-dozen warped or split ones, re-tenoning some, putting new white plastic points and fresh tips on all of them, sanding and buffing the leather edges so they fit perfectly and would not bulge out in use. It was tough work, but satisfied something in him that needed satisfaction. He had not worked this hard since the first month of owning his own poolroom.

Mayhew made no further comments and Eddie spoke to him only when necessary. There was usually a dead hour after the lunch crowd left, and now Eddie spent the time practicing, taking his Balabushka in its case from under the counter. He used Number Eight, enjoying the smooth, long roll the Simonis gave to the balls. He had cleaned the light fixtures over the tables and polished all eight sets of balls, had thrown away all the used chalk and put fresh blue cubes out. The light was clear and bright; the balls shone crisply on the green; Eddie drilled them into pockets with quiet precision. What he was practicing, for the first time in his life, was nine-ball.

He would rack the balls into the little diamond with the yellow-striped nine in its center, blow them apart with his strongest break shot and then run them in rotation, starting with the one and working up to the money ball – the nine. It was different from the straight pool he knew: you had to make tougher shots, and play position differently, running them out in the numbered sequence. Maybe the most important thing was that you had to work the entire green. A good straight-pool player kept the balls at the bottom of the table and did most of his scoring on tight shots. In nine-ball you had to go from one end to another, sometimes making the cue ball travel by two or three cushions to settle down for position. He would miss some of those long, difficult shots, or get so badly off-angled that he couldn't give himself position on the next ball. The pressure built as you approached the nine. If you missed on the seven or eight it would give the game away.

Arabella worked from nine to five at the magazine's office on campus. Her salary was twelve hundred a month, only slightly less than Eddie's; it came from a government grant. With her salary, her alimony and his paycheck, they were well off. They ate dinner out most evenings, did not entertain, and went to every new movie in town. They made an odd couple – a former faculty wife and a former pool hustler – but their oddness was consonant with the times; they were invited to a lot of parties. Eddie drove them through snowy streets to suburban houses or to duplexes in older neighborhoods to drink with professors of sociology, history or art. His lack of education did not inhibit him. People talked about tenure or declining SAT scores among the students; at the homes of younger professors, pot was smoked ceremonially as a kind of testament to youth. Eddie would pass the joint without inhaling. He preferred bourbon. J.T.S Brown.

At one of these parties Eddie was talking to Arabella near the kitchen door of someone's house when he saw her staring toward the other end of the room. He looked over to see a couple who had just come in. The man was tall and youthfully middle-aged; he wore a gray turtleneck under his parka. The girl with him was much younger. She wore tight faded jeans and a sweater like the man's, also under a parka. The man's boyish face looked familiar to Eddie; he was noisily stamping packed snow from his hiker's boots and did not seem to mind the commotion he was making. 'It's Harrison,' Arabella said softly.

'Who's the girl?'

'Some graduate student.'

Eddie had seen him on television years before. It seemed he had worn the same sweater, the same boots, while talking about disadvantaged children or New York artists or whatever it was. He was tanned and muscular-looking; his shoes and sweater looked expensive, as did his heavy corduroy pants and the long, matching scarf. He had one of those faces that manages to appear modest and smug at the same time, as if he knew he was important and did not want to imply that he knew it.

A half hour later Eddie found himself talking with him. Arabella was not in the room at the time. Frame just came up, and said, 'You're Felson, aren't you?' and Eddie said, 'That's right,' and they talked casually for about five minutes. It was simple; neither mentioned Arabella. They talked about the recession.

For the occasion, Arabella had bought Italian white wine and California Burgundy, together with a quarter-wheel of Brie – the runniest Eddie had seen. During his first weeks with

Arabella he had felt he was finally entering the modern world of American style and had responded to it happily enough: dry wine, French cheese, English biscuits to put the cheese on, Perrier, rare lamb, sushi. Sometimes Arabella cooked osso bucco or couscous – dishes he had never heard of before. He had not shown any surprise at this kind of living; it went with her appearance, her accent. Sometimes she put liver pâté on wholewheat English muffins for breakfast and served them with espresso from her stout little Vesuviana, in white cups with baroque silver spoons. It was like a certain kind of movie, or pages seen in Arabella's *New York* magazine or the magazine section of her Sunday *Times*.

One of the striking things about university life was its amiable ostentation of taste, and not just in food. It included furniture, paintings, bric-a-brac – glass ashtrays from Venice, nineteenth-century prints showing views of Brussels, antique chess sets. Not everyone was involved in this; some were either oblivious to it or scorned it. Their apartments were furnished cheaply and their cuisinary embellishments were those of the early sixties: flaky Cheddar, mushrooms, and pepper mills. But half the homes Eddie had seen were exemplars of careful, *au courant* taste, mixing antiques with high tech. If the apartment you were in for Sunday brunch had track lights over a walnut highboy and a piece or two of industrial metal furniture, you knew there would be croissants – served with unsalted butter on a plain white dish from Scandinavia – and the eggs would be undercooked.

The best thing about all this was Arabella's ease with it. It was as though she knew her British accent and the delicate, clear structure of her facial bones gave her an edge. There was no strain on her part and no uncertainty; she knew without hesitation which cheeses, which fresh pasta and which wines to order, just as she had known what spare, simple pieces of furniture to buy for the new apartment. She was sure, swift and without snobbery. Coming from a world of backyard barbecues, Eddie slipped with surprising ease into this ambience, pleased with Arabella's confidence, pleased with the way she never talked about such things.

Roy and Pat were delayed; by the time they got out of their duffel coats and were handed glasses of wine by Eddie it was four o'clock. He wheeled Arabella's little Sony in front of the sofa and turned it on. Arabella put the cheese and the Carr's wafers on the high-tech coffee table; Roy Skammer held his wine glass aloft and said, 'To the champ himself!' and the television picture shifted from a movie preview to a rack of pool balls in closeup and the superimposed words, THE GREAT SHOOTOUT – DENVER. An overhead shot showed Fats breaking the rack. The cue ball caromed into the bottom and the side rail; its path, seen from above, was like a geometric diagram. A voice-over began, calling the two players 'legendary' and the game 'demanding the most a player can give.' It was mercifully short and it mercifully omitted saying that Eddie, had already lost three matches in the series. Now Eddie, seen from overhead, stepped up to play safe. Pat and Roy applauded. Now in profile, Fats made a shot, and then another. His run would be in the twenties. This was the game where Eddie made sixty-three, but Fats had the floor now. A whispered commentary – whispered needlessly, since it had been added after the game – spoke of the difficulty of shots that were not difficult and passed over ones that were; the tape had been edited so it all went faster than in reality. Every now and then the camera picked up Eddie wearing his glasses and sitting in his chair waiting for Fats to miss. When Fats did miss, Eddie stepped up and went to the table. It was a relief to see it: he was far less slow and uncertain than in the Miami game on Enoch's monitor. He looked all right, even with the glasses. Eddie watched himself pocket a dozen balls and then play safe. His stroke was sharp and smooth.

Much of the midgame was cut; while Arabella was pouring more wine the tape abruptly segued to Eddie's big run – already thirty balls into it. He was shocked to see the change in himself on the screen. His stroke had been good before, but now it had a control that was visible even on television.

His body was relaxed. His movements were as graceful as those of Fats or of Billy Usho. He looked sharp in his clothes. He could remember the good, near-dead stroke he had felt at the time of the run, could recall the sense of inevitability in the way the balls fell in, but he had no idea that he looked so good.

'Eddie,' Pat Skammer said, 'You look *wonderful*!' and some obscure, uncertain part of himself assented. It was a revelation. He looked as good as any pool player he had ever seen. The small Eddie Felson in front of him pocketing pool balls with precision and flair, walking confidently from shot to shot was *him*. He sipped his white wine and watched himself. He would lose the game 150-112, but he could have won it.

'Do you play any more matches?' Roy asked.

'One. Next week.'

'What about 'Wide World of Sports'?' Arabella said.

'Nothing.'

Finally Eddie missed, on the Sony in front of them. '*Aww!*' Pat Skammer said. Fats stepped up and began what would be his final run.

'I'll beat him in Indianapolis,' Eddie said. 'I'll beat his ass.'

On Monday in the Rec Room, several of the players said they watched the game on TV and he looked great. One of them remembered shots that had been especially impressive. But when Mayhew came in and a student asked, 'Did you see Mr Felson on TV Saturday?' Mayhew scowled at him.

'I see more games in *here* than I want to see,' he said.

The airplane landed in a hush of snow – airport runway snow not yet soiled. Even the passengers were muted by it, waiting in wombish quiet for permission to stand and retrieve their luggage, then standing mute in the aisle as though the white outside the plane's baby windows had charmed them to silence. This mood remained until assaulted by the Formica, Orlon and Muzak cheeriness inside the terminal building, bright as a liar's smile. Eddie tucked his cue case under his arm, walking through this fluorescent limbo to Baggage Claim. Through windows framed in pitted aluminum, he saw giant toys of airplanes bearing familiar heraldry – Trans World, Delta, United – being tended in a field of white. He hurried. It was December 12; he was to meet Fats in two hours. He found his bag on the carousel, and then a taxi.

Despite the gray slush in the parking lot and the dense rows of cars whose owners filled the mall, his driver zipped along without delay. Eddie was over an hour early. The driver stopped at the entrance to an enormous J. C. Penney's; on his way there he passed a restaurant with a sign reading TONY'S PIZZA – COCKTAILS. Eddie carried his bag and stick through Christmas-crowded aisles and tinkling music to the side of the store that faced the mall itself, a wide gallery with huge Christmas trees and an artificial creek. On the other side of an enormous aviary was a sign that read PARCEL CHECK and a row of lockers; he walked past sleeping macaws and a cockatoo, the floor of their cage littered with yellow popcorn, and put his things in a locker. Far down to his right, above the heads of a shifting multitude, a banner read FAST EDDIE MEETS FATS. He was pleased to see the top billing. This time he was ready. He would lock up Fats with safeties; and when he got a shot, would bear down on him as he had not borne down on him throughout this tour. Eddie turned and headed toward Tony's. Fats was no unbeatable genius, no benevolent father either; he was an old man and, like anyone else, he made mistakes. Eddie would beat him.

Tony's tables were full of women and the bar empty. Eddie sat in the middle of it and ordered a Bloody Mary. There was, fortunately, no music in Tony's; it smelled pleasantly of oregano and hot bread dough. The bartender was a good-natured young woman in a red sweater. He had drunk nothing on the airplane, and the pepper from the Bloody Mary burned pleasurably on his tongue. He liked the warm, pungent anonymity of this American place – liked being unidentifiable among middle-aged women. He sat in a suburb of Indianapolis but could have been anywhere at all; there was probably a Tony's Pizza in Bangor, Maine, or in Honolulu that would be indistinguishable from this, with no character but what its designer had given it and a manufactured ambience that could have made it all: the women with their children in booths eating pizza, the Budweiser clock on the wall over the bar, the red-sweatered blonde who served him drinks – part of some jolly TV commercial for, say, the telephone company.

In his jacket pocket was a page torn from a Rec Room copy of *Billiards Digest* that morning. He took it out now, spread it on the bar in front of him and read over the ad:

EASTERN STATES CHAMPIONSHIP
NINE-BALL EVENT
$7,000 IN PRIZES!
FIRST PLACE: $2,500
ENTRY FEE: $350 DECEMBER 13, 14, 15
MABLEY'S BILLIARDS
NEW LONDON, CONN
DEFENDING CHAMP:
GORDON (BABES) COOLEY

He would show it to Fats and ask him what he thought. He finished his drink and ordered another, letting the sweet warmth in his stomach spread, thinking of pool.

He was whistling when he got his cue case from the locker. He began moving through the crowd of Christmas shoppers down toward the banner.

When he arrived it was time to start, but Fats wasn't there. The table was set up and ready – a Brunswick table for a change, with an honest green cloth. At least a hundred people were seated in the stands and another hundred were hanging around waiting for something to happen. But time passed and Fats did not show up. Eddie called the Ramada Inn and they rang Fats' room, but no one answered. The shopping-mall manager tried Enoch Wax's office in Lexington; Enoch had heard nothing from Fats. Eddie waited an hour, shooting a few trick shots to hold the audience and to give himself something to do. At three-twenty there was still no Fats and the bleachers were nearly empty. Eddie told the manager he was leaving, went back to Tony's, had a drink and called a taxi to take him to the Ramada Inn.

'Mr Hegerman checked in about noon,' the clerk at the desk said.

'Could you let me in the room?' Eddie said. He had tried the house phone and let it ring five times. Then he checked the bar, the restaurant, the coffee shop and came back to the desk.

'You're Mr Felson?' the clerk said. 'Mr Hegerman's partner?'

'Yes. Could I have a key?'

'Sheryl will let you in, Mr Felson.'

Sheryl, it turned out, was the woman with dyed hair at the cashier's window. Eddie followed her across the lobby and down a long hallway. At Room 117 he took the key from her and opened the door himself.

Fats was in bed. He was dressed and in a sitting position, with his eyes open and his face frozen like that of an elegant waxwork. He was clearly dead.

On the plane back to Lexington, Eddie had four Manhattans. When he arrived at the apartment he was drunker than he had been in years, even though it didn't show. When Arabella let him in it was after midnight and she was wearing the white panties and T-shirt she sometimes slept in.

'Fats is dead,' he said as soon as he had set his bag and cue case down. 'He made it to Indianapolis but he died before the match.' He went back into the kitchen and got himself a beer.

'It's a shock,' Arabella said. 'A real shock.'

Eddie poured beer into a glass and watched the foam settle. 'Even dead,' he said, 'the son of a bitch looked good.'

Arabella smiled faintly. 'I wish I'd met him.' She hesitated a moment. 'Something came while you were gone.' She walked to the Korean chest in the living room and took a large, thin package from it.

It was postmarked Miami. In the upper left was a return address but no name. Eddie opened it and slid out a big color photograph. He held it near a lamp and looked.

Against matted trees on a white beach two roseate spoonbills stood on alarmingly thin legs. One of them had begun to hunch its wings up from its body. It's bill inclined upward; its eyes looked toward the sky. The other bird, slightly behind, watched, as if waiting to see what would happen when those pink-tipped wings began to beat the air.

Babes Cooley was a small young man, thin-hipped and thin-wristed, but his nine-ball break was like a sledgehammer. Balls spun themselves, ricocheted, caromed off rails; three fell in. He looked at the spread with contempt, thought a moment and began to mop them up. He nudged the one into the side, clipped the two into the far corner, sliced the five down the rail. His position for each was impeccable. When it came to the nine, he drilled it into the nearby corner pocket as though with a rifle. There was applause. As the woman referee racked them up, Babes looked at the man he was playing and said, 'You're troubles have just begun.' The man looked away.

Eddie sat on the top row of the three-level bleachers, his cue on his lap, watching. Beside him an old black man was chuckling at Cooley's arrogance, clearly liking it. Four games were going on at the tables below, with the first eight players having their first round. There were four rounds this opening day; each of the thirty-two entrants was slated for one match of ten nine-ball games. By midnight sixteen would be in the losers bracket and sixteen in the winners. It started again the next day at noon, with losers playing losers; after two rounds of that, eight men would be permanently out of the tournament. Then, after dinner, the winners from this evening would begin their matches. The system was called double elimination; it required a man to lose twice before he was out of it.

This was the first pool tournament Eddie had entered in his life. When he was young, the great hustlers – Wimpy Lassiter, Ed Taylor, Fats – would not have dreamed of going public. Nine-ball tournaments hadn't even existed. Straight pool for coverage by newspapers had been left to the Willie Mosconis and Andrew Ponzis, superb players too, who donned evening dress and played in hotel ballrooms in New York or Chicago. They made a living from that and from a few endorsements, from a salary as showmen for the Brunswick Company, from giving exhibitions in colleges, publishing slim books with titles like *Championship Pocket Billiards*. While they tried to dignify the game of pool, to obliterate the memory of whatever smoky rooms they had learned it in – rooms that were always in the worst part of the worst towns – another network of professionals known only to a few had moved around some of those very rooms and others like them, in affable anonymity, men capable of as much pool-table dazzle as their tuxedoed counterparts, but dressed in brown suits like salesmen or in laborers' dark green, travelling, looking for action. Eddie had joined that incognito fraternity and had, for a brief time in his life, been its finest player.

In front of him, Babes Cooley moved from shot to shot with tight-lipped assurance, lit by bright fluorescents set into a ceiling of gritty Celotex. Babes was dressed gorgeously in a slick blue nylon running outfit, with red racing stripes on the pants and blue Nike shoes, as though he were a basketball player warming up. His opponent was a stolid local man in a brown sweater; he seemed assiduously to ignore the flash of his opponent as he sat in a chair against the far wall and waited to shoot. From the looks of Babes' game he would have a while to wait.

On each side of this table, other matches were in progress. Two intense young men in tight blue jeans were at one; at the other, a weary man, older than Eddie, watched a youngster in his late teens who was taking a maddeningly long time between shots. The older man had looked familiar when the players were drawing their first-round positions a half hour before, and Eddie saw now with a start that he knew him. It was Gunshot Oliver from Kansas City, a legend from Eddie's earliest days. When Eddie was fifteen, Gunshot had come through Oakland and played for two nights at Charlie's; he was the first travelling hustler Eddie had ever seen. This man, waiting with a kind of bleak irritation for the high-strung younger man to shoot, was the first player Eddie had ever seen who exerted the professional's quiet control over the cue ball, easing it off rails and ducking it between other balls to arrive at position in new and shocking ways. The way he bent to shoot and the steadiness of his stroke had opened Eddie's eyes. Oliver shot all night against the best local hustler, a man Eddie would not be able to beat for another year, and by three in the morning was playing him at odds of one fifty to a hundred balls. By that time, Gunshot's name was being spoken reverently by the dozen people watching and Gunshot himself was running seventy or eighty balls at a time with unwearied precision. It had thrilled Eddie's young, ambitious soul.

The kid playing Gunshot now finally shot the three ball down the rail and missed. He shook his head and grimaced, probably blaming the table or the cloth or the lights, telling himself one of the weary stories of how he had been cheated of the ball. Oliver stood and walked slowly over to the table, limping slightly. When he bent to shoot, his back was to the bleachers; his unshined black shoes were run over at the heels; and there was a small hole in one of his socks. The kid had been lucky and left him safe. Oliver tapped the three ball lightly, trying to snooker the other player behind the five But the tap was too strong, and the white ball bounced off the rail and out from behind the five, leaving the other man open on the three, Oliver scowled and seated himself.

Suddenly Eddie remembered something. That night in

Oakland thirty-five years ago, after Gunshot Oliver had collected the last of the fifty-dollar bills – had broken the bank, such as it was – the man who lost him said, 'You shoot the best straights I've ever seen,' and Oliver had smiled faintly at him. 'Have you ever seen Minnesota Fats?' he asked quietly. It was the first time Eddie had heard the name.

'I've heard of him,' the loser said.

'The best in the country,' Oliver said.

Fats was dead. It had seemed impossible then that a player like Gunshot Oliver – a man who calmly pocketed balls that Eddie had thought could not be made, a man who played position by moving the cue ball around as though it were a chesspiece to set where he wanted it – would, by invoking a name, imply a level of play even beyond his own. Eddie had never played Oliver, had never seen him since that time, but in a few years he had moved beyond him, had learned to make his own chessman of the cue ball. Oliver was right about Fats. There were levels above levels, and Fats was at the top. Now he was in a fresh grave near Miami, probably under a headstone that read George Hegerman and gave dates, with no indication of the lovely stroke that had died with him.

Babes Cooley clipped the nine into the side, making it register in the pocket. He looked innocently at the seated man whom he was playing and said, 'It just keeps on getting worse.'

Eddie wanted to shout at the arrogant young bastard, imagining him for a moment in his brash blue nylon playing straight pool against Minnesota Fats, being ground to helplessness by age and skill and experience. He sat there on the narrow bleacher seat, crowded in by a rapt audience of men, furious at Fats for being dead.

Cooley slammed the nine in on the break, said, 'Ohhh *yes*!' and broke again after the balls were racked. He pocketed two on the break, but the one ball took a bad roll and froze itself to the bottom rail. The cue ball stopped at the top of the table. The one was nine feet away and the cut required was paperthin. He would have to go for a safety. *Okay, you son of a bitch*, Eddie thought.

Cooley frowned, stepped to the end rail, set his bridge hand down on the wood, set the cue down decisively and stroked. The concentration of his thin body was sudden and remarkable. He took one practice stroke and then speared the cue ball. It flew down the table, whispered against the one ball and flew back up, dying in a cluster of balls. The one slid along the bottom cushion and plopped into the corner pocket. Someone in the crowd whistled and then there was loud applause. Eddie did not clap; he merely gripped his cue case harder. He would have avoided that shot and Fats might have missed it.

On the other table, Gunshot Oliver had begun to shoot. Eddie turned his attention back to that game. Oliver ran the four, five and six. When he made the six he brought the cue ball off the cushion and split the nine ball away from the seven beautifully, setting it up for the run-out. It was a straight-pool player's shot, the kind of thing Eddie himself did almost instinctively. Oliver pocketed the seven, eight and nine. There was polite applause. But on the eight and nine his stroke lacked something; the cue ball, though it found places where the next shot could be made, did not have the sureness of movement that Eddie remembered from Oakland. Oliver stroked stiffly and the ball looked somehow dead as it rolled into positions that were barely adequate.

The referee began to rack the balls. Abruptly Eddie rose and stepped down from the bleachers. He tucked his cue case under his arm and walked away.

'The kids make me nervous,' he said into the phone. He lay on the freshly made bed in his Holiday Inn room, by his unopened suitcase.

'They don't have your experience,' Arabella said.

He hesitated. 'I'm fifty years old, Arabella. I watched Babes Cooley playing a half hour ago and I wanted to kick his punk ass. I'm old enough to be his father.'

'You're still upset about Fats, aren't you?'

She was right. 'I thought I was going to learn some things from him.'

'Maybe he didn't have anything more to teach you.'

'Maybe not.'

The poolroom was something like his own had been, but larger. It sat between a Big Bear supermarket and a fabric store in a faded shopping center directly across the interstate from the Holiday Inn. You drove over a cloverleaf, parked in front of the supermarket and pushed through glass double doors. On a gray, cigarette-burned carpet sat two rows of eight pool tables. In the aisle between them, three rows of temporary bleachers had been erected to face the tables on the right. The two tables at the far end were for the players to warm up on; the two near ones were covered with heavy plastic. The four in the middle were where the tournament games were played.

The eight tables on the left as you came in were in regular service, with the poolroom's ordinary customers shooting their games and pretending to ignore the men who came in the door with expensive cue cases and sharp clothes. The tournament tables had a white card on the side of each facing the bleachers. Most of the evening spectators were crowded in the bleachers near the table whose card displayed a '1'; Eddie's first game was on Number Four. Eddie took his Balabushka out, slipped the empty case under the table and began to warm up. One bleary-eyed old man watched him dispassionately; no one else paid any attention.

After five minutes a clean-shaven young man with glasses and a white shirt came pushing through the space between the bleachers. He held out his hand to Eddie. 'I'm Joe Evans,' he said politely. 'You must be Mr. Felson.'

Eddie shook the hand. 'Do you want to warm up?'

'A little,' the young man said.

There was a wooden chair for each of the players against the wall, separated by a small table that held a pitcher of water, an ashtray, a plastic shaker of baby powder and a towel for sweating hands, and a few fresh cubes of chalk. Eddie sat in one of the chairs and watched Evans.

The young man spread out the balls and began to run them in rotation, starting with the one. He was not very good; that was apparent immediately from his tight stroke and the self-conscious grimace on his face when he missed. He was playing as if for an audience, although no one was watching except Eddie and the old man in the bleachers. Eddie had seen this kind of player before: Evans' emotional concentration was on not making a fool of himself. He was not thinking about winning, only about looking good. It would be simple to beat him.

It was simple. A few times during their match Evans had opportunities, but he blew them. Eddie could see his mind working from watching his face, trying to talk himself into shots, trying not to think about what he was leaving for Eddie if he missed, generally letting his head get in the way. A few times Eddie felt genuinely sorry for him, at the way he beat himself; but most of the time he was annoyed. Eddie played him methodically, shooting nine-ball as though it were straight pool; he beat him ten to four. During the last few minutes, a half-dozen latecomers, unable to get seats near the hot game on Table One, came to the bleachers near their table and watched. There was mild applause when Eddie won the tenth game. That was it until tomorrow; he was now one of the sixteen winners.

'I'm glad you're off to a good start,' Arabella said.

'The kid was terrible.'

'He must have been good enough to get the entry fee.'

'I've got someone named Johannsen tomorrow. I don't know who he is, but he'll be tougher. How're things at the magazine?'

'There isn't much to do right now. I spend a lot of time with the secretary, drinking coffee.'

'It sounds better than typing.'

'Eddie,' she said, 'I wish I had a talent like you have. I don't want to spend the rest of my life working in an office doing what some man tells me to do.'

'I'll teach you how to play nine-ball.'

'It isn't funny, Eddie. If I could shoot pool like you, I'd be rich.'

Somehow that annoyed him. 'Buy yourself a cue stick,' he said.

'I mean it, Eddie. You sat on your talent for twenty years.'

'I'm not sitting on it now.'

There was silence on the line for a moment. Then she said, 'Beat that man tomorrow, Eddie. Beat him bad.'

Johannsen was chubby and wore a plum-colored sweater over blue jeans; he appeared to be about thirty. During the warm-up he was unself-conscious and accurate. It was two in the afternoon, and they were playing on Table Three, with a dozen people watching when the referee stopped the practice, racked up the nine balls and put two extra balls out for the lag. Eddie won the break by lagging his ball to within a quarter inch of the cushion, but when he smashed them open nothing went in. From behind him he heard a whispered voice in the stands say, 'Straight-pool player,' and he knew, grimacing, what it meant: in straight pool you never had occasion to hit the balls that hard. It took practice to learn to do it. He turned to look at the man now breaking in the match starting on their right; the young player drew his cue back, hesitated, and slammed his whole body forward against the table as he rammed the stick into the cue ball. The diamond of nine balls flew apart so hard that the nine, from the center of the rack where it was always placed, spun off two cushions and narrowly missed a pocket before coming to a stop. On Eddie's break the nine ball had barely moved; and Johannsen, despite the cluttered position of the balls, ran them out.

It looked for a minute to Eddie – furious with himself and able to do nothing but wait – that he would run out the next rack, but he made a mistake on the seven ball and missed it, dogging it into the rail near the bottom corner.

Eddie stepped up icily and ran the seven, eight and nine. On the break he tried to slam them harder, but only one ball fell in and the nine barely moved. But the way it moved left it lined up dead with the three ball for the corner pocket, and Eddie took advantage of that. He ran the one and two, and made the nine on a combination. That got him applause. On the next break he hit harder, ending with his belly against the table and his cue stick extended in front of him; this time the nine stopped near the corner pocket, with the four a few inches on the other side of it. He felt better about the break shot now. But the two ball was at the far end of the table; and when he came off the one, his position on it was wrong. He bent, stroked twice, and slammed into it, giving the stick a forward fillip with his wrist, for strong drawing English. And crammed the two ball into the pocket and back out again, dogging it. Eddie turned away, to see Babes Cooley on Table Four pocketing the nine-ball to applause. He sat down and looked at the floor. He heard Johannsen getting up to shoot, heard the tap that would send the two ball into the pocket and the cue ball back down to a simple position on the three, heard Johannsen shoot the three ball in, and looked up in time to see him line up the four and nine and make the easy combination – scoring the nine ball, winning the game and the break. Johannsen had him three to two and had the break coming up. It was a son of a bitch, especially because this imperturbable man in the sweater was one of the weaker players in the tournament. He had won a college nine-ball championship somewhere once in the Midwest, and that was it. If Eddie couldn't blow him away, he had no business being here.

He had come to see that there were only four or five serious contenders in this tournament: Babes Cooley and a few other young men who played the circuit. The others – some of them lured by the spreadout prizes that went as far as two hundred dollars for twelfth place, and some of them wanting to play for once in their lives against the top players – had no real hope of winning. If Eddie had a problem it should be with Cooley and his near-equals – not with people like this aging college boy who played nine-ball as thought he were in a library.

But the aging college boy was persistent; he capitalized on Eddie's mistakes and after an hour was ahead by eight to six. Cooley was finished by that time, with a score posted ten-three in his favor, and some of the spectators came down to Eddie's table.

It was a critical point and Eddie was sweating it. Johannsen was in the middle of a wide rack; if he ran this one out, it would give him nine and the momentum to win the match. The one hopeful sign was that he'd begun taking a long time between shots, was being studiously careful, frowning now over even a simple position and chalking up with great care. He might be beginning to choke.

He made the seven ball with agonizing deliberation, getting good position on the eight. All he had to do with that was shoot the eight straight in and stop his cue ball; the nine sat near the opposite pocket and would only require a simple cut. But Johannsen was sweating it. He frowned and shot the eight in with a lot of draw. The cue ball rolled too far; he still had a shot on the nine, but not as easy as what simply killing the cue ball would have given him. 'Shit!' he said morosely, 'I don't deserve that.' Eddie looked up at him; he might just miss the nine, with that kind of crap in his head.

Johannsen bent to shoot, frowning in concentration. He cut the nine ball so badly it was embarrassing; it bounced off the rail a foot from the pocket. The cue ball went around the table and came back, leaving a simple shot. Eddie looked away from Johannsen, got up and carefully shot it in. Eight-seven. From then on, Eddie knew he had him. He let himself loosen up a bit, ran the next game out as though it were part of a rack of straight pool. He stroked the nine into the pocket with a firm *click*. There was applause. Eight-eight.

This time, he slammed them harder and made three on the break, leaving the nine near the side pocket and the four nearby. He ran the two and three and left the cue ball exactly right for the carom shot. He glanced at Johannsen's face before moving up to the shot; the man looked like a sulking child. Eddie bent, took very careful aim, and stroked. The cue ball hit the four ball, bounced off it and tapped the nine. The nine ball rolled over twice and fell in the side pocket. The applause was loud. Johannsen got up, came over, and with a forced smile shook his hand. Eddie unscrewed his cue.

The pairings were posted by the cashier's desk where you first entered the room. Eddie stopped to check it when he was leaving. It took him a moment to figure out the difference between the losers' brackets, on the left, and the winners', on the right. He had never done this kind of thing before and it still seemed strange to him. While he was studying it, the tournament manager came up with a felt-tip pen. 'Here you go, Mr Felson,' he said, and printed FELSON on one of the empty lines to the right – the top half of a bracket with the bottom empty.

'Who do I play next?' Eddie said.

'You're not going to like this,' the man said. He reached out and printed the name in the blank space; COOLEY.

No one answered when he called Arabella, even though he waited until five-thirty, when she was usually home. He did not feel like eating out and ordered a hamburger with coffee from Room Service. He turned on the television. But he didn't watch and didn't finish the overcooked hamburger. His head ached and his palms were sweaty. He felt jumpy. If only Fats were around, or somewhere he could be called. He would like talk to Fats about Babes Cooley.

Eddie's lag was very good, but Cooley froze his ball to the end rail and won the break. They were on the first table, and every seat in the bleachers was filled, with a row of standing men craning to watch from behind the bleachers and another row squatting in front.

Babes Cooley wore shiny black pants that fit his narrow butt as tight as elastic, draping with a Las Vegas crease to the tops of alligator shoes. His shirt was collarless and of pale blue silk; around his neck hung a slender gold chain. His black hair was feathery from blow-drying; his face electric from cocaine. He stepped up to break and, just before swinging his cue, looked over at Eddie, who stood leaning against the covered table next to theirs. 'This is a privilege, Fast Eddie,' he said, and slammed into the cue ball. The break was magnificent: four balls fell in and the yellow-striped nine ricocheted completely around the table. Babes was thin and small; it was astonishing to see such power coming from his body.

'Thanks,' Eddie said. Some people in the stands laughed.

'It seems rude,' Babes said, 'to do this to a living legend.' He made the remaining five balls with elegant dispatch, firing the nine ball into a corner pocket with finality. The referee racked the balls and Babes smashed them open again, made three this time, ran the rest. His body seemed to be wired with a quiet, electric arrogance, and his position play was immaculate. Eddie stood and watched, knowing that to seat himself would be weakness.

In the middle of the third rack, with the score two--nothing, Babes got an unlucky roll on the five ball and was forced to play safe. He did it neatly, leaving Eddie snookered behind the seven with the five completely out of sight. Eddie walked to the table; it was his first shot of the evening and he would be lucky just to hit the ball. What he had to do was clear: the cue ball must be banked off two rails, through a cluster of balls and into the five. Eddie bent and shot it and – to his surprise – did it perfectly. When the white ball hit the five it sent the orange ball up the table and stayed where it was. There was applause. He had not only avoided giving Cooley the ball in hand but had played him safe.

Cooley raised his eyebrows but said nothing. He stepped up and shot a safety without hesitation, leaving eight feet of green between cue ball and five. The five might be cut in, but it was a killer. Eddie sucked in his gut and stepped up to shoot it, not wanting to but knowing he had to. He could not go on playing safe, not on a shot like this, without giving Cooley control of the game. He had to spring for it.

Eddie adjusted his glasses, took his stance behind the end rail, glared at the distant five ball and stroked hard. The cue ball clipped the five and the five arrowed into the centre of the pocket. The white ball continued to carom around the table, coming to rest in position for the six. The bleachers behind burst into applause.

'A legend in his own time!' Babes Cooley said.

'You got it.' Eddie bent and shot in the six. Then the seven and eight, giving himself a cinch on the nine. He drove it into the pocket without hesitation and waited, through applause, for the referee to rack the balls.

But on the break he could not get the power he wanted and no balls fell in. There was nothing to do but stand back and watch Babes size up the layout. It was terrible to dog the break, to lose his momentum; that was one of the infuriating ways this game differed from straight pool. In straights, if you were hot you kept right on going; in nine-ball you had to get over this goddamned hump of a break shot.

Babes had a tough lie on the one, but he made it and sent the cue ball around the table in a way that Eddie would never have thought of, for position on the two. From there it was simple; he had to separate the six and eight, frozen together near the side pocket, but he tapped them apart on a carom and then cleaned up, firing the nine in smartly and then stopping to tuck his shirt in while the referee racked them. He looked over at Eddie and smiled faintly, with cold eyes.

Just as he stepped up to the head of the table and drew back his cue for the break, someone in the stands shouted, '*On the snap, Babes*!' and Babes, his face distorting with the effort, slammed into them like a sledgehammer, bellying up to the table as the balls rolled crazily. The nine, heading sideways into a rail, was pursued by two balls. They hit into it and seemed to shepherd it toward the corner pocket where, almost out of power, it hesitated a moment and then fell in. Eddie looked away. The score was three-one.

As Babes got ready for the break the same voice shouted, '*One more time*' and Babes rammed them open just as hard but the nine did not fall. Two others did, though, and the one ball stopped near the side for an easy shot. Eddie watched with furious impotence as Babes took them off the table one at a time. It was not like straight pool; Babes played a kind of position that was extravagant and unfamiliar, sometimes stopping his cue ball for surprising angles on the next shot. But the positions made sense and they worked. He ran out without even getting close to trouble. Four-one. Eddie sat down.

The whole crowd was clearly with Babes, and he flirted with them between shots, going to one person or another and whispering something brief, with a tight smile, looking at them boldly while they applauded. He was like the MC of the game and Eddie himself only one of the minor performers. Eddie saw it and felt it and could do nothing about it. Babes kept making balls, avoiding trouble, playing elaborate and deadly positions. He moved around the table fast and certain, as though his small feet hardly touched the carpeted floor, sometimes running the fingers of one hand through his fluffy black hair. Eddie overheard someone in the stands say, as Babes was doing this, 'He sure is pretty.' It was said with admiration.

Babes *was* pretty, and his nine-ball game was more than pretty. It was beautiful and lethal. The next time Eddie had the table, the score was eight-one and the shot was unmakable. Wanting to kill somebody, Eddie held his breath and played it as safe as he could; but the safety Babes came back with was devastating, and on his return Eddie missed the object ball. Babes took the cue ball in hand, palmed it a moment, looked at Eddie and said, '*Coup de grace* city.'

'Shoot the balls,' Eddie said.

'On my own time, my legendary friend,' Babes said, 'on my own time.' Someone in the crowd laughed.

Babes set the cue ball down and made the shot, and then another. He ran them out as easily as breathing, not even bothering to chalk his cue or study the table, plunking in the nine ball at the end of it as though it were child's play. Eddie's feet hurt and his shooting arm was tired, but he was hardly aware of these things. He was being beaten remorselessly; he would have given his soul for Babes to miss.

'*One more time, Babes honey*!' It was the same voice. Babes shotgunned the rack apart like a clay pigeon. The nine careened around the table but did not fall in. However, the three, five, seven and eight did fall. The one ball had to be banked across the side. Babes did not hesitate; he rifled it in, stopped cold for position on the two and had the two ball pocketed before the applause from the bank shot had died out. He could not be stopped except by a miracle, and no miracle occurred. He tapped the remaining balls in, hesitated a moment before shooting the nine, looked behind him at the bleachers and then back to the nine ball. He drove it in hard, stopping the cue ball dead. The applause was very loud.

Ten-one. Eddie kept a tight hold on himself, walked up to Cooley and extended his hand. Cooley took it. 'You shoot better than I expected,' Eddie said.

'My friend, I always do.'

'I felt like a fucking fool.' Eddie said on the phone. He lay on the bed with his cue beside him and a Manhattan in his hand.

'He's the best nine-ball player in the country, Eddie.'

'If they came any better I'd cut my throat.'

'You still have a chance to come back.'

Eddie wasn't sure he wanted to come back from the losers bracket and play Cooley again, but he did not say that. 'I play in an hour. If I lose I'm out of the tournament, and if I win there's another game at noon tomorrow.'

'Then take a shower and relax. It's no disgrace to lose.'

He did what she said and showered. Then he put on fresh

clothes, drove across the interstate and arrived exactly on time to play Gunshot Oliver.

Oliver clearly did not recognize him, and Eddie did not identify himself. The older man seemed to be in some kind of meditative daze, coming out of it only for the time it took him to shoot. He shot well, but his break was weak and he seemed to have disdain for the game.

During the middle of the match Oliver set his cue stick against the wall and walked slowly back to the men's room. Eddie sat down, poured a glass of water and waited. On all four tables, losers' games were being played and the crowd watching was slight. Eddie waited a long time, not really caring, until the old man came out again, looked around himself and ambled back toward the tables. But he hesitated at the first one he came to, where Evans was playing, watched a moment and then, shockingly, sat down in the empty chair at the wall behind that table, waiting to play. The old son of a bitch didn't even know who his opponent was. He sat there in his baggy brown pants with his belly hanging over the leather belt and his lined face puffy, wathing Evans play pool with a kind of weary disregard. He looked as though he'd just got out of bed.

The referee was standing near Eddie. Eddie touched his elbow and said, 'You'd better get Oliver,' and pointed to him.

'Jesus!' the referee said. 'He's really out of it.'

The referee had to lead him to the table like a seeing-eye dog. Oliver looked lost and angry, and when he came close Eddie could smell whiskey on him as strong as perfume. It was his turn to shoot. He made two simple shots, missed the third and sat down with a sigh. Eddie looked away. The score was five-three in Eddie's favor. He finished off the table, broke hard and ran the rack. He felt uncomfortable and wanted to get this over with; he bore down carefully and won four of the next five games, getting scattered applause when the match ended. Ten-four. Oliver just sat there. Finally he got up and shambled off without shaking Eddie's hand.

His game the next day was with a young black man named Cunningham. Eddie bore down hard, but the man was good. He was the third-rated player in the tournament, the man Cooley had beaten just before beating Eddie, and he controlled the game. His position play was like Cooley's – elaborate and sweet – and although he fought him hard, Eddie knew by the middle of the match that he was being outplayed. The man did not make any better shots than Eddie did, was in fact a shade less accurate; but he knew his nine-ball. And Eddie was being forced to see that there was a lot to know in nine-ball. Cunningham won the match ten to eight. That was the end of it. He could pack up and go home or wait and watch the semifinals and the finals.

As he was unscrewing his cue stick, he looked up to see Babes Cooley elbowing through an aisle between the bleachers, screwing his cue together. Babes nodded curtly in his direction and stepped up to the table Eddie had just lost on. He began to warm up for the semifinal match.

Eddie slipped his cue stick into its case, pushed through the crowd and left. There was a plane from Hartford to Cincinnati at ten-thirty, and a flight to Lexington at midnight. He could take his time and eat dinner in Hartford. For a moment he felt as though he should stay, should watch Cooley and study the ways he played position. But it didn't make any difference; nine-ball was a young man's game.

Eddie handed her a cigarette and she lit it from his, tilting her head back to blow the smoke toward the ceiling. They were in the living room. She had waited up after he called from Hartford. 'I know it's upsetting,' she said, 'but coming in fifth isn't the end of the world.'

His prize money was four fifty – enough to pay the entry fee and the hotel bill, but not the airplane tickets and rented car. 'It was a second-rate tournament.'

'It was your first tournament, Eddie.'

'And last.'
'You'll feel better in the morning.'

But he didn't feel better. When he got to the Rec Room and saw he had to begin the day by sweeping up, he felt worse. He cleaned up the bathroom, polishing the chromium and the two small mirrors with Windex. It was eleven o'clock by then, and still no customers had come in. This was the week before Christmas break, and there probably would be few students around anyway. He decided to cover another table with a rubber-back cloth. If he was going to be doing this for a living from now on, he might as well do it right.

By the time Mayhew came in Eddie had the rails off Number Five and he working on the slate. Mayhew said nothing; when Eddie stood up from his work the old man was behind the counter looking bleakly around the near-empty games room. Eddie turned back to the slate he was leveling.

For twenty years of his life there had been no excellence. Working for himself, running his own business, he had never worked as he was working now for the grim, detached Mayhew and for the college students with whom he almost never spoke. There was desperation in his covering of the tables, repairing the split cues, getting the faucet washers replaced in the men's room, installing brighter bulbs in the light fixtures. Arabella asked him once why he worked so hard at such a job, and all he could say was, 'I need it.' It was true. He needed something *right* about his life – if only a properly covered pool table, its fresh green cloth tight and clean, its rubber cushions firm, its surface level. By starting to play again, to put his skill and nerve on the line, he had awakened something in his soul that was not easy to stifle.

Sometimes in bed with Arabella, he found himself making love with energy close to ferocity; but the release when it came was never adequate to the demands he was making on himself, on his fifty-year-old body. Once she said, 'Take it easy, love. It's not a contest.' Finished with sex, he would fall back in bed with his heart pounding and his mouth dry, satisfied and not satisfied. It had never been that way with Martha, as he had never run his own business with the energy he was putting into this anonymous, university recreation room. Only as a young man playing pool all night for money had he been able to find what he wanted in life, and then only briefly.

People thought pool hustling was corrupt and sleazy, worse than boxing. But to win at pool, to be a professional at it, you had to deliver. In a business you could pretend that skill and determination had brought you along when it had only been luck and muddle; a pool hustler did not have the freedom to believe that. There were well-paid incompetents everywhere living rich lives. They arrogated to themselves the plush hotel suites and Lear jets that America provided for the guileful and lucky far more that it did for the wise. You could fake and bluff and luck your way into all of it: hotel suites overlooking Caribbean private beaches; blow-jobs from women of stunning beauty; restaurant meals that it took four tuxedoed waiters to serve, with the sauces just right, the lamb or duck or terrine sliced with precise and elegant thinness, sitting just so on the plate, the plate facing you just so on the heavy white linen, the silver fork heavy, gleaming in your manicured hand below the broadcloth cuff and mother-of-pearl buttons. You could get that from luck and deceit, even while causing the business or the army or the government that supported you to do poorly at what it did. The world and all its enterprises could slide downhill through stupidity and bad faith, but the long gray limousines would still hum through the streets of New York, of Paris, of Moscow, of Tokyo, though the men who sat against the soft leather in back with their glasses of twelve-year-old Scotch might be incapable of anything more than looking important, of wearing the clothes and the haircuts and the gestures that the world, whether it liked to or not, paid for and always had paid for.

Eddie would lie in bed sometimes at night and think these

things in anger, knowing that beneath the anger envy lay like a swamp. A pool hustler had to do what he claimed to be able to do. The risks he took were not underwritten. His skill on the arena of green cloth – cloth that was itself the color of money – could never be only pretense. Pool players were often cheats and liars, petty men whose lives were filled with pretensions, who ran out on their women and walked away from their debts; but on the table, with the lights overhead beneath the cigarette smoke and the silent crowd around them in whatever dive of a billiard parlor at four in the morning, they had to find the wherewithal inside themselves to do more than promise excellence. Under whatever lies might fill the life, the excellence had to be there. It had to be delivered. It could not be faked. But Eddie did not make his living that way anymore.

Chapter Seven

When he came home late one Friday in March, Arabella was gone and the place felt empty. Annoyed, he made a Manhattan in the kitchen and then walked into the living room. Something was wrong there too; it took him a minute to realize that the metal sculpture of the woman and dog, bought on that goddamned trip to Connors, was gone. It had sat beside Arabella's green Korean chest since November. He had become fond of it, had bought a bottle of chrome bumper cleaner and shined it up. Originally, even five hundred seemed too much for the thing, but he had come to be proud of owning it. He looked now in the other rooms of the apartment, but it wasn't there.

He was making his second drink when he heard Arabella come in and hang her coat in the hall closet.

'Where in hell's my statue?' he shouted.

'Take it easy.' She came into the kitchen. 'Fix me one of those and I'll tell you.' Her face was flushed and her eyes bright.

'He added more whiskey and vermouth to the pitcher and poured two drinks. 'Let's hear it.'

'I sold her.'

'What the hell? That was my statue.'

'It was a gift for me.'

'Maybe. How much did you get?'

'I'll tell you in a minute. Do you remember Quincy Foreman?'

Eddie thought he remembered. An English professor, built like a linebacker. 'How much did he give you?'

'Eddie, there's a lot of money in things like that.'

She was wearing a corduroy skirt with pockets. She reached into one of these and pulled out a folded-over check. She unfolded it, glanced at it to make sure and then looked at Eddie.

'Damn it,' Eddie said, 'let me see the check.'

She held it out. He took it and looked. It was made out on the Central Bank for twelve hundred and fifty dollars.

'I tried for fourteen,' she said.

'My my,' Eddie said. He was holding his drink in one hand and the check in the other. He set the drink down. 'If we leave early in the morning we can get there by lunchtime.'

'Get where?'

'Deeley Marcum's junkyard.'

She was looking at him in frank surprise. 'To buy another piece?'

'To buy three pieces,' Eddie said. 'Four, if we can get them for twelve fifty.'

After stopping at the bank for Arabella to cash the check, Eddie drove out the Nicholasville Pike. 'I'll carry the money.' he said, and she handed the bills to him. Twelve hundreds and a fifty. He folded them over and stuffed them into his pocket, not taking his eyes from the road.

In Delfield he stopped at the A&P for a six-pack of Molson's, then headed straight for the junkyard. It was a quarter to twelve when they pulled up.

He had decided what pieces he wanted before going to bed the night before. There were two short women that would fit in the trunk of the car and two that could go in back – one on the seat and one on the floor. Size wasn't his only consideration; there was also weight. And he was fairly sure he knew which ones were better-looking than the others.

There was another woman with a dog, standing just where his had stood. The old man had taken his suggestion. Eddie stopped to look at it a moment, noticing that the welds were better than on the first. Then he took the beers back to Marcum's shack.

This time Arabella tried to stay out of it while he dealt with Deeley – who, apparently, had just gottten out of bed. The old man washed his face at a dirty sink that sat next to his welding equipment, dried off with a handful of paper towels and took a beer from Eddie without thanking him. He took a long draw from the bottle, holding his head back and chugalugging, and wiped his mouth off with his forearm. He blinked at Arabella, ignoring Eddie. 'I got a Heliarc coming down from Louisville,' he said.

'Terrific!' Arabella said.

'They say it's a beauty. I'll wait till I see it.'

Eddie said nothing, opening himself a beer and taking a drink. It was a raw February day and it seemed strange to be drinking cold beer.

Finally Deeley deigned to notice him. 'How do you like that woman and dog? I mean the one you bought?'

Eddie looked at him. 'The dog could be better, but it's all right. It should have had more balls.'

Marcum raised his eyebrows slightly. 'The dog was hard to do,' he said. 'I've got more experience with women.'

'Get yourself a dog,' Eddie said, 'if you're going to do dogs.'

'A dog's more trouble than a woman.'

'Sometimes it's trouble just to get out of bed.'

Marcum stared at him a moment and then he began to laugh. He looked at Arabella. 'Stay with this one,' he said. 'He knows a thing or two.'

'I'd like to buy four more,' Eddie said.

Marcum blinked. 'Four?'

'Four more of your women. I'll show you.' He led Marcum out into the yard and pointed out the ones he wanted: the Las Vegas Model, the Statue of Liberty, Little Bo Peep, and a cartoonlike one called Olive Oyl. When they came to this one, Eddie said, 'I'll give you a thousand for all four.'

Marcum stared at him. 'I can't do that.'

'I'm going to finish my beer,' Eddie said. He had left it in the shed. He turned and began walking that way.

Marcum followed him silently, and when Eddie was drinking from the bottle he said, 'Why do you want *four*?'

Eddie said nothing.

'Some people want to buy one of them, but when I tell

what I expect to get, they get nervous. But nobody wanted four before.'

'We're going to try selling them.'

'Shit!' Marcum said. 'I thought you were up to something. I'm the one ought to be selling them to people, not you.'

Eddie shrugged. 'Maybe you're right.'

'You're goddamn fucking correct I'm right.'

'Who would you sell them to?'

'Rich people in Louisville,' Marcum said. 'Museums and galleries.'

'Is that so?'

'Original works like these don't come cheap.' Marcum, still holding his empty beer bottle, gestured grandly toward his yardful of metal women.

'How will you get those rich people in Louisville to come here and buy?' Eddie said.

'I'll go to *them*.'

'From door to door?'

'I'll sell them to a gallery, if I sell them.'

'A gallery won't pay you as much as I will. They've got to make their profit and pay their overhead. You'll have to get a truck to take them to Louisville.'

Marcum's face had developed a pout. 'If I sell them, I won't have anything here to show people. That's my livelihood, charging admission.

'One dollar,' Eddie said, looking out at the yard. 'I've been here twice and nobody's come in while I've been here.'

'They come in,' Marcum said. 'Sometimes whole families at a dollar apiece. And I charge another dollar to take pictures.'

'Then you're doing all right.'

'I've never touched a welfare check or a food stamp in my life.'

'That's a good thing,' Eddie said. 'A man ought to be independent if he's got a talent.'

'In spades, Mister.'

'I appreciate how you feel,' Eddie said. He reached down

into his pocket and took out the folded stack of hundred-dollar bills, most of them new and began counting them silently. He put the fifty into his jacket pocket, set the stack of twelve hundreds on the metal-topped table beside them and put a chunk of scrap metal on top of it to keep the bills from blowing off. 'This is my last offer,' Eddie said.

Deeley looked at the money and then at Eddie.

'When you get that Heliarc,' Eddie said, 'you can make more women. You've got plenty of raw material.'

'And plenty of imagination,' Arabella said.

'What about that fifty you put in your jacket?'

'All right,' Eddie said, 'it's yours.'

'We could go into the business,' Arabella said.

'We are in the business. This car is a travelling museum.'

'I mean we could open a gallery.'

Eddie was silent for a minute while passing a truck. They were halfway back to Lexington, the sculptures in the seat behind them wrapped in the blankets and towels he had the foresight to bring along. When he got back into his own lane again, he said, 'There wouldn't be enough customers. We'll be lucky to sell the four.'

'They'll sell,' Arabella said. 'People have more money than you think.'

'Wouldn't we saturate the market with a dozen?'

'I've thought about that, Eddie. There are other artists out here in the boondocks – or craftsmen or whatever. We could have variety. I've worked for that magazine three years, and I know about every Deeley Marcum in the state.'

'Lexington is no art town. You have a few hundred possible customers at most. It's like pool.'

'It's better than pool, Eddie. There's a lot of money in Lexington, and people came down from Louisville and Cincinnati.'

'I don't know,' Eddie said. But a part of him was beginning to believe it.

'There's a folk-art boom just starting. You should see the ads I get from New York. They sell *reproductions*, Eddie, and they sell them for plenty.'

'Lexington isn't New York.'

'There are a lot of people there who wish it was. Folk art is getting to be like croissants and pasta. There's a whole class of Americans who want to get into the act, want to be *au courant*.'

'I don't speak French.'

'But you know what I'm talking about. With what I know about the people who make things like these,' she reached back and put her hand on the head of a metal woman that protruded from a green blanket 'and with your ability to drive a bargain, with what you already know about running a business . . .'

He thought about it a minute. He had only planned to sell the four pieces from his living room. It had been fun bargaining with Deeley, and he liked the excitement of markup – of buying a thing for three hundred dollars and selling it for twelve. It was a lot like gambling on pool when you knew you were going to win. 'Could we sell these in New York? To a dealer?'

'That would be like Deeley selling them in Louisville. The thing about Lexington is low rent and low overhead.'

It was beginning to sound good, although it still seemed foolish – dealing in art when he didn't know a goddamned thing about art. 'How much money do you have?'

'Not much.'

'How much would it cost to rent a place?'

'Four hundred a month. Five, maybe.'

'How long a lease in case we fizzle?'

'I don't know. Six months?'

'A year, at least. We'll have to paint the walls and put ads in the paper. Then there's insurance and taxes and all those goddamned forms from the state and city and from Washington. And collecting the sales tax.'

'You've been doing that kind of thing for twenty years, Eddie. You know how to handle it. I'm a good typist, and I'm good at filling out forms.'

'If I put twelve thousand into it, can you find me enough art to buy?'

'Oh boy, can I ever! We can get handmade quilts and carvings. There's an old black druggist near Lancaster who does visionary carvings on wood panels.'

He thought awhile before he spoke. 'There's an empty store a block off Main Street. Mandel Realty has it, and I know Henry Mandel. I'll call him.'

'Sweet Jesus!' Arabella said, staring at the road in front of them.

'It might work,' Eddie said, 'it really might.'

'Holy cow!' Arabella said.

They had been passing Holiday Inn billboards, and now up ahead of them on the right he saw the green sign for the motel itself. They were about an hour out of Lexington. When they got closer he could read the words HEATED INDOOR POOL. He began to slow down. 'Let's get a room.'

'*Eddie*,' she said, 'we'll be home in an hour.'

'I like the way things are right now.'

He hadn't felt like this in bed for years. They had a back room with a view of a snowy field and trees. He opened the draperies while she began taking her clothes off. It was a king-size bed. They lay on it and kissed. He found himself laughing for a while and she laughed with him. 'A couple of art hustlers,' he said, and began kissing her again. Afterward, they rented disposable bathing suits at the front desk and had the pool to themselves for a half hour. She was a good swimmer – almost as good as he, and she did not worry about getting her hair wet. Then they got drinks at the bar, took them to their room. Eddie called Information in Lexington and got Henry Mandel's number.

'It's silly,' she said while he was putting in the call. 'You can call him free in an hour.'

'Go dry your hair,' Eddie said. 'I know what I'm doing.'

Henry wanted five seventy-five a month for the place, plus the cost of heating it. The lease would be eighteen months.

'Too much,' Eddie said. He had dried off and was sitting naked in a chair. 'I'll give you four fifty on a twelve-month lease renewable for twenty-four at a ten percent increase.'

'No way,' Henry said. 'That's a choice location.'

'It's one room and it's been empty half a year.'

'There are other people interested, Mr Felson.'

'Then rent it to them.'

'They have problems right now. I'd like to do business with you.'

'If you paint it I'll give you four seventy-five.'

'*Paint* it! For Christ's sake, do you know what labor costs for that these days?'

'Henry,' Eddie said. 'this is still a recession and you know it. If you don't rent that place to me, it's just going to sit there while you pay taxes on it.'

Henry was quiet for a moment. Arabella, who had been running the hair dryer, came back into the room. She was stark naked. She seated herself in the other chair and looked at Eddie.

'Eddie.' Henry said, 'I can buy you a few gallons of paint, but you'll have to do the painting.'

He took a deep breath. 'I'll come by Monday and pick up the keys. If the place is all right, we'll sign papers in the afternoon.'

'For eighteen months?'

'Twelve, Henry. Twelve months.'

When he hung up Arabella said, 'You're amazing.'

'You look great in that outfit. Let's stay over.'

'What for?'

'Honey,' Eddie said, 'up till now we've just been engaged. This is our honeymoon.'

The best thing about it was the downtown location. He liked that with the same liking he had felt toward Arabella's small apartment. It was a sizeable room with a couple of closets, a countertop and a two-piece bath. There was a lot of light, with the glass front of the building and windows over a small garden in back. The garden was littered with rusted coat hangers from the dry cleaners that had occupied the place before; and it had an incongruously large brick barbecue over in the center of it, surrounded by trampled-down grass; but it might make a good place to put out some of Marcum's steel ladies in the spring. When he suggested this to Arabella, she was excited by the idea and began picking up the coat hangers. The walls inside were grimy, and there were big pipes that would have to be painted over. The green linoleum on the floor would have to go. Bending to lift a piece of it away, Eddie could see that the floor beneath was good oak in need of sanding. You could probably have it done for two hundred, and then use polyurethane, which he could put on himself.

He made a deal with Henry to rebate a hundred fifty from the first month's rent – for paint, brushes, rollers and a ladder, along with the polyurethane for the floor. Eddie knew where to get the supplies at a discount, and he had them assembled by mid-afternoon. He used a pay phone on the corner to call the telephone company to get a business line put in. Then he called the electric company to turn on the current.

'Maybe we ought to be locating our stock,' Arabella said.

'We have to have the place ready before we put it in.' He was feeling terrific and he knew what needed to be done. He was wearing old jeans and a worn flannel shirt. He got down with a broad putty knife and began peeling up big flakes of linoleum, throwing them into a cardboard box. 'I'll get this crap off today. I've already talked to a floor refinishing place and they'll be in with sanders tomorrow morning. We'll scout out your artists the next day, while the varnish is drying, and then see what we'll need in the way of stands for the sculpture, and track lights, and rods to hang quilts on the walls. We'll figure out ads for the papers and a sign for out front.'

'Eddie,' she said, 'you're a one-man band.'

'Wait'll you hear me do "Stars and Stripes Forever".' The trick with the putty knife was to slide it in one smooth motion under the old linoleum. 'This is going to be a first-class floor,' he said, working, pleased with himself.

Ellen Clouse ran a one-pump gas station in Estill County, an hour and a half from Lexington. There was a three-room wooden house, badly in need of paint attached; and all three rooms were full of quilts in dizzying patterns. A sign over her front door read 'QUILTS FOR SALE – GENUINE KENTUCKY CRAFTS.'

'I don't make 'em myself,' Ellen said, 'but there's a half-dozen women do it for me. My mother quilted, but mostly I pump gas.' She was a broad, unsmiling woman in her fifties, with steel-gray hair and untied Adidas on her feet. 'Some of these quilts is trash, but some are dazzlers. Look here . . .' She led them to one on the far wall. 'This quilt is a Bible pictorial. There in the middle is the Hebrew children in the fiery furnace and that's Abraham and Isaac in the bottom-right corner.'

'Appliquéd,' Arabella said.

'It's the best way to do it, honey,' Ellen said. Her voice seemed surprisingly gentle for such a mannish woman. Eddie studied the quilt. It was divided into five brightly colored panels, with cloth cutouts of people and trees and a Noah's ark and the curving flames from the furnace in the middle. The stitches that held it all together were fine and even. It was a good-looking thing once you got past the gaudiness, and it would take a lot of hours to make it. He looked at her. 'How much is it?'

'That quilt was made by Betty Jo Merser over at Irvine, and she's dead. Died last year of cancer of the Fallopian tubes. She wanted five hundred for it.'

'It's a valuable quilt,' Arabella said.

'Let's see some more of the best ones, Miss Clouse,' Eddie said.

She took them through the three rooms, where the walls were covered with quilts. In the third room there was a pile of them twenty or thirty deep, on an old wooden bed. There were coverlets and pillowcases too. Most of the decorations fell into one of two kinds: patriotic and religious. A few mixed the two of them; one of these had Jesus in a manger with the American flag overhead. One patriotic quilt showed crudely cut-out airplanes, with the legend REMEMBER PEARL HARBOR. It was signed, and dated in 1943.

By the third or fourth one, Eddie felt he could look at them and pick out the ones that were genuinely good. It was partly a matter of design and partly of construction. Some of them were cheap and random, but others – especially those made by the dead Betty Jo Merser – had a lot of energy to them and good, tight workmanship. But he had no idea how much money they were worth.

Just as this was beginning to bother him, there was the sound of a car horn outside and Ellen excused herself to wait on a gas customer.

When she had left, Eddie walked over to the Bible pictorial and felt its cloth. 'How much could we sell this for?' he said.

'I'm not sure,' Arabella said.

'Do you know anyone in Lexington who has some of these, or some like them?'

'The woman who lays out the magazine has quilts. I don't know where she got them.'

'And she'll have books?'

'She must have.'

'That's good enough. We can go see her after I varnish the floor.'

With the finish dry, the floor looked even better than he had hoped. He had bought good interior white and a heavy roller. He put out drop cloths, set up a ladder and did the ceiling. It might need touching up after the lights were put in, but he could do that easily. The ceiling was done by noon and he started the walls. Arabella bought Windex and paper towels at the corner drugstore and started on the windows.

The telephone had come and now sat on the drop cloths in the middle of the floor. During a break Eddie sat by it with coffee and a Big Mac and called a sign-painting place from the Yellow Pages. It would cost four hundred for a board sign to hang over the door, and a hundred thirty to have KENTUCKY FOLK ART GALLERY painted in gold letters on the window. He told them just to do the window. Then he got his roller and went back to the walls. Arabella did the rest of the windows and then started picking up trash in the yard. After Eddie finished the second wall his shoulder was aching; he rested it while he scrubbed up the lavatory bowl and toilet. The money would go out alarmingly for a while; but you had to be prepared to put up money when you gambled, and that didn't bother him. He got some of Arabella's Windex and polished up the bathroom fixtures, cleaned the mirror over the sink. He began to whistle. There would be furniture, and stands for display, and the lights and installing them. But Arabella was right. A place like this could really go. With Arabella talking to the customers, with her looks and her accent, and with her connections at the university, they might take off. Even if they didn't it would be exciting for a while. And it beat trying to get back his lost pool game or working for Mayhew at the goddamned university recreation room.

Jane Smith-Ross had a big pictorial on the wall over her fireplace, with lambs and cows in a field. Eddie looked closely at the appliqués and at the stitching. The stitches were not as small or as neat as Betty Jo Merser's. Maybe they could get an old photograph of Betty Jo and have it blown up and put it on the wall, with her birth and death dates. Make her into a kind of quilt celebrity. Who knew anything about such people, anyway? Looking at this one over the Smith-Ross mantelpiece, he felt a proprietary feeling about Betty

Jo's work. It was better than this.

'Can you tell me what you paid for it?' he asked.

'My husband bought it for my birthday four years ago. It's from the nineteen thirties and I think he paid eight hundred dollars.'

'Do you know where he bought it, Jane?' Arabella asked.

'I sure do,' Jane said with a little laugh. 'It's ironic. It's a Kentucky quilt, but Dalton bought it in Cincinnati, at Shillito's.

Eddie looked at it again. The figures were not as good as Betty Jo's; the sheep were stupid-looking and there was no imagination to the cows. Betty Jo's fiery furnace had looked hot, and each leaf of flame had character. It wasn't as old as this one – Ellen Clouse had said it was done in the fifties – but if this was worth eight hundred, Betty Jo's was worth a thousand. At Shillito's, anyway.

Jane Smith-Ross had two picture books on quilting to lend him; that night he studied them carefully. There was no doubt about it: Betty Jo Merser was a find. The whole problem would be marketing. He would hire someone to install the track lights and to put shelves along one wall; he wanted to start dealing with Ellen Clouse for all the Betty Jo Merser quilts she had. The fiery-furnace one would look terrific on the freshly painted white wall on the left as you came in the door. They could hang two or three of them and store the rest on shelves, like pool-table cloths. If you put Deeley Marcum's statue of the Las Vegas Model on the floor – that newly varnished oak floor – to one side of it and a few feet out from the wall, the two of them would go together just right. Thinking about it, his heart began to beat faster.

He had no difficulty getting a carpenter and an electrician. Everybody needed work, and it was winter-time. But when he talked to the electrician about an alarm system for the windows, the man said he didn't know anything about that. Eddie called a place from the Yellow Pages, but no one answered. He decided to worry about it later and left the man installing track lights in the ceiling while the carpenter was cutting boards for the shelves. Arabella got license applications at City Hall and began calling her friends to tell them about the shop, starting the word-of-mouth. He left the men working and went to the newspaper office to talk about advertising. He had run a few ads for his poolroom from time to time, but they had been simple cuts. He needed something for the gallery opening that would look elegant. And there was radio and TV. Enoch – or his secretary – might be able to help with that. Maybe he could get Arabella on the morning show, to talk about Kentucky folk art. And then they had to look into the other artists: they would need to stock more than metal statues and quilts.

It did not seem crazy, or even strange, for him to be doing what he was doing. Art had never meant anything to him, and he had never been in an art gallery or museum in his life. But what he was doing felt like a hustle and he liked the notion of a hustle, liked putting his mind into it. It was in the service of money, and he loved money – loved dealing with it, loved making it, using it, having a dozen or more large denomination bills, folded, deep in his pocket. So much in his life did not make sense. But money did.

'We could take the quilts on consignment and not have to put up any money,' Arabella said. They were driving toward Irvine.

'That means we don't pay Ellen in advance?'

'Right.'

'How does she know we have a better way of selling than she does?'

'You talk her into it.'

He drove silently for a while, pushing the two-year-old Toyota pretty hard. He had been thinking of a panel truck or Microbus, with KENTUCKY FOLK ART GALLERY on the side, along with a logo of Marcum's woman-and-dog in profile. He thought about Arabella's idea for a moment and then said, 'We'd have to give her at least half, and I want to go for broke. I want to buy a quilt for three hundred and sell it for nine. Otherwise it's not worth our time.'

'What about poor Ellen?'

'Poor Ellen? In the first place Ellen didn't make the quilts, and in the second she hasn't been able to sell them at that dump with the Esso pump and the kerosene stoves. If you want to feel sorry for somebody, make it Betty Jo Merser, Ellen's the robber baron of this enterprise, not its victim.'

'You should be teaching economics at the university instead of shooting straight pool.'

'A person learns about money shooting straight pool.'

'Eddie,' Arabella said, 'You're driving too fast.'

He said nothing but did not slow down.

'I'll give you twenty-seven hundred for all nine.' Eddie had that much in cash and he set it on a little table with a doily on it near the fireplace.

'You're being *silly*,' Ellen said. 'That's the whole lot of Betty Merser's life's work, and any five of them's worth that much.'

'They're not making you anything hanging on the walls here.'

'Let me get you folks some tea,' Ellen said. She went into the kitchen. She didn't even look at the money.

'Eddie,' Arabella whispered, 'You're going to have to pay more or get fewer quilts.'

'We'll see.' He had his eyes on the fiery furnace above the fireplace, with the three black-haired children tied with ropes about to be shoveled in. He could get twelve hundred for that quilt if he could find the right buyer.

When Ellen came back carrying a tray with mugs of tea on it, Eddie said, 'What do you think all nine of them are worth?'

'You're downright serious about those quilts, aren't you?'

'I like the workmanship.' He took a cup from the tray.

Ellen nodded but said nothing. They sat with their tea for a while and then, abruptly, she stood up, smoothing out her heavy corduroy skirt. 'Maybe you'd like to see what her mother did.'

Eddie looked up at her. 'Her mother?'

'Betty Jo's. She passed away before the war.'

'And she did quilts?'

'She's the one taught Betty Jo. Leah Daphne Merser was the best quilter around.'

'Where are they?' Eddie said.

'In the bedroom.' She walked through the door to the right of the fireplace. 'There's only three.'

There was a wooden chest at the foot of the bed. Ellen opened this and took out a sheet that covered what was inside. Under this was a quilt wrapped in a clear plastic garment bag. She took it out of the chest with care, set it on the bed, eased it out of the bag and began unfolding it. As it opened up Arabella began to hold her breath.

'I've had these a long time,' Ellen said. 'There was a dealer from New York going to buy them back when Betty Jo was alive, but I never heard from him. I wasn't all that fond of selling. Don't know if I am yet.'

Eddie stepped closer to look. He had spent several hours with Jane Smith-Ross's books, looking at the detailed illustrations carefully. This quilt was the real thing. It was trapunto, with flowers and birds in appliqué, and the stitching was as delicate as that in any of the pictures. He remembered one in the book that the legend said belonged to the Museum of American Folk Art in New York; the book gave it two pages, in color, and another page to show details of the stitching. This one was better. He picked an end of it up gently; the cloth was smooth and light, and the quilting of flower petals was flawless. He looked over at Ellen. 'I'd like to see the others.'

'Seven thousand dollars!' Arabella said.

'In for a dime, in for a dollar,' Eddie said. He was driving just at the limit. In back of him, wrapped individually in plastic, were the nine quilts of Betty Jo Merser and the three exquisite ones of her mother. He felt fine. He always like raising the bet.

'If you get sprinklers in, I'll write it. Otherwise I just can't.'

'*Sprinklers?*' Eddie said. That was one thing he hadn't thought of. 'How much is that going to cost?'

'Plenty. But I can't write you a policy without them. Not on those quilts. Not on any of these things.'

'I'll look into it,' Eddie said, shaking his head.

'I need to take two weeks off.' Eddie was standing by the newly covered Number Four. Mayhew had just come in.

'Can't do it,' Mayhew said.

'You ran this place without me before I came.'

Mayhew looked at him and said nothing.

Eddie wanted to hit him, but instead he lit a cigarette. Then he said, 'I've earned it.'

'There was a lot of wear in those old cloths,' Mayhew said, not looking at him. 'I didn't ask you to put new ones on.'

Eddie looked at him. 'They were worn out.'

Mayhew opened up the cash register and began counting the bills.

'I'll see you in two weeks,' Eddie said, turning to leave. There was only one pool game going on, on Number Three. Two silent young blacks were shooting nine-ball.

'No you won't,' Mayhew said, not looking at him.

Eddie said nothing and walked to the door.

'If you're not back tomorrow, you're not coming back,' Mayhew said.

Eddie walked out the door and past PacMan and Space Invaders. Outside it had begun to snow. He would have to go back sometime; his Balabushka was there.

'Eddie,' Arabella said, 'I'm scared.'

'Scared?'

'It's all been so fast. We don't know if we'll be able to sell these things.'

It was almost midnight; they had just come from painting the wooden stands and trying out the track lights. The lettering on the glass in front had been finished that afternoon. They would open Saturday.

'It's going to work,' he said.

She sat heavily on the white sofa. 'I hope so,' she said. She leaned her head against the back of the sofa and closed her eyes. 'Sometimes you go at it in a way that scares me. Headlong.'

He didn't speak for a minute, looking at her tired face with the eyes still closed. 'I held back all the time I was married and running the poolroom. I just sat tight and watched television a lot. It wasn't any good.'

She opened her eyes wearily. 'Maybe not.'

'It wasn't any good at all. Martha and I didn't *do* anything. We drank too much and bought things for the house and every now and then we had a fight. I went out to the poolroom every morning and brushed down the tables and put out fresh chalk and after a while I was fifty years old.' He stubbed out his cigarette in the ashtray by the chair. 'There aren't many things I can do. I don't know if I'll ever be able to play pool again well enough to make money from it; and even if I can get the money to buy another poolroom, I don't know if that's what I want. It'll just be more of the same.'

She was looking at him. 'You're nowhere near burned out. Even if this fails you'll find things to do.'

He looked at her. 'Name two.'

'Eddie,' she said, 'I'm going to bed.'

After she had left the room he got out the blue-covered journal that he used for business expenses and began going over the figures: the cost of installing lights, the money in quilts and metal sculptures, the two-months' rent deposit on the gallery, the cost of operating the car. He had about five thousand left in the bank. It was all that was left from twenty years of running the poolroom. It was less than he had made several times in his twenties from a single night of shooting straights.

He set the book on the table and lit another cigarette. On Saturday they would go to Madison County to see that druggist and his wood panels. Arabella had written the man up two years before for the magazine when Greg was running it; she had shown Eddie the article, with photographs. They were Biblical things, forceful and direct, like Betty Jo's quilts. He went to the closet and took one of the plastic bags from a shelf, and got the quilt out. He spread it over the couch and adjusted the lamp shade so the light fell brightest on the center, where the Hebrew children were ready to be put into the fiery furnace.

He would never have found the quilts without Arabella, nor the metal sculptures that stood against the living-room wall now like an audience. There were plenty of people in Kentucky who called themselves craftsmen and folk artists, but most of them were second-rate. It was only through Arabella's experience with the magazine, the fact that she had already gone around the state with Greg and seen dozens of the people who tried to make a living from work like this, that he was able to avoid wasting time with junk. She had provided the judgment and knowledge; he had only contributed money and nerve. Desperation, maybe. He looked at the bright appliqué flames under the light – red, orange and yellow, coming from the furnace door. For days the picture had been in his mind at odd times, as persistent as an advertising jingle or the desire for money. The three dark children were strapped by a red surcingle to a broad shovel, like the thing bakers used. They lay rigid, their wide cartoon eyes open in fright, their mouths little dark lines. A huge hand gripped one end of the shovel, ready to push them in. Of all the things he had looked at in the past week, this was the one that held his attention the most.

He made up his mind. He would take the quilt to the shop

tomorrow, but it would not be for sale. He would keep it for himself.

He spent the afternoon installing wooden brackets and rods for hanging the quilts – three along one white wall and two along the other; it was dark outside by the time he hung Betty Jo's Fiery Furnace in the middle of one wall. He climbed the ladder and aimed two floodlights directly at it. Against the white, the colors of the quilt were brilliant, and its five pictures, centered by the Hebrew children, were like a mystical comic strip.

He had the two smaller metal statues in the trunk of the car, which was parked outside. The Little Bo Peep was made from bumper parts welded together, partially covered with a blue cloth pinafore; her head was two small hemispherical hubcaps fastened together and painted with a pouting face. She carried a shepherd's crook made from a tailpipe.

He positioned her on a wooden pedestal to the right of the quilt and adjusted the track lights to spotlight her. When he came down from the ladder, he stood at the far wall and looked at them together. The effect was striking. He seated himself on an empty pedestal and began to decide which quilts he would display and which keep folded on shelves. He knew them all by now.

He did not like the wooden carvings at first, and the old black man who made them was difficult; but he had to admit a lot of work had gone into them. There was a series of eight panels called THE EMERGENCE OF AMERICA INTO THE WORLD OF MEN that must have taken years to do. The wood was dark, close-grained walnut. Each of the panels was roughly a yard square and each was carved with figures in relief in the manner of the drawings of a precocious child. The man who had done them was lean, very old, and so black that he was nearly purple. Like Marcum, he had a song and dance about museums and galleries in Louisville and Chicago; when

Eddie questioned him about his claims of being an important artist, he began pulling newspapers and magazines out of an old metal cabinet in his shop behind the pharmacy. There were columns in old newspapers – several with pictures of him and of one or another of his wooden panels – but the clippings were old and yellowed. His real triumph was a two-page spread from the Sunday *Courier-Journal* showing several of the panels in color and a picture of the artist in a white smock at the counter of his drugstore. The caption read, 'A KENTUCKY WOODCARVER INTERPRETS HISTORY.' The date on the paper was September 1961.

'The university has displayed that set,' the man said. His name was Touissant Newby and his demeanor was grave. 'People arrive from Chicago and want to buy. But I don't make my prophecies to hang in somebody's apartment.'

Eddie nodded and said nothing. The panels were fastened to the wall and poorly lighted. He put on his glasses and started with the one on the left, studying them one at a time. The first showed a sailing ship on a bright blue ocean, with a cluster of what were probably Pilgrims lined up on deck, their wide-open eyes heavenward. Over them a dark cloud hovered with streaks of yellow lightning in deep relief. The faces of the people were childishly drawn but carved vigorously. The sea had painted whitecaps and the the yellow of the lightning was paint; everything else was natural wood. The whole thing had a crazy, urgent force to it, but it made Eddie uneasy.

The next panel showed Indians bowing before a stern white man on a rocky shore. The ship was in a cove in the distance. Carved in relief into the sky were the words MAN'S MISUSE OF MAN. In the next panel a dozen Indians were shooting arrows into the Pilgrims while a Pilgrim baby looked on, its face distorted in fright. The final panel showed a conventionalized city skyline, with dark skyscrapers and the wasted bodies of children lying in the street at the foot of them, their eyes shut and their faces twisted. This one had a wooden frame carved around it; on the frame were painted the words AMERICA AS WE HAVE MADE IT. The idea was clear enough and Eddie did not exactly disagree with it. He had seen this final panel reproduced as a photograph in Arabella's journal article. The anger was unsettling, and he wasn't sure you could sell things this grim – not for the kind of prices they would require. Deeley Marcum's work was so blunt as to be nearly comical, but there was nothing comical about these panels. The were like dark spiritual graffiti. They reminded Eddie of bag ladies on the street who hated whatever they saw.

'If you're going to sell, I suppose it'll be only the whole set,' Eddie said.

'I didn't say I wanted to sell,' Newby said.

Arabella said nothing; she looked from one of their faces to the other and jammed her hands into the pockets of her coat.

'If I'd made those I wouldn't want to sell them,' Eddie said. 'Maybe one like this.' He pointed to a single panel that showed a church with the devil seated – horns and trident painted red – on its front steps. 'Or The Three Graces.' That had been the first one Touissant Newby showed them; it had three fat black women on their backs asleep on a brass bed with three chamber pots under it.

Newby looked at the floor. 'Five hundred dollars.'

'For both.'

'Apiece.'

Eddie said nothing and walked out of the shop. It was a raw March day and there was ice on the sidewalk. A minute later Arabella came out. She was wearing a knit cap pulled down over her ears. Eddie had his scarf over his chin and his own cap pulled down.

'I don't think we should buy anything more,' she said as she came up to him.

'I didn't like that set at first, but I like it now.'

'He'll want thousands for it, Eddie, and we haven't even opened the shop yet.'

'Those titles grab you after a while.' Eddie jammed his hands deeper into his pockets. 'The old son of a bitch.'

'Once we begin selling the quilts, and Deeley's women – '

'I don't want to wait,' Eddie said. 'If we put that eight-piece set on the wall facing the quilts – and get the old man to lend us that newspaper article. Somebody's going to want to buy it.'

'Eddie,' Arabella said, 'I'm scared to risk any more *money*. What if the business doesn't go and nobody wants to buy anything?'

He looked up at the dead white sky, feeling the deep chill. 'I don't want to play it safe. I've never won anything playing it safe.'

Arabella looked at him a moment as if she were going to say something, but she didn't speak.

'Let's go back inside,' Eddie said. 'It's too damned cold out here.'

He paid with a combination of a check and cash. It left him less than two thousand in the bank. Arabella had twenty-three hundred in savings and the alimony on the first of each month. That was it. He felt all right. In his twenties, playing against Fats in Chicago, he had put every penny he had on one game, doubling the bet in the face of losses, They had shot straight pool for five thousand dollars and Eddie had never played better in his life, amazing even himself with what he could do with that much money riding on a single game – while Bert and Charlie, the cautious ones, had watched as he pocketed the balls one after another.

Now, with the eight panels of the set and three others with them in the backseat and trunk, he felt the old sense of control. Going back to Lexington it had begun to snow and the road was white with fresh powder over ice patches. Eddie drove like a dream, handling the little car effortlessly, his whole nervious system relaxed and precise, spiritually enhanced by the presence of risk.

It was almost midnight when they arrived in Lexington. Eddie drove them to the shop and they carried the panels in. He wanted to see them under the floodlights. And he was too wide awake to go to bed yet.

While Arabella made coffee with the hot plate on the countertop, he measured off the right-hand wall with his tape, marking it into eight equidistant sections, and then drilled holes with his quarter-inch drill and put in Molly bolts. Each of the panels had a heavy ring screwed to the back; he hung them in order across the wall. He climbed the ladder and re-aimed the lamps, dividing them between the two walls. Against the fresh white, the colors seemed incandescent. The Levelor blinds had been installed the day before; he went over, lowered and then tilted them, to make the window wall now white. He walked back to the center of the room; his footsteps on the bare floor were shockingly loud.

'It's spooky in here,' she said. 'I feel frightened.'

'Look at the things on the walls,' he said. 'For Christ's sake, it looks *good.*'

She raised her head and looked around herself. She faced Touissant Newby's walnut panels for a long time. Then she turned to Eddie and smiled. 'Yes they do. They really do.'

Arabella went to bed as soon as they got home, but Eddie stayed up for an hour in the living room, surrounded by his quilts and wooden panels, with the row of insolent metal women – like a small angry choir – against the wall facing him. It was three o'clock before he turned in, and even then he had difficulty getting to sleep. He kept seeing the gallery as it would be with all the stock in place. They had nothing small or cheap for sale; if they could sell only one piece a week, it would pay the rent and support them. Everything beyond that would be profit.

On Saturday morning Arabella had coffee and croissants ready to serve to as many as forty people, but no one came in. She had sent out announcements and made phone calls. Several professors had promised to drop by, but they did not. Eddie put a simple notice in the window saying 'OPEN' and his ads had run in the evening paper on Thursday and

Friday, but no one came in the doors. People passing looked in, and some stopped to stare for a while at the Las Vegas Model and the Olive Oyl that stood there facing out, with the REMEMBER PEARL HARBOR quilt behind them. It would take a while. If a week passed and no one came in, that would be the time to panic. He left the shop for a while in midmorning to go up Main to Alexander's Photo and get the black-and-white blowups he had ordered to be mounted on plastic. He brought them back and fastened them to the walls with brass round-headed screws. They were big grainy pictures, copies from old photographs, and they looked properly artistic on the walls; Betty Jo Merser, unsmiling, with her gray hair in a bun; Deeley Marcum, bald and squinting, from one of his old newspaper clippings; and the double-page spread on Newby from the *Courier-Journal* enlarged to twice its original size. It was eleven-thirty by the time he had them all up.

At one-thirty a couple came in. He was from the university, from one of the science departments. Arabella did not know him. He held his hands behind his enormous camel-hair overcoat and she kept her arms folded in front of her, placing her weight on one foot while studying the quilts and the metal sculptures and then going from one wooden plaque to the next. Both of them were self-conscious; both more interested in looking at things in the right sort of way than in the things themselves. At one particular moment when the woman was studying the middle panel of Newby's set, she held her fingers to her chin and pursed her lips in an exaggeration of discriminating thought.

'You certainly have some interesting pieces here,' the man said. 'Unusual.'

'If they weren't so . . . ' the woman said, ' . . . so *exaggerated*.'

Eddie looked at her. He knew how Deeley Marcum felt about women and he felt that way now. 'That's folk art for you,' he said.

'I guess *so* . . . ' the woman said. Then she smiled with forced brightness. 'We'll be back. Thank you so much.' The man nodded apologetically and they left.

'Deeley could make her out of bumpers,' Eddie said when they had gone.

But the couple had started something, for other people began to come in. Arabella had reheated the coffee, and she served it in plain white mugs and gave them croissants with butter on plastic plates. It was while there were six or seven strangers in the gallery that Roy and Pat Skammer came in, both in puffy down coats and heavy scarves.

'Fast Eddie,' Roy said, 'your talents never cease to amaze me.'

'It's easier than nine-ball.'

'How's it going?' Pat said. 'Have you sold anything yet?'

'Not yet.'

'The cheapest thing we have,' Arabella said, 'is four hundred dollars.'

'I'll take it,' Roy said. 'What is it?'

'The quilt next to the bathroom, with the flowers.'

'We don't have enough money to pay the heating bill,' Pat said.

Roy smiled benignly. 'We can sleep under the quilt.'

'You're being an idiot,' Pat said in exasperation. Then she looked at Eddie and smiled. 'We just dropped by to look you over and wish you luck.'

It wasn't until five-thirty that a dean from the college of education came in, studied the Marcum sculptures for several minutes and then said to Eddie, 'I'd like to buy the Las Vegas Model if you'll take a check.'

It was as simple as that. Eddie figured the sales tax, took the man's check and helped him load the piece into the back of his Volvo across the street. The price Eddie had put on the sticker at the base of the sculpture was nine hundred fifty dollars; he had bought it from Marcum for less than four hundred. Their profit was well over five hundred dollars.

On Monday and Tuesday there were no buyers, although several people seemed interested. On Tuesday morning, a woman from Channel Three called; and at two in the afternoon, while a few customers were looking over the things, she came by with a camera crew and spent a half hour making a tape for the Monday-morning talk show. She had her cameraman pan the room and then do closeups of the quilts and sculptures while she did a commentary into the microphone. Her manner varied from earnestness to superciliousness. She called the quilts 'items of Americana' but raised here eyebrows helplessly when the camera was on her and Olive Oyl together. Then she had the camera make a quick pan of the eight wooden plaques and did an interview with Arabella. Arabella was pleasant but reserved; her British accent seemed more pronounced than usual. When the woman asked her about Marcum's pieces, she said they were indigenous American folk art; that they were comic, satirical and original. Eddie stayed out of it, liking the way Arabella handled the woman. He did not want to be asked questions about how a pool player could become an art dealer.

Eddie had seen the kid hanging around. The day before they opened, he stood in front of the window a long time, staring at the display. Another time he stood across the street for nearly half a day. But he had never come in the shop before. A gloomy-looking young man with fiercely black hair and eyebrows, he had the pale skin and hairy forearms of a certain Appalachian type. You saw them at country gas stations, with the sleeves of their green workman's shirts rolled to the elbow and the black hair on their arms distinct against the white skin. They drank Orange Crush and R. C. Cola.

Eddie had just come back from lunch and was parking the car when the kid came bursting out of the shop and slammed the door behind him hard enough to break the glass. Eddie watched him head down the street, turn and go from sight.

Eddie went on in and hung his coat up. Arabella was standing by the cash register, her face cloudy. He walked over and put his hand over the back of hers. 'Something wrong?'

'That dammed kid.'

'I saw him stomping off. What happened?'

'He wanted me to meet him for a drink when I close up.'

'He looked pretty young.' Eddie did not say anything about Greg, who had not been much older.

'That's what I told him,' Arabella said, 'but he was persistent. He said age didn't matter to him as long as everything else was right. That's when I told him to get lost.'

Eddie got a cigarette from his shirt pocket and lit it. 'Don't worry about it. You did the right thing.'

She reached into the pocket and took a cigarette for herself. She smoked rarely, and only when upset. 'I suppose so,' she said.

The morning show on Monday gave them six minutes. Eddie timed it. The pictures of Marcum's women looked bright and good, and when Arabella came on she was very professional, smart and relaxed. It should help a lot.

By eleven there was a good crowd of people there – at least a dozen. Several mentioned the TV show, and a few seemed interested in buying, saying they would think about it or mull it over. But nobody bought anything. By six the shop was empty, and at six-thirty Eddie and Arabella locked the door and left. He was beginning to feel worn out.

'Well,' Arabella said, 'we're merchants. Two weary merchants.

'Let's eat at the Japanese place,' Eddie said. 'I'm not ready to go home.'

The restaurant was two blocks away; they left the car in front of the gallery and walked. After dinner they decided to go to a movie and then they walked around downtown for a while. It was eleven before they got back to the car. As they crossed the dark street to the gallery, Eddie saw something on the window; it became clearer when he got closer.

Using white spray paint, someone had covered the glass over the gallery sign and then written below it, in glossy white, KENTUCKY FUCK ART GALLERY.

'Son of a bitch,' Eddie said between his teeth. 'That god-damned son of a bitch.'

'I'll call the police,' Arabella said.

The police were no help, although the sergeant who came by a half hour afterward said he'd have his men keep an eye on the place, Eddie was able to get the paint off with a razor blade, and since the gold lettering was inside the glass, no real harm had been done.

He was an unprepossessing man in a gray tweed overcoat with a button missing. He appeared to be about sixty. When he came in he went immediately to the quilts and looked at them at great length, especially studying Betty Jo's Fiery Furnace, which had a small not-for-sale sign on the wall below it. Leah Daphne Merser's bird-and-flower design was next it, and he studied that for a long time too, tilting his head this way and that. Eddie sat on the stool at the counter drinking coffee. There was no one else in the store.

Suddenly the man broke the silence. 'Remarkable trapunto,' he said. 'The stitching is flawless and the stuffing is tight.'

'Leah Daphne Merser,' Eddie said. 'She was one of the best.'

'I believe you,' the man said. 'Nineteen thirties?'

'She died during the war.'

'I see you are asking eighteen hundred dollars.'

'I know it seems like a lot,' Eddie said.

'It's a museum piece,' the man said. 'I have no problem there.'

Eddie finished his coffee and said nothing. The man began looking at the metal sculptures. After a few minutes he came over to the counter. He was carrying a checkbook. 'I'll take the trapunto quilt,' he said, 'and the Statue of Unliberty. I think you were exactly right in putting them together.'

The statue was eleven hundred. Eddie had the sales tax figured in a moment and made out a receipt. He was wondering about the reliability of the check when the man spoke. 'Can you deliver?'

'In Lexington?'

'We're a few miles out. Manitoba Farm.'

Eddie kept his surprise from showing. Horses from Manitoba Farm ran in the Kentucky Derby; at least one of them had won it.

'I'm Arthur Boynton,' the man said.

'I can bring them out tomorrow morning.'

'That's fine. I'll be there at ten.' He handed Eddie the check.

'You should have seen it,' Eddie said, pleased. He set the car keys by the register. There was no one in the store but the two of them. 'They have marble statues in the foyer and abstract paintings in the living room. There's nothing horsey about it.'

'Just rich,' Arabella said.

Eddie looked at her. She was frowning as if in concentration. 'Yes,' he said, 'rich.' He felt suddenly uncomfortable. 'What are you pissed about?'

'I don't know.' She had just finished showing one of the less expensive quilts and it was laid out on the counter to display the pattern; she began folding it now. 'I'm sorry if I was mean-spirited, Eddie,' she said, 'but I'm beginning to feel as if I'm working for you. You make the decisions and take the responsibilities.'

He seated himself on the stand where the Statue of Unliberty had been. 'You took us to Marcum and the others,' he said. 'You've put up money.'

'It's not the same. I was the one who was supposed to know folk art, but you chose the pieces to buy. You've taken over.'

He understood her problem, but he was getting annoyed. 'You don't have to be a second-class citizen.'

She was silent for a moment. Then she said, 'Maybe you're right. You caught me off balance at first. I hadn't expected you to move so fast.'

'I was making up for lost time.' He took a cigarette from his shirt pocket and lit it. 'Still am.'

She finished folding up the quilt, carried it to where the others were kept and set it on top. Then she came back and stood by Eddie, putting her hand on his shoulder. 'I could gather the articles I've done over the past few years, add five or six more, and I'd have a book. I've talked to some people at the Press, and they like the idea.'

He looked up at her and then held up a cigarette. 'Sounds fine to me,' he said. 'Now that we're beginning to roll, we don't both have to be here.'

She took the cigarette and lit it. 'The trouble is there's no money in a university press book, and a lot of work. I have to get photographs, and do interviews. I don't know if I'm ready for it.'

'I thought that's what you like doing.'

She took a deep puff from her cigarette, and let it out slowly. 'I'm good at it. But it's like shooting pool is for you. I'm not sure about it anymore.'

He pictured his Balabushka, still locked in its rack at the Rec Room. 'Wait a minute,' he said, suddenly angry. 'It's not that I don't want to play those kids. I just can't beat them.'

You don't really know that, Eddie.'

'I know it well enough. 'Babes Cooley made me look like a geriatric fool.'

Her eyebrows went up. '*Geriatric*? Don't be silly. Your problem is that you aren't committed to pool any more than you are to me.' She took a quick, angry puff from the cigarette and then stubbed it out unfinished. 'You were never committed to beating Fats either, Eddie. Never.'

He stood up angrily and walked over to Betty Jo Merser's Fiery Furnace, with its Not for Sale sign, and studied it for a moment. He liked the quilt more every time he looked at it; it helped calm him down. Then he turned to Arabella and said, 'Maybe you're right. But it's a stand-off between you and me.'

'A stand-off?'

'If what's between us means so much to you, why do you keep a drawerful of obituaries for Greg Welles?'

She stared at him silently for a moment. Then she said, levelly, 'That's goddamned competitive of you, Eddie.'

'I suppose it is,' he said. 'I hate those newspapers.'

Arabella shrugged. 'All right. It's a stand-off. There are worse things.

They were civil but distant at breakfast. When he said it was time to leave for the shop, she suggested he go ahead while she cleaned up the breakfast things. She would be over in an hour or so. There was nothing wrong with it, but they hadn't done it that way before. He took the car and drove over alone.

When he got out of the car he knew immediately that something was wrong. The pieces in the window were gone, although the glass wasn't broken. He unlocked the door and opened it. There was a heavy smell of cold, wet smoke. He flipped the light switch, coughing. Through a haze he saw, where Newby's work had hung, the words KENTUCKY FUCK ART – this time in huge, skewed, blue letters – sprayed carefully, the letters gone over and over again until the paint dripped in tears down the empty wall. There was not a single piece of art in the room.

He knew where to look. A hole the size of a saucer had been smashed through the sliding glass door right beside the lock. All the son of a bitch had to do was reach his arm – with its goddamned black hair – through the hole and flip the lock down before sliding the door open. The room was freezing cold. The door was still wide open.

It was all out in the little garden, in the brick barbecue oven, still weakly radiating heat. A black sodden mass of burned quilts. It would be impossible to tell which was the Hebrew Children in the Fiery Furnace, which were the delicate, intricately wrought trapuntos of Leah Daphne Merser or the appliqués of Betty Jo Merser. He had burned them and then, just to make sure, doused them with water from the garden hose. Amid the quilts, Deeley Marcum's women lay in a crumpled heap, dismantled, smashed and charred. The son of a bitch must have worked all night at it.

An arm of Little Bo Peep had fallen to the ground. Eddie picked it up and poked at the mess. Underneath everything else were pieces of charred wood. The goddamned son of a bitch had used Newby's magical carvings for kindling. For kindling.

Chapter Eight

The carpet was a deep forest green; it extended halfway up the walls. In the center of the room a sunken bed rose six inches from the floor, covered with burnt-orange suede cloth; near it stood a huge circular bathtub of beige imitation marble. Surrounded by bright mirrors, a black marble sink glittered in a far corner. Its basin and faucets were gold. On a shelf above the toothbrush holder sat a small white television set. This was on when Eddie checked in; a closed-circuit show was explaining the rules of baccarat, as played at Caesar's Tahoe. Lamps were everywhere, their chrome bases bright as the polished mirrors. It was a big room, a winner's room.

The bellboy pulled the cord that opened heavy green drapes; outside was deep blue sky and a segment of a bluer lake – Lake Tahoe itself, mostly hidden by the Sahara Hotel across the highway. A Roman sofa upholstered in the green of the rug and walls sat facing the window. There were no paintings on the walls. There was no art at all.

He tipped the bellboy generously and, when he had left, stripped to his shorts and seated himself on the Roman bench for a while, looking at the sky. There was nothing of university life in what he saw outside the window or inside; he felt a kind of youthful excitement just to know that. He had a stack of one-hundred-dollar traveller's checks on the night-stand beside the bed. He no longer had a marriage, a business or a job. It didn't matter. He did not have to think about any of that for two weeks. This hotel and this view had been made for him; twelve floors below were a gambling casino, four restaurants, bars, a theater, and a huge ballroom with five pool tables in it. It was a world he understood more than he would ever understand life, and he sat here at the high edge of it, high himself to be West, rich enough for time and place.

He stood, then padded barefoot to where his suitcase was

and took the cue case from beside it. He slid out the solid, beautifully wrought Balabushka, walked back to the window and stood there screwing the two pieces together, looking at the sky and a distant row of dark pines behind the Sahara.

He had flown to San Francisco, picked up a rented car at the airport and had driven the two hundred miles across California, starting with the Bridge and then a four-lane highway through Oakland. There was miles of Oakland, the city where he was born, and yet none of it meant anything to him. There was not even the name of a familiar street on the exit signs, no tall building seen from the road that he had seen before. Only the light in the morning sky and the glimpses of the bay caught through heavy traffic on the Bridge were familiar. The house he had lived in was off the road somewhere, behind gas stations and gritty buildings, He had no idea where. Despite this, driving a bypass that was like any other American bypass, he knew he had come home for a moment at least. On the backseat were his suitcase and his cue stick; in his pocket was money. He had nothing to do for two weeks except play pool as well as he could.

At the hotel now he took a long, slow shower, standing in the tub in the center of the room with only half the curtain drawn, letting hot water run down his body for a long time before soaping up. He had turned on the huge TV that faced the bed, and as he showered he could hear the voice-over detailing the ways of placing bets on a roulette table; 'Each player is given his own color of chips,' the plausible voice explained, as though to children, 'and he keeps them throughout his time at the table. Your croupier will answer any questions.' The picture on the screen showed a young woman croupier handing chips to a bettor. Money was not mentioned. Everything was cheerful. It was just the thing to be watching while taking a shower in the middle of the bedroom. The Balabushka lay on the bed, its bright chrome-plated joint gleaming in the light from the bright Nevada sky, ready for use.

★

Just keeping the glass clean could have occuped the labors of half the Mafia. The elevators were walled with mirrors, and when you stepped out on the main floor you found yourself walking along a hallway lined with hundreds of large, diamond-shaped mirrors without a spot or a grain of dust on them. Then you turned left, went down a few carpeted stairs, and you were in the casino, facing an acre of chromium-and-glass slot machines – all clean, polished, in immaculate condition despite the hordes of glassy-eyed people who moved among them, wandering from the nickel slots to the dollar ones, threading their ways past the fifty-cent and quarter machines. All the machines had fronts of colored glass lit brightly from inside. Some people stood fixed before one machine for hours at a time, taking silver from a paper cup, dropping it in the slot, pulling the handle, letting the coins that sometimes fell into the chute at the machine's bottom accumulate until the cup was empty and then refilling the cup. Terrible odds, Eddie thought, but they didn't seem to care. Maybe they were afraid of doing something stupid or wrong in front of the croupiers and dealers at the games where you had a better chance. The only blunder with a slot machine was deciding to play it.

Powerful air conditioning sucked smoke from the air faster than the crowds could produce it. Not one ray of natural light penetrated the casino from sunlit Nevada outside; a million watts of electricity spread itself around the enormous room in luminous blue, gold and red glass like the setting for an endless, vaguely pornographic, musical.

Beyond the acre of slots sat the tables – craps and blackjack, covered in pool-table green. Off to the left in a quiet backwater cordoned by velvet ropes and monitored by men and women in tuxedoes and stage makeup, with frilled electric blue shirts, was baccarat. No sheiks or movie stars sat at those tables, but that was where they were supposed to be if they ever came to Caesar's Tahoe. The sounds of slot machines, hushed by the thickness of the red and blue carpet, penetrated to this quieter area as a kind of atonal

Muzak. The only loud noises came from the odd crapshooter instructing his dice.

Beyond craps and baccarat were restaurants and a sushi bar. Eddie headed for the sushi bar.

He started to seat himself at an empty table that overlooked the casino when he saw a Reserved sign. Annoyed, he went on through the drinking crowd and found himself a small table against the wall. He ordered a Manhattan from a waitress with fishnet hose and a skirt about three inches long; the name on her tag read 'Marge.' The sushi sat in crushed ice on a buffet table in the center of the room where a piano would have sat a few years ago – before sushi joined the croissant as chic.

Just as Marge returned with his drink, he looked up to see a familiar face coming across the room toward him. It was Boomer. 'You still got that electronic Balabushka?' Boomer said.

'In my room.' Eddie signed the check for the drink. 'Sit down.'

'Let me have a Drambuie on the rocks, Marge.' Boomer seated himself with a sigh. 'If I draw you in the first round I'm complaining to the management.'

Eddie took a sip from his drink, which turned out to be far too sweet. 'Have you seen the tables yet?'

'I just got here.' Boomer did not seem to be putting on one of his acts. His voice was genuinely morose. When his Drambuie came, he drank it off fast and ordered another. Eddie's eyes followed Marge's legs idly as she headed for the bar, until he saw three slim young men, brightly dressed and looking wired, coming up the steps from the casino. The one in front was Babes Cooley. With him was Earl Borchard. Under his breath Boomer said, 'The sons of bitches.'

The young men were laughing together. They walked to the table marked Reserved and seated themselves. Two waitresses came over, all smiles, and began taking their orders for drinks.

'Fucking kids,' Boomer said morosely.

Eddie said nothing, turning back to his Manhattan.

The main floor of the hotel was laid out like one of those supermarkets where it is impossible to buy what you want without being given opportunity to buy what you do not want: you had to go through the entire casino to get anywhere else. The ballroom where the tournament would be was at the end of a long hallway; and to get to the hallway from the elevators of the restaurants, you had to walk past the slot machines, the crap tables, the baccarat, twenty-one, roulette, chuck-a-luck and wheel of fortune. Keeno, of course, was everywhere; its numbered boards caught the eye wherever one happened to stand, and its green-skirted runners were ubiquitous.

The ballroom was not so big as Eddie expected, but it was big enough. The five tables were surrounded by rows of wooden bleachers. At the far end of the room was a platform with a speakers' table holding microphones.

The pool tables were beautiful and new. A few well-dressed young men with leather cue cases were standing near them; one was rubbing the palm of his hand over the clean green as Eddie came in, but no one was shooting. A few dozen people sat in the bleachers. A man at the speakers' table was adjusting a microphone with one hand while holding a drink in the other. There would be no games today, but a ceremony was scheduled for nine-thirty; some players had not arrived yet and it wouldn't be necessary to attend it. It was seven-thirty now.

Eddie stood between two sets of bleachers for several minutes, looking at the tables. Several younger men entered the room, pushing eagerly past him. He looked to his right; beyond the bleachers was a sign reading 'PRACTICE AREA: PLAYERS ONLY; and just as he looked, seeing the corner of a pool table and a patch of its new green, he heard the sound of a rack of balls being broken. Someone was beginning to practice. For a moment, in his stomach, he felt ill. He turned and left the room.

*

He ignored the telephone and switched on the big TV set. He had told Arabella he would call when he got there, but he did not want to call anyone. It was dark outside the window now, except for the neon on the Sahara. He should go eat supper, attend the opening ceremonies and then practice, but he did not want to do any of those things. He did not want to shoot pool or watch it being shot. He did not want to hear the names of the other players or hear about their trophies and titles and championships, hear the names of the referees, the expressions of gratitude to the pool-table manufacturer who had supplied the equipment, the officials who would keep score, the man who was directing the tournament and his assistants. But most importantly – dismayingly – he did not want to take his Balabushka and shoot pool with it.

A cop show had appeared on the TV screen, with pale blue cars screeching around corners in San Francisco and then roaring downhill in low, bouncing undulations toward the Bay Bridge, The sound on the set was low – barely above a whisper. Eddie picked up the phone, dialed Room Service and ordered a medium-rare hamburger with two Manhattans. He lay back in bed watching the screen. There was the bay from closer now. There was Alcatraz, pale in the distance, shimmering and insubstantial.

One problem with Babes Cooley was he reminded Eddie of Arabella's dead lover. So sure of himself. So young.

Halfway through the second Manhattan, he fell asleep. He awoke with a sore throat at six-thirty, with pale light in the sky outside the still-open draperies. The air conditioner had been set high and he had not gotten under the covers; he still lay on the burnt-orange bedspread with his Balabushka beside him. A teacherly woman on TV was lecturing in Spanish. He felt stiff. He was catching cold.

For a moment he felt like getting under the covers with his clothes still on and going back to sleep. He was drugged already by sleep, had probably slept for ten hours, but he could sleep more. It was too early in the morning to be up. He had done this kind of thing before, on weekends when married to Martha – sometimes sleeping for sixteen hours at a stretch and then taking the rest of the day to wake up on coffee and cigarettes.

He shook his head sharply at the memory of that, and sat up. It was visibly brighter outside. He took off his wrinkled shirt, walked to the bathroom and began to shave, soaking his face awake with hot water. It was time to get on with it. Maybe he could get into the ballroom and practice.

But the ballroom was closed and locked. The casino certainly wasn't. Although the action was light at seven in the morning, it was still action. Five weary crapshooters were huddled around one of the tables; there were a half-dozen blackjack games going; and a crowd circulated among the slot machines – most of them women, most of them motherly. Eddie pushed past them, found the coffee shop and had breakfast. After that he explored the main floor of the hotel, which was like a city in itself. He found a long mirrored arcade of shops; some were just opening up. Expensive clothes were displayed in windows: bathing suits from France, tweed jackets from Italy. One shop sold Krön chocolates; another, Cartier watches. He kept walking, carrying his cue case. At the end of the arcade, a sign over a doorway read HEALTH CLUB AND POOL. He walked in.

The pool was huge and free-form, under a sky-light. It was surrounded partly by gray boulders, to give the effect of a grotto – in fact, there was a real grotto entrance across the water from him, with the boulders making an opening like a cave, where you could swim in. There were a few small palm trees. Off to one side was a tiled whirlpool bath big enough for a dozen people at once. Behind this stood a row of trees; through them was a glimpse of a glass door and a tiny bit of sky. It was the only natural light he had seen from the main floor of the hotel. On the other side of the pool was a restaurant, closed now, with pink cloths on its poolside tables. From speakers somewhere came classical music.

To the left of the restaurant was the entrance to the health club; through the glass door he could see a woman at a desk. He walked along the concrete margin of the empty pool and pushed open the door.

There was a gym – also empty – a few yards past the desk. In it sat a half-dozen new Nautilus machines, their chromium glistening, their leather seats and benches polished, deep red. Beyond the gym a sign read MEN'S LOCKER ROOM AND SAUNA.

He turned and loooked at the women. 'Can I get trunks?'

She smiled like a stewardess. 'Sure.'

He showed her his room key and she handed him a pair of disposable shorts with the same houndstooth pattern he and Arabella wore at the Holiday Inn the day they had decided to go into business. There was a pile of big yellow towels on the counter. He took two, headed back to the locker room and changed. The supporter in the trunks was no good. He left his Jockey shorts on under them, stowed his clothes, padded out to the concrete, took a deep breath and dove into the pool. There was still no one else there. He began doing laps, swimming in long, powerful strokes.

After twenty minutes of that he dried off and worked his way slowly through the Nautilus machines, using the same weights he used at the gym back in Lexington: the hip and back machine, the leg curl, the leg extender, the triceps and biceps, the chest and shoulder. They were better machines than he had ever used before, just as the pool was the best indoor pool he had ever seen. Their gears worked quietly; the weights moved smoothly and did not clank. He kept at each machine until he had exhausted the muscle group, sweating profusely. The music from the speakers stopped and a cultivated voice announced the Overture to *The Marriage of Figaro*, and Mozart music began. Eddie pumped the weights up and down, wearing his wet bathing suit, sweating. Only on the overhead press did he cut back on the drag, reducing it by twenty pounds from what he was accustomed to. He did not want to overwork his shoulders; they had to be smooth for shooting nine-ball.

The tournament would start at one, but the ballroom opened at ten. At a quarter till, Eddie was in his room exchanging his wet shorts for dry ones; he was at the ballroom door when it opened. He went to one of the practice tables, put the fifteen colored balls out on the green, screwed his cue stick together and began to shoot. His stroke was crisp and sharp, his eyesight clear. His body – clean, exercised and purged of its long sleep – felt tireless. He ran the rack, and then another. Some young men began a practice game on the other of the two tables behind the bleachers; he ignored them, clipping balls into pockets.

'. . . one of the all-time greats, Fast Eddie Felson!' the announcer said with forced enthusiasm. There was scattered applause. Someone whistled through his teeth.

This was the low bracket of the tournament, and Eddie was matched with a jeweler from Alameda who looked deadly earnest but could barely make three or four balls in succession. He wore steelrimmed glasses, had a potbelly, and seemed never to have considered winning. Eddie beat him handily but without doing anything especially well. He needed more practice.

He hesitated several times before picking up the telephone and quickly punching out the Kentucky number. When she came on, the lack of tension in her voice surprised him; he was surprised again by the ease in his own. Maybe the distance in miles was working for them. He asked if there had been any word from the police.

'They say they're looking,' she said. 'But I don't know what they can prove. If they catch him.

'I don't want to think about it.' He reached across the bed for a cigarette. 'I won my first round.'

'That's good news. How many do you have to win to be in

the money?'

'If I beat the next man it'll pay back the entry fee. Fifteen hundred dollars.' He hesitated a moment and then said, 'I've got to get back down there and practice.' He could not think of anything else to say.

'Sure,' she said, too quickly. 'Give me a call in a day or so and let me know how you're doing.'

When he came into the ballroom, the second round had started. Babes Cooley was playing on Number One, and most of the crowd in the room filled the bleachers near that table. Eddie got as close as he could and watched for a moment, standing on the back row and seeing as well as he could over the heads in front of him. Babes was running a rack, concentrating quietly on his position. When he broke the balls the power in his lithe body was phenomenal; the rack of nine exploded like a meteor, like a firework, like a heavy atom split to fragments by a neutron. Babes waited for the remaining balls to stop moving, chalked up, bent down, stroked, shot them in.

Eddie turned, climbed down the back of the bleachers. He found a practice table. He put the fifteen balls on it and began shooting them in.

After a half hour, he looked up to see Boomer watching him.

Boomer was no longer dressed in workman's clothes; he had on a bright yellow shirt and tight designer jeans. He was freshly shaved.

'Fast Eddie,' Boomer said, 'don't shoot the fifteen balls. Shoot nine-ball.'

Eddie stood up from the table and looked at him.

'I don't know why I'm telling you this,' Boomer said, 'but it's no good to shoot straights when you're going to be playing nine-ball. Different games.'

'I know they're different.'

'You stroke different, too. You don't coddle the balls in

nine-ball. You got to be firm with 'em.'

'I know that, Boomer,' Eddie said.

'Then get your head out of straight pool. Straight pool's a dying game. I shouldn't be telling you this. You want to be a gentleman straight-pool player, go right ahead.'

Boomer walked off to the other practice table, just left empty by another player. He racked the balls into the diamond and then took his cue from its case. 'And when you break, forget your dignity.' Boomer said. 'Don't protect that Balabushka. Smash the fuckers.' He tightened his cue stick with a final twist. 'Beats me why I tell people things like that.' He drew back and smashed the rack open.

Boomer was right. He had been protecting his cue stick while hardly being aware of it. He put away the six high-numbered balls and racked the other nine. Then he set the cue ball down on the line, gripped his Balabushka tightly at the butt, holding it farther back than he usually did, hesitated a second and let go. The balls spread wide. Two of them fell in. It was a good break, better than any he had made in New London. He could feel the power of it in his right shoulder as he swung.

When he was racking again he heard applause from the playing area and then the amplified announcer's voice: 'Mr Cooley wins the match by a score of ten-three.' Eddie gritted his teeth and slammed into the rack. The balls flew apart. The nine rolled across the table and stopped just short of the corner pocket.

Something had gone wrong with the air conditioning in the ballroom. When Eddie left the practice table behind the bleachers and came around to the playing area, a heavy layer of cigarette smoke hung below the ceiling; the spotlights pierced it like sunshine through clouds. It was evening of the tournament's first day. The bleachers were at last filling up. Cocktail waitresses circulated, taking orders for drinks. Eddie pushed through the people standing between the bleachers and looked over the playing area.

Above each of the five tables hung a yard-long metal lamp shade with a red Budweiser logo in the center and card holders on each side. A white-sleeved man stood on a stool and changed the cards at the middle table while another brushed the cloth with a heavy brush, cleaning off the chalk marks and talcum powder. The man on the stool put up a card that said MAKEPIECE, and then on the other side. FELSON. Eddie walked up and waited, holding his cue.

A moment later a tall black man in an impeccable brown suit walked up. He held out a huge hand to Eddie and Eddie took it. 'I'm Makepiece.'

'Felson.'

'Fast Eddie?'

'That's right.'

The referee put the stool away, slipped on his tuxedo jacket and straightened his tie. He put two white cue balls on the table and looked at Eddie and the black man. 'We're ready to lag.'

From loudspeakers came the announcer's voice: 'On table three, from Orange, New Jersey, runner-up in the Eastern States Nine-Ball Championship of 1983, Mr Brian Makepiece!' There was a mild applause. 'His opponent will be the star of the Mid-American television series along with the late great Minnesota Fats – from Lexington, Kentucky, Fast Eddie Felson!'

The applause was slight. Earl Borchard was playing on Table One, and most of the crowd's attention was fixed on him. 'Star of Mid-American television.' Was that the best they could do? But he had no titles, not even as a runner-up in some regional tournament. All he had was the name, and sometimes when he heard it like that on a loudspeaker, he did not picture himself as being that person – Fast Eddie.

He bent to lag, and overshot. Makepiece won the break, stood erect at the head of the table, bent, and in a kind of swooping motion pounded the cue ball into the rack. The seven ball fell in. He pursed his lips in a scholarly way, studying the lie, then bent and shot in the one. A cool, detached black man. Eddie felt no threat from him. The idea was to keep calm, shoot the balls remorselessly, play safe when necessary and grind him out. Makepiece ran them up to the eight and missed. When the eight jarred back and forth in the corner pocket and then hung up, he scowled at it and looked away. Eddie did not need to be an expert at nine-ball to see the man was a loser. He chalked up carefully and pocketed the eight. Then he dropped the nine in the side. On the break for the next game, remembering Boomer, he slammed into them with all his strength and made the nine. Two-zero. For the first time in nine-ball, he began to feel good, to see the multiple ways of winning a game not as a confusion but as an asset. He could make the nine on the break. He could make it after the break on a combination and, that failing, he could run the other eight balls from the table much as he might in straight pool and then pocket the nine. Looked at that way, the game was simple. He ignored the crowd that was ignoring him and bent to work. In an hour he had won by a score of ten games to two. His playing was not brilliant but solid. Makepiece lost his nerve during the fifth game, and the rest was mechanical.

The applause, when the referee announced the score, was better than before. Two down. One more win would put him in the money.

In the evening he played a kid on Number Two, in the corner to the left of the official's table. The kid's name was Parsons; he was some kind of boy wonder of seventeen. He had come in third in the World Open at straight pool, but this was his first nine-ball tournament. He was pretty good – far better than Makepiece – but not good enough. Eddie stayed ahead of him throughout, and the final score was ten-seven. A kid like this was no problem. Out of the hundred twenty-eight players maybe a dozen would be a problem.

He unscrewed his cue, got his case from under the table, slid the two cue pieces into it, fastened the lid. He looked up. The air conditioning must have been repaired; there was no more smoke below the ceiling. He felt tired. It was good to be in the money – a real start. Pushing his way through the crowd to leave, he was congratulated by several strangers: 'Way to go, Fast Eddie!' and 'Good stroke!' As he left the ballroom he began to whistle.

It was ten o'clock and he had not eaten. That hardly mattered here, where time seemed without reference in the world and the casino never closed. He stopped at a near-empty blackjack table with a betting minimum of twenty-five dollars, bought four chips and hit a blackjack on his first hand. By the time he quit at midnight, he had won nine hundred. He tipped the dealer a chip and went to the hotel's Polynesian restaurant for dinner, sat by an artificial waterfall that burbled between enormous ferns and ate sugary pork with chopsticks. He ignored the drinks that came in coconuts and ordered a half bottle of new Beaujolais with his meal, as Arabella would have done. Good old Arabella. With the money he had just won at blackjack he could bring her out here. He thought about that a moment as the waiter poured his wine and decided not to. Being alone was all right. He did not need help, or company, or sex. He needed to roll with the good feeling inside him, the feeling that came from winning money, and he needed to practice nine-ball.

At one o'clock he went back to the ballroom, found an empty table behind the bleachers, racked only nine, and practiced until the ballroom closed at three. His game, despite the wine and the deep fatigue he felt, was even better. He could see in glimpses the entire gestalt of the table, see the nine different balls as one patterned entity. He could run out a game as a unit. It was something he once had at straight pool and then forgot. It was mystical. Intuitive. The balls fell in for him as if charmed.

Later he lay between crisp sheets, listening to the nearly inaudible deep whirr of the air conditioning, seeing through open draperies the glow in the night sky from the huge neon sign of the Sahara. He had won three nine-ball matches in two days, had worked out each morning in the gym alone, had swum a dozen laps in the huge pool, eaten in the hotel restaurants, played blackjack in the hotel casino. His soul was easing into peace. The frenetic days working for Mayhew and then buying quilts and sculptures and wood carvings, then painting, wiring and cleaning the gallery were all past him, along with the confusions of middle age: sex, money and love. He belonged here, in this room. He belonged in the ballroom downstairs, in the casino, in the long mirrored hallways like a maze running by unwordly shops. He had not stepped outdoors and he did not plan to. This hotel was like an anthill or a starship, a dwelling offering everything in life that Eddie wanted. This week was like a religious retreat. Between these sheets at four in the morning, his shoulder faintly throbbing from the swing of his splendid cue, he let his heart experience the fine old ecstasy of the gambler's life: his dedicated life, lived at the edge of the world and partly in dream, where polished balls spun across a brilliant green, where his skill shone in a room beneath layers of smoke. He could see himself now as a monk, a sleepwalker in life. As a monk was drawn by God – or was in those moments in which he was permitted to be – Eddie was drawn by money. He played pool for money and he loved money deeply and truly – loved even the dark engraving on the splendid paper of fresh bills. He could love the game of pool and the equipment of the game, the wood and cloth, the phenolic resin of the glossy balls, the finish of his phallic cue stick, the sounds and colors of pool. But the thing he loved the most was money.

On the next day the losers had come to dominate the tables, and Eddie, if he won, would play only once. It worked like this: after the first round there were sixty-four winners and the same number of losers; after the second, thirty-two winners remained; and after the third round, sixteen. That would become eight, then four, then two, then one – requiring one day for each reduction in numbers, each narrowing of the winners' field.

That would not end it. Whoever survived would have to play the winner of the losers' bracket in the finals, since this was double elimination. The losers' play-offs were going on from ten in the morning until midnight, each of the five tables continuously in action, like a chorus to the dwindling stars of the winners' bracket. Eddie was one of the sixteen undefeated, as were Borchard and Cooley. So, for that matter, was Boomer – although Boomer was barely hanging on.

His game was at ten that morning. Downstairs, he ate, swam, worked out lightly with the machines, swam more laps, and had coffee while he lay in the whirlpool bath and let the jets of hot water massage his shoulders. It was nine by then. He got out after fifteen minutes, dried off and had scrambled eggs in the restaurant at a poolside table, watching a couple of young women in bikinis who had begun swimming. Nice small breasts; nice asses. He had a second cup of coffee and watched them as they climbed out of the pool and stood, knowing they were being watched, laughing and pushing the wet hair out of their faces. The speakers were playing Mozart. Eddie finished his toast and left.

The match was very, very tough, and to win it he had to be lucky. He was. On the third rack the young man made the nine-ball but scratched on an unlucky kiss; on the fifth, Eddie was left a simple combination when the cue ball made a long, unexpected roll. And twice, when Eddie simply missed a ball he left the table safe by luck. The final score was ten-seven, and this time the applause was loud. The crowd had been watching his game more than the others, and they clapped loudly and whistled when he pocketed the nine for his tenth game. He was now one of eight. The luck didn't matter for now; he was getting there.

As he started to leave he saw Boomer coming in, still morose, screwing his cue together.

'Good work,' Boomer said. 'I'm next.'

'Who's your man?'

Boomer grimaced. 'Borchard.'

'I'll pull for you.'

'Just break his arm when he comes in.'

Eddie managed to crowd in at the bleachers; they made room for him. It didn't last long; Boomer didn't have a chance. Borchard shot like a wizard, clipping balls in with a nerveless placidity while Boomer sweated and grumbled under his breath and chalked his cue and cursed and missed. The score was ten to one and the applause was thunderous.

After the match Eddie shook Boomer's hand.

'Son of a bitch,' Boomer said. 'Bastard blew past me like a *monsoon.*'

Eddie went back to a practice table and began to shoot. Watching Borchard, he had noticed some things about the way the younger man played position, shooting the cue ball without English and at medium speed, letting the cushion control the rolling far more than a straight-pool player would. He wanted to try it himself. It was tricky; it violated things Eddie had learned thirty years before; but he kept at it, thinking *if you can't beat 'em, join 'em*, and shooting the cue ball without English and at medium speed, trying to kill it in corners and off the side rail. It took awhile but he was getting it.

He practiced three hours before going to lunch. On his way to the French restaurant he stopped at a blackjack table for twenty minutes and won six hundred dollars, drawing the right card every time he hit. It was luck again, and he was wise enough to know it was only luck, since the odds of the game were against him. He took his money and had the best lunch on the menu, drinking Perrier instead of wine. He wanted his head clear for practice afterward. He was getting a grip on nine-ball; he could feel it in his stomach. He wanted to keep shooting, watching the way he could make the cue ball set itself down for position on the next ball, and the next.

On his way back to the ballroom he walked past the blackjack tables without looking for a seat, and as he approached the final gambling area on his way to the tournament he heard a familiar gravelly voice shout, '*On the come, Sweet Jesus*!' and looked over at a crap table and there was

Boomer throwing the dice, putting his whole body into it.

Eddie stopped. Boomer was no longer wearing his nine-ball clothes. The silk shirt and tight pants were gone; he had on wrinkled brown corduroys, a tan work shirt and scuffed lumberjack boots. On his head was an olive drab Aussie hat – an Anzac hat with a safety pin in the side of the brim. His sleeves were rolled up over hairy arms and his broad, ugly face was fervid. 'Do me *now*!' he shouted as the dice came to rest, and then his face twisted sourly. 'Craps,' said the man in the tuxedo behind the table. 'Pass the dice.' Eddie went on to the ballroom.

He racked the balls and broke them as hard as he could, going for the nine. It moved only a few inches. He racked them again, broke again. The nine went to the side rail and bounced, then stopped. He racked again and broke, and then again. This time the nine fell in. The swing had to be controlled and yet be as strong as he could make it. He broke with top English and with draw, and with no English at all, and kept breaking until he felt he had the stroke right. In a game of straight pool you would never hit anything that hard, but this wasn't straight pool. After getting the break down to where he wanted it, he began spreading the balls wide with his hand, setting them up for a run that required the cue ball to make a tour of the table. He was weak there too, because you didn't play three-rail position in straight pool, chasing colored balls from one end to the other and back again. He kept at this until eight o'clock. His shoulder was killing him, but he had learned something. He looked up as he was taking his cue apart and there was Boomer, wearing his nine-ball clothes again and carrying his cue stick. Boomer's silk shirt was electric blue and his pants were white. The hat was gone.

'You're a virtuous son of a bitch,' Boomer said, 'You been here all day. Or night, or whatever it is.'

'How'd you do?'

'Let's have a drink.'

Eddie felt his right shoulder. 'I need the Jacuzzi.'

They got one of those?'

Eddie nodded.

'Let's get a drink and go to the Jacuzzi.'

As they went through the casino Eddie said, I saw you shooting craps.'

'So did the whole fucking world. I make a godamned spectacle of myself at a crap table. Always did. I was born to be an engineer. Gambling is no work for a man of my gifts.'

'How'd you do?'

Boomer stuffed his hands into his pockets. 'I got eliminated.'

'At craps or at pool?'

'At both.' He nodded his head contemptuously toward the crap table they were passing. 'That Makepiece, the one you had sitting on his hands, shot nine-ball against me like a fucking sorcerer.' He shook his head. 'I'm broke.' They headed down the hallway that led to the pool. 'When they play against me they play like demons. I'd do better assembling radios.'

Eddie reached in his pocket and took out two of the hundreds he had won at blackjack. 'Here. You can pay me back next time'

'Thanks,' Boomer said, scowling.

'I owe you,' Eddie said. 'You were right about nine-ball.'

They had the whirlpool bath to themselves. Boomer was wiry, hairy and pale, and he got into the water with finicky care. They leaned against the tiles side by side with a few feet of space between them, and Boomer drank Drambuies one after the other while Eddie nursed a single Manhattan. The water eased Eddie's shoulder and the drink relaxed him.

'After his third drink Booker had cheered up a bit. He stretched out his legs under the frothy water, stuck his toes up out of it and began wiggling them. 'I need to quit this life,' he said, 'this goddamned gambling foolishness. I'm too old for it.'

'How old are you?'

'Thirty-seven.'

'I'm fifty, Boomer.'

Boomer rolled his head over to look at Eddie. He was still wiggling his toes. 'We're different,' he said. 'I like gambling, but winning isn't all that much to me. I like to fool around.'

'What about me?'

'Well,' Boomer said, 'you may not be comfortable with it, but you're a winner.'

Eddie looked at him a moment. 'Have another Drambuie,' he said.

The next morning he lost. He did as he had the day before; slept soundly, worked out, swam, ate breakfast and arrived at the ballroom feeling strong and ready. The young man he was paired with was named Willy Plummer; he was the third-place winner from last year and the titleholder of this year's West Coast Nine-Ball Open. He was small and thin, and he shot pool like a machine. He seemed unable to miss. Eddie played a better game of nine-ball than he had played before in his life and he lost the match ten-seven. There was nothing to do but shake the man's small hand and then go to the chart on the wall behind the bleachers and see where his name came up on the losers' bracket.

He would have one match that evening against someone named Hastings, and then, if he was still in it, three more the next day. And three after that. He took a deep breath. He had been pushed back into the swamp; he would have to fight his way out to get back in the air. A lot of people like Boomer had been eliminated, and all the easy marks were gone, even from the losers' bracket. It would be uphill all the way, and very tight at the top.

Chapter Nine

He lay back and tried to focus his attention on the hot water coursing across his shoulders and on the bank of ferns along the wall in front of him, but the memory of the lost match would not go away; it was in him like an infection. He could see Willy Plummer at the table making shot after shot, in control of the game, imperturbable, while he himself sat at the little table a few feet away and watched helplessly. He had never heard of Willy Plummer before. Willy Plummer was not the player that Earl Borchard or Babes Cooley were, and he dressed like a pimp. Green sharkskin pants and a gray silk shirt with brown squares on it. Narrow Italian shoes. Pale cheeks and pale hands. Plummer made the nine once on a combination that brought the bleacher crowd to its feet applauding; he made bank shots and kick-ins, sent his cue ball flying around the table to stop on a dime.

'Don't let it tear you apart.' It was Boomer's voice. Eddie looked up. There stood Boomer in shorts, slightly bow-legged, a Drambuie in one hand and another drink in the other. 'I brought you a Manhattan,' Boomer said.

'The son of a bitch forgot how to miss.'

'It happens,' Boomer said. 'The best thing for it is a drink.'

Eddie took the drink and Boomer got into the whirlpool. 'The game of pool,' Boomer said 'has been the despair of my middle years. When I was twenty I thought it made me a man. I thought that beating other men at eight-ball was the meaning of life.'

Eddie sat up and took a swallow from his drink.

'Maybe you were right.'

Boomer seated himself on the ledge beneath the water and stretched out his arms along the tiles at the side of the pool. 'To tell the truth,' he said, 'I've never found a philosophy to replace it.'

'I haven't learned much since I was twenty,' Eddie said.

He finished the drink and set the glass on the edge of the pool. 'I've got to practice.'

'I'm going to the Golden Triangle,' Boomer said. 'Why don't you come along?'

'What's the Golden Triangle?'

Boomer raised his eyebrows. 'Where the action is.'

Boomer, who seemed to belong in a Mack truck, drove a dusty Porsche. It was strange to be outside again, although at night the main street of Lake Tahoe was something like a casino, with the lights, and the crowd on the sidewalks. Boomer drove them a mile or so and then abruptly pulled off onto a side street and parked. Neon on a plain brick building read THE GOLDEN TRIANGLE: BILLIARDS. They walked in.

It was a small, smoky place with eight pool tables and a short bar with beer signs behind it. At the back of the room a crowd surrounded the corner table, blocking it from view. On the one next to it, Makepiece was somberly shooting pool against someone Eddie did not recognize. Two other players from the tournament were playing bank pool on the front table. Each barstool held a man with a cue case. One of these smiled when he saw Boomer. 'Hello, Boomer,' he said. 'How's the eight-ball game?'

Boomer frowned at him. 'Play you for fifty,' he said.

The man unfastened his leather case and stood. One of the front tables was empty. They walked over to it. Boomer could not have much more than fifty dollars. He had better not lose the first game. Eddie followed and watched for a few minutes until Boomer sank the eight ball and racked them up for the next game. Eddie took two fifties out of his pocket and unobtrusively handed them to him. 'Just in case,' he said, and went to the back of the room, where the crowd was. Two of the people watching recognized him and made way. He was able to push in far enough to see what was going on. Babes Cooley was bent over a shot; standing at the side of the table carrying his stick and watching was Earl Borchard. They were playing nine-ball. Both men were silent, intense, concentrated. Babes shot out the rest of the rack, pocketing the nine with care. Someone racked the balls. Eddie turned to the man next to him. 'What's the stake?'

'Five hundred,' the man whispered.

'For how many games?'

'Five hundred a game.'

Babes broke and made the nine. The man racked them again, Babes broke again, left himself snookered, played a delicate and perfect safety.

Eddie watched for an hour, while the lead went back and forth. He felt a growing dismay. They both played beautiful pool; both were in dead stroke. But even that wasn't so bad. What made Eddie more and more uncomfortable was that not only did both of these men look unbeatable – these kids who seemed to own the room they were in as they seemed to own the ballroom back at the hotel – but it seemed to him that they both shot pool better than Eddie himself had ever shot it. Even at his best, when he was in his twenties and pool was nearly all he knew in life.

During the second half of the hour Borchard started pulling ahead, making the nine more frequently on the break or running the balls out, clipping them in and nudging them in, shooting fast and loose and never missing. Finally Cooley said, with uncharacteristic softness, 'That's enough for now,' and unscrewed his cue. Eddie looked at his watch. It was a little after midnight.

As Eddie approached the front table, Boomer cut the eight into the side. He looked up to see Eddie, winked, reached into his hip pocket and pulled out a roll of money. He peeled off two hundred dollars and handed Eddie the bills. 'I'm recovering my health,' he said.

The other front table was empty now. Eddie told the man behind the bar to put him on time and then got his cue out and racked the balls for nine-ball. He broke them open and began running. It would take him five more matches to pull out of the losers' bracket, and if he could do that he would still have to play either Cooley or Borchard. He shot hard, ramming the colored balls into the backs of the pockets. A couple of men came over, leaned against another empty table next to him and watched. He finished the balls, racked them, broke, ran them out. When he was racking again, he looked up to see Earl Borchard leaning against the other table, watching him. 'You shoot them in pretty clean.' Borchard said in a country-boy voice as cold as ice.

Eddie took the wooden rack away from the balls and slid it under the table.

'Would you like to play nine-ball?'

Eddie looked at him. 'I don't know.'

'I understand you're a straight-pool player. Maybe I could give you some weight.'

'How much weight?'

'I'll play you ten to eight.'

It was like a slap in the face. Eddie had never been offered a handicap before in his life. 'For how much?'

'Five thousand.'

'I don't have it.'

'Maybe your friends'll help.'

'What friends?'

'Tell you what,' Borchard said, smiling coldly. 'Ten to seven. How can you lose?'

'I don't have it,' Eddie said. The man's smile made him furious.

'I have.' It was another voice. Eddie looked behind him to see Gunshot Oliver. He was better dressed than he had been in New London, and did not seem drunk. He had his billfold in one hand. 'I'll back you.' he said. 'I've seen you play nine-ball.'

Eddie stared at him. He had thought of Gunshot as a broken-down old bum; here he was with a fat billfold, offering to put up five thousand dollars.

'If you win,' Oliver said, clearing his throat, 'I'll split with you. If you lose you don't lose anything.'

Other people in the room had become silent, and what

games were going on had stopped. Boomer was walking over to see, cue in hand.

Eddie did not want to play Borchard, but there was no way to back out. He looked at him, at his heavy mustache, his chalk-smeared white shirt, his small hands. No one was unbeatable. 'Okay,' he said.

'Let's lag for the break,' Borchard said.

Eddie won the lag and smashed them open hard, but the nine didn't fall. He ran five balls and then had to play safe, leaving the cue ball behind the seven and against the rail. Unworried, Borchard managed to hit the six on a rail-first and still not leave a shot. It was a pisser. Eddie looked around him for a minute. A pair of men in the crowd were making a bet, handing a pile of bills to a third man in a brown overcoat. The whole goddamned poolroom was watching the game, including the people at the bar. He bent and shot, playing safe again. The cueball rolled too far by inches. It was the thinnest of cuts and ruinous if Borchard should miss, but it was a shot. Borchard chalked up serenely, bent and stroked. His stroke was as smooth as ice; the six ball rolled across the table and fell into the corner pocket; the cue ball went completely around the table, stopping dead for the seven. Borchard clipped it in. Then the eight and the nine. A man from the crowd stepped up and began racking.

Eddie went over and leaned against the empty table by Boomer. Boomer put his hand on Eddie's arm. 'Don't let up on him.'

Borchard rifled the cue ball; the nine, kissing twice, fell in. Eddie felt his stomach go tight. Borchard needed eight games now, and he had the break. Eddie's edge was practically gone, in the first five minues. 'He'll miss,' Boomer said. 'You have to wait.'

But Borchard didn't miss. What he did was make four balls and then play safe, leaving Eddie the full table's length away from the orange five ball – and the five ball an inch off the middle of the bottom rail. It could not be cut in. But the seven ball was sitting right in the corner pocket at the top of the table. Eddie took his glasses off and checked them for dust. They were all right. He looked at the seven again. All it needed was a tap. He took a deep breath, bent, and stroked at medium speed, with no English. The cue ball hit the edge of the five, cater-cornered itself out of the bottom corner and came diagonally back up the table, straight at the seven. It clipped it. The seven fell in. The cue ball kept on going, off the top rail and halfway back down the table, as the five came to rest a foot from the bottom corner pocket. Someone in the crowd whistled. A deep voice said, 'That's the ticket!' It was Boomer. Eddie, steadier now, shot the five in and then made the rest, pocketing the nine firmly in the side.

While the balls were being racked he hefted his Balabushka, trying to concentrate on the break. Abruptly he though of something. There was a rack of house cues on the wall to his left. He walked to it, looked at the printed numbers on a few of them and found a twenty-three – the heaviest pool cue made. Coming back, he handed the Balabushka to Boomer, chalked up the club of a house cue, stepped to the head of the table and slammed into the cue ball, feeling the extra weight magnified by the speed of his stroke. The balls crashed open and the nine fell in.

On the next rack he did not get the nine; it only turned over a few times, but he made two of the others. Not looking at Borchard, he concentrated on the balls, using the Balabushka now, and smoothed them into the pockets one at a time. Dropping the nine was simple.

'Like buttering bread,' Boomer said.

'How'd you do at eight-ball?'

'Six hundred,' Boomer said. 'I put it on you.' He nodded toward the man in the brown overcoat who had been making bets.

'Good bet,' Eddie said. 'I can't miss.

For three more racks he didn't. He felt control of the game now, felt some of the clarity he had felt in bed the night before. He did not make the nine on the break again, but he made something each time and then ran them out. It was like straight pool: a matter of position, or confidence, of knowing that the game was, at bottom, shockingly easy.

But on the fourth break, even with the smash he gave them with the twenty-three-ounce house cue, nothing fell. The three ball was headed for a side pocket but at the last moment the seven knocked it away. The nine had stopped two inches from the bottom corner.

But the score was five-two. He needed only two more games. Borchard needed eight. While Borchard started shooting, beginning with an easy one ball, Eddie went to the bar, ordered a Manhattan, and looked over his shoulder to see Borchard pocket the nine on a combination. Five-four. The son of a bitch. Borchard broke, made a ball, began running. Two pairs of balls were frozen at different ends of the table; one of them should stop him, force him at least to play safe; but neither did. He caromed his cue into one pair as he pocketed the three ball, doing it with the ease of a straight-pool player, and separated the other two on the next shot. He ran out. Five-five.

In the next rack he made the nine on his third shot, from a billiard off the three. On the next he ran them out after pocketing two on the break; and on the next he made the nine on the break. Eddie and Boomer said nothing. The score was eight-five. Borchard looked unstoppable. The crowd had become silent.

Borchard stepped up, quiet and concentrated, and broke, making the seven ball. His position on the one was fine. He drove it in, made the two and then the three. The four ball was a cinch and the position on the five another cinch. Borchard looked at the four and hesitated. Then he bent and shot. He missed. He missed the four ball, hanging it in the pocket. He raised his eyes heavenward, dropped his shoulders and said, 'Son of a bitch.'

It had happened. It could happen to anyone. Eddie chalked his cue and stepped up. Borchard had left him an open table and a road map: the four, five, six, eight and nine, as easy as pie. And one more game after that. Borchard had choked or blinked or twitched or one of the things that every player sometimes did, and this was what he had left.

Eddie shot the four in, killing his cue ball for the five. He made the five, then the six and eight. His position on the nine was dead-on. He clipped it in. Eight-six.

He gripped the big cue hard and slugged with it, but the balls were sluggish and the nine barely moved. The one teetered and fell in. The two was tough – a table's length away and the kind of backward cut Eddie hated. He looked at Borchard, who seemed expectant, and then at Boomer. Boomer winked at him, unruffled. Boomer looked certain enough. *What the hell*, Eddie thought, *I'll make the two ball*. For a moment he allowed himself to think of all the ways of missing it, but then, knowing it was deadly to think that way, put the thought out of his mind. He was not fifty years old for nothing. You did not have to think about missing. He would make the two ball. It would be a pleasure to make it.

He stroked easily, and shot. The cue ball rolled down the table, hit the blue two ball with just the right amount of fullness and speed. The ball rolled diagonally away from the white ball and fell into the corner. The cue ball kept going. The three ball was frozen to the head rail. The cue ball came back up the table, slowing down, and set itself in line with the three. The room was silent.

Eddie shot the three in, loosening even more, and the cue ball settled behind the four. He shot it in. Then the five. And the six, seven, eight. The nine, striped with pale yellow, sat near the spot where it had sat ever since the break. Eddie stepped up, chalked, and drilled it into the corner pocket. The sound it made, hitting bottom, was exquisite.

'Well,' Boomer said, driving them back. 'Twelve hundred dollars can change a man's philosophy beyond belief.'

'Don't shoot craps with it,' Eddie said.

'Eight-ball. I was born to play eight-ball.'

Eddie had the twenty-five hundred in his pants pocket, and he pushed it down with his thumb. On the backseat lay the twenty-three-ounce cue stick which he had bought for ten dollars. 'He had eight games. If we'd been playing even, he'd have won.'

'Don't *you* get philosophical,' Boomer said. 'The man lost. You beat him.'

There were six rounds to go in the losers' bracket, and all of them were sudden-death. Eddie had three matches on Thursday and three on Friday. If he won. If he lost, that was the end of it. On Saturday night the one undefeated man would play the single player who had managed to come out of the loser's bracket unbeaten. That would be the finals, for first and second place. Whomever the winner had beaten the day before would be third. Third place was seven thousand dollars and second was fifteen. First prize was thirty thousand, and a trophy.

He got to bed at three, slept until eight-thirty and managed a quick swim and a whirlpool before breakfast, but there was no time for a workout. At ten o'clock he beat his man handily. It was over by eleven-thirty, and Eddie, not seeing Boomer around, headed straight for the Nautilus machines and gave himself a light session, just enough for a sweat, and then immersed himself in the whirlpool. The next game was at two. He would not practice today; he needed all he had for the two upcoming matches. He had beaten Borchard, and in the one match had made almost as much money as he had put into those quilts. For a moment he thought of Betty Jo Merser's round black face with her lips pursed, liking her. So few women could do anything. The loss of those quilts – especially of the Fiery Furnace with its three children on a shovel and its bright flames – had hurt him as much as losing a pool game could hurt. And the quilts could not be won back. They were gone forever. It was best not to think about it. He eased the back of his neck against the warm tiles and let the churning water come up to his neck and chin, relaxing his shoulders. He let his legs float out in front of him beneath the water. The music of a string quartet came across the broad pool to his right with a delicacy like that of the light coming through the ferns beside him. He closed his eyes and felt himself drifting off to near-sleep. The young men could be beaten. He had beaten Borchard. Nine-ball was only pool. He had played pool all his life.

He stayed in the whirlpool a long time and then dried off lazily and dressed. He had a sandwich for lunch, went back to the ballroom, warmed up for ten minutes on a practice table and then played and beat the man who had beaten him the day before, Willy Plummer. The score was ten-three and Eddie did not miss a shot. Plummer scored on the two breaks when Eddie made nothing, and he pulled a lucky shot out from one of Eddie's safeties, but it was no contest. The next game was at nine that night.

Back on a practice table Boomer was playing eight-ball with one of the tournament officials. When Eddie came by, he looked up from his shot and said, 'Cooley got beat. At noon.'

'Who did it?'

Boomer cut one of the striped balls into the side pocket. 'Who do you think? Earl Borchard.'

Eddie walked on to the hallway and then to the casino. To get out of the losers' bracket, he – or somebody – would have to beat Cooley. After that was Borchard without a ten-seven handicap. For a moment, walking by the filled blackjack tables and then along a bank of slot machines, he felt weary. He felt like driving to San Francisco and taking the next flight home to Arabella. He went up to the room, which the maid had just finished making, and took a nap on clean sheets, falling asleep immediately.

That night at nine, the match was close and Eddie missed two critical shots that could have cost him the game but didn't. The man he was playing was more tired than he, and rattled. Near the end of it, Eddie left him an easy lie on the six; he ran the six, seven, eight, and blew the nine. Somehow Eddie expected it and had not even seated himself. He just stepped up, shot the nine ball in and went on to win the match. It was ten-thirty. He left the ballroom and went directly to bed.

The game the next morning was also close; there was no one easy left in this tournament. More than half the players had gone home. Eddie was rested from a ten-hour sleep and a good breakfast; the kid he played looked as though he had been up all night and was trying to stay alive with Methedrine or cocaine. There were red lines under his eyes and the fingers of his bridge trembled when he shot. He kept combing his hair. Eddie beat him ten-six. There were two more to go – a game with somebody named Wingate at three, and then at nine, Cooley.

He went to the sushi bar at lunch and had wait in line. When he had gotten his food and was looking around for an empty table, a man across the room waved at him. He went over. It was someone he had seen around the tournament, although he didn't know his name. 'Have a seat,' the man said. There was another man at the table and two empty chairs. Eddie sat down. He didn't feel like talking, but there was nowhere else to sit. 'My name's Oldfield,' the man said. 'This is Bergen.'

'Good to meet you both.'

Oldfield finished what he was chewing. 'Heard about you for years. Never saw you play before last night.'

Eddie looked at him but said nothing.

Bergen was a small man with a mustache and unworldly look. His voice was almost apologetic. 'Mr Oldfield lost a bit of money. He was betting on Borchard.'

'Borchard shoots a good stick,' Eddie said.

'I know, I *know*,' Oldfield said. 'I'm backing him in this tournament. I backed him last year.'

'A lot of these kids don't have a cent,' Bergen said.

'I suppose not,' Eddie said. 'How much did you lose?'

'Twelve.'

'Twelve hundred?'

'Twelve thousand.'

Eddie shook his head. 'A lot of money.'

For a moment he felt annoyed, as though Oldfield were blaming him. Oldfield stood up, and then Bergen. 'See you around, Fast Eddie.' he said. 'Enjoy your lunch.' The two of them left. Eddie finished his food, thinking. Other people had been betting money on the match. The man in the brown overcoat was holding a fistful of it, and there was money moving around elsewhere in the crowd. An old, old system existed called 'two brothers and a stranger,' where two men would work together, one of them backing his friend's opponent and then betting against the friend – the 'brother.' If that was what Borchard and Gunshot had been doing, if they had been working together, Eddie was the stranger and his win meant nothing.

He spent an hour after lunch in the gym and the whirlpool, then went to his room and changed into a fresh shirt and jeans. In the ballroom, pushing through the crowd standing between packed bleachers, he entered the playing area and found himself for a moment face to face with Babes Cooley. Babes was wearing skintight black pants over black pumps, and a white silk shirt. His face was flushed and his eyes bright. He was standing by Table Two; Eddie would be playing Number Three.

'Good shooting last night, old-timer,' Babes said, smiling coldly. He was polishing the end of his cue stick with a white towel.

'Thanks,' Eddie said.

'Don't spend it all in one place.'

Eddie looked at him hard. 'With twenty-five hundred,' he said, 'I could hire somebody to break your right arm.'

Cooley's smile didn't waver. 'I'd beat you with my left.'

Eddie walked to Table Two and took his cue out of its case.

His opponent was a man in his thirties who looked like an Italian barber. Ross Arnetti. When the announcer introduced them to the crowd, Arnetti's titles were impressively numerous, although they were all for second and third place. He had been runner-up in the World Open at straight pool twice, was third in the U.S. Invitational– also straight pool – and second in two regional nine-ball tournaments. The announcer called Eddie 'one of the all-time greats making a fine showing at this event.'

Eddie won the lag. As he stepped up to break, he heard the crash of balls on the table next to his and glanced over to see Babes Cooley starting up. Eddie had his twenty-three-ounce battering ram with him, and he gripped it hard now and drove the rack open. The nine died near the bottom corner, and the three stopped right behind it. The five fell in. Eddie ran the one and two, sighted carefully and drilled into the combination. The nine fell.

He had been disturbed a bit by the conversation at the sushi bar, but the hatred he now felt for Babes Cooley had wiped that out. Arnetti seemed like an amiable man, a solid professional; it would be hard to hate him. Eddie accepted the diffused hatred he felt for the young man on the table next to him and kept it; it gave an edge to his stroke and a clarity to his vision. He played beautifully; by the middle of the match he could sense the inner collapse of the man he was playing. Arnetti was straight-backed in his chair, but he held his glass of water limply, trying to look uninterested when Eddie glanced his way. For a brief moment after cinching the nine, Eddie felt sorry for him – held by the balls and nowhere to turn – but he shook it off. It was no time for mercy. He made the nine on the break in the next rack. The match ended quickly. Ten-four. The applause was loud. As he was leaving, carrying both cues, applause broke out again and he heard the announcer's voice on the PA: 'Mr Cooley's match by ten-six.' Eddie didn't turn back to look.

The dressing area was right inside the door to his room. As he came in he saw a gray duffel on the carpet with the zipper open. Next to it sat a portable typewriter. Then he noticed the sound of running water and saw that the shower curtain in the middle of the room was closed. He walked over and pulled it open. Arabella was sitting naked on the edge of the tub, her feet in the water, waiting for it to fill.

'This is the biggest bathtub I ever saw in my life,' she said.

'How in hell did you get here?'

She looked up at him. 'Flew to Reno. Took a bus. The maid let me in. Where were you?'

'Shooting pool.'

'This water feels wonderful on my poor feet. Did you win?'

'Yes.'

'Oh boy,' Arabella said.

'I play Cooley at nine tonight.'

'Jesus,' Arabella said. 'Can you beat him?'

'He beat me in New London.'

She reached out and turned the water off and then slipped herself into the tub. 'That was New London,' she said. 'A lot's happened since.

'I hate his guts,' Eddie said. 'I hate him like I hate that kid lover of yours.'

She said nothing, but began soaping herself. Eddie took off his shirt and lit a cigarette. He seated himself on the padded bench and looked out the window. After a while he heard the water begin to run from the tub and then heard her drying herself off. Then she said, 'The mess at the shop is cleaned up. The police never picked anybody up.'

'What about fingerprints?'

'Nothing. It was all smears or something.'

'If I win this,' Eddie said, 'we could go back in business.'

'Eddie,' she said, 'it doesn't matter to me right now whether we go back into business or not. Just win it.'

He turned and looked at her. She was dressed now, in a gray skirt and black sweater. 'I'm *afraid* of Cooley,' he said. 'Scared shitless of him.'

They arrived early because Arabella wanted a good seat. She managed to get in the third row of the bleachers next to the quiet blond who travelled with Cooley. There was only one table now, in the center of the room. Eddie went to the practice area and began shooting. His stroke felt tight; his glasses had begun to irritate the bridge of his nose; his hands were cold. He kept shooting, softening his stroke a bit; he was getting into it when the PA voice came on: 'The finals of the losers' matches will begin in three minutes. The players will be Mr Gordon Cooley and Mr Ed Felson.' Eddie felt himself go tight. He picked up the poolroom cue from where it was leaning against the wall, gripped it in his right hand with the Balabushka and headed between the bleachers. The table sat empty under a trapezoid of light, and the people in the stands had become quiet. Cooley was approaching from the bleachers on the other side, just now walking into the lights. It was like a boxing arena before a title fight. Eddie put his free hand into his pocket so the trembling wouldn't show.

Cooley had a following. As he set his cue case on the table and opened it, someone in the stands shouted, 'You'll do it, Babes!' and somebody else bellowed, 'Kill!' Cooley smiled, looking down at the cue he was taking from its case. Then he glanced briefly up at Eddie but said nothing.

The announcer introduced them, listing a dozen titles for Cooley, including New London and this tournament itself from the year before. Eddie was 'the legendary Fast Eddie Felson.'

The referee's white shirt-front glistened in the lights; his tuxedo looked brand-new, perfectly pressed. 'The gentlemen will lag for break.' He wore white gloves and carried two white balls. He set them at the head of the table, on the line, and the two players bent and shot together. Eddie hit his ball too hard; it came back to the top rail and bounced a foot away. Cooley's lag was perfect.

Now Cooley was all calm efficiency. He set the cue ball on the line, drew back, smashed the balls open, dropping the five and eight. Not taking his eyes from the green he chalked and began running. He had the table empty in two minutes, to applause, and the referee racked. Eddie sat in his chair, watching, trying to calm himself.

When Cooley drew back his arm for the break, a voice shouted, 'On the snap, Babes!' and he plowed into them. The nine did not go, but the table opened for him. He ran it. The applause this time was louder. Two-nothing. Eddie began tapping his foot on the floor.

And on the next break Cooley made the nine. The applause was thunderous. Babes stopped in the middle of chalking up and turned to face the largest bleachers. 'It had to be,' he said. Then he turned, broke the balls, and made the nine with a combination. Four-nothing. Eddie's stomach was like ice, and his palms were wet, his lips dry. Babes flicked a glance his way and then back to the table. Eddie could hear him whisper plainly, 'By the balls.' Eddie's heart began pounding and he gripped his cue like a weapon.

Babes broke, made one, and began to roll. But on the four his position was off and he wasn't able to knock apart a trio of balls that had clustered near the foot spot. He studied the lie a moment and played Eddie safe on the five, sending the cue ball to the bottom rail and the five to the top of the table. Eddie stood up as calmly as he could. A cut was barely possible on the five ball, but you didn't go for shots like that against someone like Cooley. The thing to do was return the safety. When he got to the table he studied it a moment, more to calm himself than to decide. He could make that shot. Possibly. He had made tougher ones before. Cooley would play it safe. So would Fats. At four-nothing it would be dumb to go for it. Then he looked over at Cooley. Babes hadn't even seated himself. He was expecting to shoot again in a moment. Eddie took a square of chalk from the edge of the table and chalked his cue. And then a rough, gravelly voice rang out from the stands. '*Go for it, Eddie!*' It was Boomer. Something relaxed in Eddie's stomach. He set the chalk down, took his Balabushka at the balance, bent to the table. There was the five ball, eight feet away, its edge sharp in his vision. There were the three balls that would have to be broken apart if making the five would mean anything. He took a deep breath, stroked, and felt the solid hit of his cue tip against the white ball. The white ball sped down the table, clipped the edge of the five, ricocheted out of the corner and came back down to the head spot, knocking the three clustered balls apart. The five ball rolled to the edge of the corner pocket with chilling slowness and teetered on the edge. It fell in. Into the middle of the pocket. The crowd exploded in applause.

Eddie did not look up. He did not have an easy shot on the six, and the seven was in a bad place. Best to take another chance and bank the six, so the cue ball would go naturally to the seven. He sucked in his breath again and banked it. It went into the center of the side pocket. The cue ball stopped perfectly for the seven down the rail. He made it. The eight was gone; the nine was next. Eddie made the nine. There was applause again.

He looked up. Cooley had sat down.

From then on it was simple. Eddie's concentration and poise were unshakable. He made the nine twice more before a bad roll on the break forced him to play safe, and the safe he played was a mortal lock. Cooley could do nothing with it. Eddie wound up with the cue ball in hand and ran out the rack. On the next, he made the nine on the break and on the next he made it with a combination off the five ball. He was forced to play safe a few times, and Cooley managed another win, but that didn't matter. When Eddie was breaking them, now people would shout 'On the snap, Fast Eddie!' He could hear Arabella's strong, feminine British voice among them, along with Boomer's. *'On the snap!'*

He had entered that time zone he had nearly forgotten, where his stroke was not only dead-on but where his mind could somehow arch itself above his game and see the great simplicity and clarity of what he was doing on this green table with its spinning balls. Time passed without moving, until the PA system voice said, 'Ten games to four. Fast Eddie,' and the applause washed over him, bringing him back.

He put the Balabushka away and then took his glasses off, fifty years old again. He had beaten them. He had beaten Borchard at nine-ball and now he had beaten this brash genius kid. Cooley had already left. Arabella was coming toward him from between the bleachers and so was Boomer. Boomer got there first and was hugging him, smelling of Drambuie and saying, 'Those fucking kids, Eddie. Those fucking kids,' and then Arabella was coming toward him with her face glowing. He pulled himself away from Boomer and she hugged him.

Cooley had left, but now he was coming back. As Arabella stepped away from Eddie the young man walked up to him and held out a hand. Eddie took it. 'Good shooting, old-timer,' Cooley said, smiling tightly.

'Thanks,' Eddie said, hating him.

'Earl,' Cooley said, 'will whip your ass.'

'The last time I played Earl I beat him.'

Cooley looked at Eddie silently for a moment, his smile unchanged. 'Two brothers and a stranger,' he said.

The finals would be at two. It was Saturday morning. Arabella sat on a weight-lifting bench and watched while Eddie did his workout. Then they swam and got into the whirlpool together. It was 9:00 a.m.

In the hot water she said, 'Children in England learn a lot about America in school. The Grand Canyon, for instance.'

'So do we.'

'It's not as exotic for you. In Third Form we had a picture of Lake Tahoe in our text. I remember it well.'

'I understand it's right outside,' Eddie said, nodding toward the far wall.

'It's the most spectacular mountain lake in the world. Thousands of feet deep, and the water extraordinarily clear.' She was sitting next to him on the whirlpools underwater ledge, and now she put her hand on his arm. 'There's a house called Vikingsholm at the edge of it. I'd like to go. Maybe we could have a picnic lunch.'

He had forgotten the lake itself over the past few days. When he looked out the window of his room, it was only to see the lights from the Hotel Sahara or the sky; the small patch of blue from the lake no longer registered.

'I want to be back at one,' he said.

'Of course. Can we go?'

'How far is the house?'

'I don't know. The whole lake is seventy miles around.'

'Maybe you can get a brochure at the desk.'

'They don't have brochures at the desk. They don't want you going anywhere.'

It was a twenty-mile drive along a winding road. Several times Arabella cried out at glimpses of the lake itself, through dense pines and redwoods. He pulled over in a wide place and they got out to look. The water was bluer than the sky, and the sky, here where Nevada and California joined, was intensely blue. Snow gleamed on the mountains behind the water. The trees were so green they were almost black. The surface of the lake was like glass beneath them, a hundred or so yards down. Eddie still thinking of Borchard, lit a cigarette and watched Arabella watch the lake. The air was thin and cold; he jammed his hands into his pockets, puffed on his cigarette and waited. It was a shock to be outdoors. It was a shock that this lake was here, was this big, this perfect. Somehow he felt threatened by it; it seemed less real than the casino at Caesar's Tahoe, less real then the blackjack tables and the slots. Lakes like this belonged on postcards, with the pines, the cloudless sky, the snow on the mountains. He finished his cigarette, ground it out on the gravel at the edge of the road, looked down toward the water – at its uncluttered cold stillness – and thought of the blue Gulf of Florida and of Minnesota Fats. Fats had died a winner. It could be done. It was a question of balls.

Arabella came back from the turnoff's edge, her cheeks red from the cold air. 'It's every bit as lovely as the textbook claimed,' she said, and put her arm through Edddie's for a moment. Then she looked up at his face. 'Let go of it for now, Eddie. Think about it later.'

It was too early for the tourist season, and the sign at the little parking lot saying VIKINGSHOLM had a smaller sign below it: CLOSED TO VISITORS. 'Let's ignore that,' Arabella said. They climbed over the chain and headed down the trail to the lake's edge a half mile below. It was getting warmer now and the smell of the pines was strong. Every now and then they would pass a place near a turn in the trail where water gushed down the dark granite. Spring thaw. The way the lake was made. Two chipmunks scuttled along a fallen log, through ferns. Eddie and Arabella came round a turn and, below them, surrounded by enormous trees, was a house of stone and timber with a high, gabled roof. Fifty yards in front of it Lake Tahoe began.

'Sweet Jesus!' Arabella said, 'I want it.'

The water, colorless except for the glitter of pyrites in the sand, lapped the shore with exquisite gentleness. They turned toward the house. To the right of the doorway, a row of casement windows overlooked the lake. 'You could have breakfast in there and just look out,' Arabella said.

Eddie said nothing.

'It was built by a woman,' Arabella said.

'A woman with a rich husband.'

She looked at him. 'Two rich husbands.'

There was a simple bench under a redwood a few yards from the house. They sat there and had Swiss-on-rye sandwiches, doughnuts and coffee. She had brought two beers, but Eddie refused his, wanting to keep his head clear. He leaned against the bark of the tree and tried to relax – tried to get pool balls and the bright green of the table out of his head, the feel of the Balabushka out of his right hand, the knot out of his stomach.

'When we started together,' Arabella said, 'I think I was a help to you. You were low and you didn't trust yourself. You didn't want to tell me what you did for a living. It turned out I liked you shooting pool, and that helped you, didn't it?'

'Yes.'

'The problem with me, Eddie, is that I'm good with men but not with myself. When I left Harrison, I was terrified.'

She looked over at him, holding her plastic coffee cup. '*Terrified*. I'd had an easy marriage and enough comfort and I stayed in it for years after I ceased to give a damn about Harrison. Then I was in love with Greg for a while and that gave me a lift. Just to be able to attract a man as young and as bright as Greg. And then there was the accident.'

'I know.'

'I don't know if you do, Eddie. His chest was crushed. His family hated me and I wasn't asked to the funeral. For several months, with my knees bandaged, I felt that I could not leave Harrison, no matter what.'

Eddie was lighting a cigarette. 'Let me have that,' she said, and took it. 'I didn't have any bloody *money*. I had a C D worth three thousand dollars. There was four hundred in my checking account. It took a year to work up the courage to walk out. I'm scared to death of not having money.'

Eddie lit another cigarette. 'Me too,' he said.

'I know.'

'Do you want to run the folk-art business, while I travel?'

'Are you going to travel?'

'I don't know,' he said. 'After tonight things will be clearer. Right now I'm unsure.'

'About pool?'

'I still don't know if I can make a living at it, by playing tournaments.' He looked at her sitting by him, at her cheeks, bright red from the cold. 'I'm not sure about us.'

She frowned and blinked. 'I wasn't sure either, until I bought the airplane ticket to Reno.'

'And you're sure now?'

'I threw those newspapers away.'

He thought a long moment before he spoke. 'If I had some, I'd throw them away too.'

She looked at him. 'It sounds like a deal.'

Even from the doorway, with the bleachers between him and the one pool table, it was different. The lights were twice as bright as before; and when he pushed through the crowd that packed the space between bleachers, he could see the reason for the lights: television. There was a twenty-foot steel boom above the playing area, with a camera and floodlights hanging from it. Two strangers stood talking to each other by the table, oblivious of the waiting crowd. They both wore blue nylon jackets with a shoulder patch circle reading ABC. It was 'Wide World of Sports.' They had never picked up the show with Fats, but here they were now. The sons of bitches. Three cameras sat on wheels around the table, each with a man in a nylon jacket by it. On the speakers' table was a row of TV monitors.

He did not see Borchard. It was one-fifty. Arabella had asked Cooley's girl to save her a seat, and she went to it now. Eddie walked out to the table, squinting as he came under the warm spotlights. Clearly the TV people weren't ready, but it might be good to get used to the brightness. The men in blue jackets ignored him. The two at the table were bent over a clipboard; when Eddie came near they looked up and then back, preoccupied. He was just getting annoyed when he saw Borchard pushing through the crowd between the bleachers. People began to applaud. The TV men stopped what they were doing. One of them waved at Borchard and the two walked over to him and huddled in conversation. The applause became louder. Eddie opened his case and got out the Balabushka.

Twenty minutes passed, during which Eddie seated himself in one of the two swivel chairs set up for the players, drank a glass of water and tried to be calm. The TV people in their glossy jackets acted as though they were the stars. Their boom, their rubber-wheeled mounts with the heavy gray cameras on them, their thick rubber cables, their monitors and their clip-boards had become the show. Eventually one of the jacketed men came over to him and checked the pronunciation of his last name, and then said, 'It's Fast Eddie, right?' Eddie said yes. The boom was only a few feet above the table. The young man in jeans stood by the supports at each end; they began cranking metal handles. The boom slowly rose higher, as if readying for a circus act. After it stopped a foot below the ceiling, someone at the desk worked controls and the camera moved, pointing its lens down toward the table. Borchard, who looked like a stage-hand himself in his jeans and workshirt, had been talking with some women in the front row of the bleachers; he came over now and sat on the swivel chair by the little table that held water, two towels, an ashtray and pool chalk. He did not look in Eddie's direction.

The camera on the book began wiggling, pointing off toward the wall. Eddie looked at his watch. Two-thirty.

The PA sputtered and came on. 'We apologize for the delay. The television people tell me their overhead camera must be replaced and we won't be able to start for about an hour. We're sorry for the inconvenience.'

'Shit,' Borchard said.

Eddie stood up. Arabella climbed down from her seat and walked over. 'Let's get a cup of coffee,' she said.

Eddie looked at her. 'I need to be alone for a while.' She shrugged. 'Sure. I'll get a drink.'

There were about a dozen people in the swimming pool and more working out in the gym, but the whirlpool was empty. Eddie eased himself into it, rested his back along the edge, let his chin lie on his chest and gently closed his eyelids. It didn't work. He still felt the knot in his stomach, the sense of powerlessness. It was the TV people, with their pre-occupation and delays, their arrogant busyness. They weren't taking any risks, putting themselves on the line. The sons of bitches. His head ached with it.

He would have to be back there in forty minutes, and he did not want to go back. For a moment he lay in the whirlpool feeling frightened and old. The hot water gushed and foamed over his body. Gradually the knot in his stomach eased a little. He listened to the water surging, began to hear the music from ceiling speakers, let his body go limp, feeling himself bob to the movement of the water. For a few minutes, miraculously, he fell asleep – or so near to sleep that he would not have known where he was.

When he walked back into the ballroom, the nine balls were in the wooden rack and the referee had put the lag balls out. Borchard was standing by the table. As Eddie took out his cue and put it together, the announcer introduced them to the crowd. Eddie barely listened to the words. His hands with the cue were steady.

His lag was perfect and his break overwhelming. The nine came off the bottom rail and rolled the length of the table. Although it did not go in, two other balls did. As he studied the layout a cameraman wheeled closer, while another kneeled a few feet away, pointing a camera up at Eddie's face. Eddie ignored them. He ran the balls and pocketed the nine. The crowd was huge and its applause loud. Eddie lit a cigarette, watching the referee rack. Borchard was seated, looking at nothing in particular. Arabella sat in the stands, her face intent on the table; up above her, in the back row of the bleachers, sat Boomer. Eddie put his cigarette in the ashtray, picked up the twenty-three-ounce cue, and broke. The nine fell in the corner pocket. He went back to his cigarette while the referee racked. If you hit the balls right, they fell into the pockets. He broke and ran the rack, sending the cue ball around the table when necessary the way the younger men had done, not worrying about the speed of it or the possibility of a scratch. It stopped each time exactly where he wanted it to stop. Three-nothing.

But on the fourth break, though his power was there and the balls rolled energetically, nothing fell into a pocket. Nothing. Even worse, the cue ball stopped where the one ball was easy. Eddie stared at the table for a moment. There was nothing to do about it. He walked over to the chair and seated himself. Borchard got up.

The thing about pool was that no matter how up you were for it, no matter how ready your soul – as Eddie's soul was ready – and no matter how dead your stroke, if the other man was shooting it made no difference. His arm ached to be making the balls himself but he had to sit, had to watch another man play pool.

And the other man's game was inspired. Borchard – that delicate, quiet Eastern country boy with his heavy, drooping mustache and his crepe-soled shoes – seemed to have the balls on a string. He didn't look at the crowd or the referee or at Eddie, but bent his entire attention on the nine balls and eased them one after another into the pockets with his cue ball always stopping exactly where it should stop. He chalked after every shot and his small eyes never left the table. The cameramen danced their slow dance in and out and around him and the table; the audience applauded louder and louder after each sinking of the nine ball; and Borchard's expression and concentration did not change. He made the nine six times before a bad roll on the break made him play safe. The score was six-three. Borchard needed only four games. Eddie needed seven. Eddie stood up.

The position was terrible. The cue ball was snookered behind the seven. He would be lucky to get a hit on the one ball, let alone a safety. He looked at this, and for a moment felt like walking out of the room. Borchard stood a few feet from the table with a cold, inward smile on his youthful face, waiting for him to miss. It was a nightmare position and there was nothing he could do about it but poke at the cue ball and pray.

Eddie gritted his teeth, tightened the joint of his cue and looked at the shot. The lights on the overhead boom went out.

Someone in the crowd applauded and a few laughed. Eddie stood and waited. He looked at the speakers' table; the tournament director sat there with a frown, talking on a telephone. After a minute he hung up and picked up the microphone and his voice came on the loudspeaker, 'They say we've blown a fuse,' it said. 'There'll be a ten-minute recess.'

Several people in the crowd began to boo.

'We apologize for the delay,' the director's voice said.

Borchard was making his way roughly through the standees. Men in the crowd were saying things to him, but Borchard did not look at any of them; his mouth was set in a hard line and he pushed through the mass of people with a kind of heedless urgency, as though late for an important meeting.

Eddie left his cue on the table and walked to the players' restroom behind the bleachers. No one else was there; he stood alone in front of the wide brightly lit mirror. His eyes were dull and his hair limp. He looked down at his hands: greenish pool-cloth dirt outlined the fingernails; a ground-in smear darkened the heel of his left hand. He turned a faucet on and watched the sink fill with hot water while he peeled the wrapper from a cake of soap. He turned off the faucet and began to work up a lather over the palms and backs of his hands, over his wrists. He began to rub hard, lathering each finger separately, abrading the dark stain on his left hand with the fingers of his right. He filled the basin, rinsed, washed again and rinsed again. He took the soap and worked it into his face, lathering around his nose and eyes, then did the back of his neck and under his chin. It was a relief. He let the water out, refilled the bowl, ducked down and began rinsing.

While he was drying with paper towels, the door opened and Earl Borchard came in. Borchard did not even look at him. He walked to the urinal against the wall on the other side of Eddie and stood there using it loudly, blankly facing the tiled wall a few inches from his nose. Eddie began combing his hair.

At the sound of flushing, he turned to see Borchard head into one of the marble stalls, slamming the door behind him. Eddie finished combing his hair.

He was putting the comb back in his pocket when Borchard came out of the stall, still not looking at him. He walked to the mirror, stopped next to Eddie, looked at himself, took out a comb. In the bright fluorescent lights, pink blotches were visible on his face.

Borchard was only a vain, edgy kid. Without his pool cue that was all he was. Eddie turned toward him and said, 'Sometimes it's a bitch.'

Borchard turned sharply. 'I'm not your friend,' he said, barely moving his lips.

He looked away from Eddie and took a paper cup from the wall dispenser, half filled it with water, abruptly turned to Eddie again. 'I'm going to beat your ass.' He looked down at the water in his hand and smiled, then turned back to stare unblinkingly into Eddie's face. '*This* is going to beat you.' He parted his lips. On his tongue sat a wet drug capsule, green and black.

Eddie's response was like a reflex. His open hand came up immediately, slapping Borchard full on the cheek, the way a parent slaps a smart-assed child. Borchard dropped the water.

The pill hit the floor, spun, and stopped a few feet away. Borchard stood transfixed, caught stupidly in his act. Eddie walked to the pill and crushed it with his heel. His back was to Borchard, but he felt no alarm. The kid would not hit him. He walked to the door.

'I've got more,' Borchard said as Eddie pushed the door open.

'Take a dozen,' Eddie said.

'Play will resume as soon as the players return,' said the voice on the PA. Eddie walked through the crowd and up to the tournament table where the lights now flooded the green again. The referee was standing with his hands behind his back, in position. Eddie stepped up to the table, elevated the butt of his cue stick and gently tapped the cue ball into the rail. It bounced out, rolled softly, clicked into the edge of the one and stopped. The one rolled a few feet and came to a stop exactly where Eddie wanted it to, leaving Borchard no shot at all.

It was a moment before Borchard walked up and the referee told him it was his shot. He came over to the table and frowned at the position for a moment. He did not look at Eddie. He grimaced, shook his head, and played the ball safe. Eddie returned it, leaving the cue ball far from the one.

Someone in the crowd shouted, 'Go for it, Earl!' Borchard stepped up to it, bent and concentrated. He shook his head and then let go with his cue stick, shooting hard. The cue ball sped down the table, clipped the one ball but rolled too fast. It raced back up and split apart a pair of balls before stopping in a place where Eddie could make the one. It was difficult, but it could be made.

Borchard turned quickly, walked over to the little table and sat down.

Eddie, suddenly feeling young, leveled his Balabushka and, without hesitation, sliced the one in. Then the two and three. He could not miss. He bent to the four ball, cut it thin as a whisper and made it. He shot the five, six, seven, eight and then the nine, hardly hearing the applause as the nine ball fell. He leaned his Balabushka against the chair and took the heavy factory cue. The referee racked the balls. On the break Eddie made two and ran the rest. The referee racked and Eddie broke again. He shot them in one after the other. He seemed to float from ball to ball, and his vision of them beneath the white lights of television was as sharp as the edge of a steel blade. The balls rolled the way they should and fell into pockets the way they should. There was nothing to it.

As he stood ready to break, voices shouted, '*On the snap, Fast Eddie*,' and 'Nine ball, Eddie, *nine ball*!' and he thundered the cue ball into them knowing the nine would go. It did. The referee racked again while the applause continued. Again he made the nine on the break and the crowd, distant from his mind but enveloping a part of his spirit, exploded in applause. He broke, made two balls, ran the rack. Again, with the nine on a combination. No one could touch him; nothing could make him miss these balls – these bright, simple balls. He broke again, watched the cue ball settle behind the one; made the one, the two, the three, on up to the nine, slipping the nine ball itself down the rail into the corner pocket. And then, shocked, he heard the deep voice on the PA speaker saying, 'Mr Felson wins match and tournament,' the voice almost buried by applause. He blinked and looked around. The people in the bleachers were applauding, some of them whistling, some shouting. They began to stand, still applauding.

Eddie dove into the deep water, going straight down until, by reaching out a hand, he could feel the rough concrete of the bottom at twelve feet. He let himself rise slowly to the surface and bob. He shook his head, opened his eyes, saw Arabella sitting at the edge of the pool looking toward him. He flipped his body around in the other direction, and with long, slow strokes swam across the pool and into the stone-lined grotto at the far end of it. Stopping there, he could smell the wet stones. The water was shallow and warmer. There was soft flickering light from a lamp underwater. He could not see Arabella now.

Thirty thousand dollars. He had beat them. First Cooley and then Borchard. There was a stone ledge near the water. He pulled himself out gently and sat there with his feet and calves in the warm water, his wet thighs solid against the rough stone, his body dripping. Fifty years old. He had beaten the kids. He let himself relax now, uncoiling the last bit of the knot that had filled his stomach throughout this day, and let the pleasure of it touch his whole body like a warm garment. There were goose bumps on his upper arms. He stretched and yawned, a winner. He had never felt better in his life.

'I'd like to drive all the way around the lake before we go back,' Arabella said after he swam over to her.

'First thing in the morning.' He eased himself out of the pool and sat beside her.

After a while the music on the PA stopped and a woman's

soft voice said, 'The pool area will be closed in five minutes.' Eddie looked behind him at the clock over the doorway to the gym; it was five minutes to one. He was beginning to feel tired.

Arabella stood and began drying herself with a towel. 'This place is like a church,' she said, looking around her at the huge concrete circumference of the pool and up at the broad, black skylight.

'I like it.' Eddie lazily took his feet out of the water and held his hand out for the towel. 'Let's get dressed.'

They came around a corner and there was the casino, its lights garish and somehow comforting. Three crap games were going strong; all the blackjack tables were in play; a crowd milled about in the vast area of the slot machines. It was, after all, Saturday night. 'Do you want to try your luck?' Eddie said.

She folded her arms and hugged herself nervously. 'I don't know. I'm still in a daze.'

'Then let's go to bed.'

She looked at him smiling faintly, still hugging herself. They were standing at the top of a wide and shallow stairway that led down to the still-empty baccarat tables. 'You really did win, didn't you? You really *did*.'

They walked through the casino, where people and money circulated freely and at ease. Arabella put her arm through his. Tired as he was, his step was light. As they passed the last of the crap tables, a very old man was shaking the dice fervidly; now, with a broad, sweeping movement he threw them powerfully from the side of his hand out onto the long green. Eddie and Arabella stopped to watch them bounce and glitter under the bright lights. The number that came up was eleven. '*Natural*!' cried the old man joyfully, leaning forward to pull in a pile of bills.

V. S. Anderson
King of the Roses £1.95

Chris Englund, five times winner of the Kentucky Derby, knows that he could be on the way to his sixth and greatest win with Knidos, a thoroughbred with the promise of a champion. But someone doesn't want Knidos to win – someone with the money to stop him. Courage and honesty battle against bribery and corruption in a race where the stakes are appallingly high.

'An impressive debut by a superb writer' PUBLISHER'S WEEKLY

Noel Behn
Seven Silent Men £1.95

You couldn't find a seedier bunch of small-time burglars than River Rat, Windy Walt and their friends. But present them with the chance to pull off America's biggest ever bank job and just look what happens. Their spectacular getaway is followed by an even more spectacular capture. But still nothing's solved; the FBI aren't just puzzled, they're totally perplexed. At least some of them are.

'Inspired caper-telling . . . high humour alongside ingenious complexity' ROBERT LUDLUM

Norman Katkov
Blood and Orchids £2.50

It began one balmy September evening when a young Navy wife, savagely beaten by her sadistic lover, accused four local Hawaiian boys of rape and assault. Her lie let loose a storm of outraged passion and prejudice. A brutal murder followed a bloody vigilante beating and the stage was set for a final awful confrontation.

'Violence, courtroom battles, steamy tropical ambience – a long and gripping read' IRISH TIMES

William J. Coughlin
The Twelve Apostles £1.95

No law firm stands higher or more proud than Nelson and Clark – so awesome, so prestigious that its senior partners have come to be known as the Twelve Apostles. Now, with the death of a partner, the battle is on to fill his chair, the fight between a beautiful woman and the man who loves her. An epic confrontation played out in the walnut-panelled offices and glittering restaurants of London and New York.

David Brierley
Big Bear, Little Bear £1.75

It is 1948, and the Russians have their eye on Berlin. As Stalin plans to swallow the city, Orris, only survivor of the British underground network in Czechoslovakia, is out to track down the mole in British intelligence. But there was one thing Orris hadn't bargained on. Her name was Rahel.

'If you want espionage in the le Carre class this is it' OBSERVER

'An authentic winner' SUNDAY TIMES

Derek Robinson
Piece of Cake £2.50

Their flying was breathtaking, they played God in the sky. They lived as they flew – reckless, flamboyant, no time to lose. For Hornet Squadron even dying was a piece of cake. From the early days of the war in France to the Battle of Britain's 'finest hour' the squadron fights on through terrible losses and triumphant victories.

'Destined for a place in the literary clouds' PRESS AND JOURNAL

Fiction

☐	**The Chains of Fate**	Pamela Belle	£2.95p
☐	**Options**	Freda Bright	£1.50p
☐	**The Thirty-nine Steps**	John Buchan	£1.50p
☐	**Secret of Blackoaks**	Ashley Carter	£1.50p
☐	**Hercule Poirot's Christmas**	Agatha Christie	£1.50p
☐	**Dupe**	Liza Cody	£1.25p
☐	**Lovers and Gamblers**	Jackie Collins	£2.50p
☐	**Sphinx**	Robin Cook	£1.25p
☐	**My Cousin Rachel**	Daphne du Maurier	£1.95p
☐	**Flashman and the Redskins**	George Macdonald Fraser	£1.95p
☐	**The Moneychangers**	Arthur Hailey	£2.50p
☐	**Secrets**	Unity Hall	£1.75p
☐	**Black Sheep**	Georgette Heyer	£1.75p
☐	**The Eagle Has Landed**	Jack Higgins	£1.95p
☐	**Sins of the Fathers**	Susan Howatch	£3.50p
☐	**Smiley's People**	John le Carré	£1.95p
☐	**To Kill a Mockingbird**	Harper Lee	£1.95p
☐	**Ghosts**	Ed McBain	£1.75p
☐	**The Silent People**	Walter Macken	£1.95p
☐	**Gone with the Wind**	Margaret Mitchell	£3.50p
☐	**Blood Oath**	David Morrell	£1.75p
☐	**The Night of Morningstar**	Peter O'Donnell	£1.75p
☐	**Wilt**	Tom Sharpe	£1.75p
☐	**Rage of Angels**	Sidney Sheldon	£1.95p
☐	**The Unborn**	David Shobin	£1.50p
☐	**A Town Like Alice**	Nevile Shute	£1.75p
☐	**Gorky Park**	Martin Cruz Smith	£1.95p
☐	**A Falcon Flies**	Wilbur Smith	£2.50p
☐	**The Grapes of Wrath**	John Steinbeck	£2.50p
☐	**The Deep Well at Noon**	Jessica Stirling	£2.50p
☐	**The Ironmaster**	Jean Stubbs	£1.75p
☐	**The Music Makers**	E. V. Thompson	£1.95p

Non-fiction

☐	**The First Christian**	Karen Armstrong	£2.50p
☐	**Pregnancy**	Gordon Bourne	£3.50p
☐	**The Law is an Ass**	Gyles Brandreth	£1.75p
☐	**The 35mm Photographer's Handbook**	Julian Calder and John Garrett	£5.95p
☐	**London at its Best**	Hunter Davies	£2.95p
☐	**Back from the Brink**	Michael Edwardes	£2.95p